Unnatural Causes

Thomas T. Noguchi, MD, is the world-famous former chief medical examiner of Los Angeles County whose cases have included the deaths of Marilyn Monroe, Sharon Tate, Janis Joplin, Robert F. Kennedy, William Holden, and John Belushi. He is now a professor in forensic pathology at Los Angeles–University of California Medical Center.

Arthur Lyons is the critically acclaimed author of more than eight Jacob Asch mysteries.

Thomas T. Noguchi, MD
and Arthur Lyons

UNNATURAL CAUSES

Pan Books
London, Sydney and Auckland

First published 1988 by
G. P. Putnam's Sons Ltd, New York

First published in Great Britain 1991 by
Pan Books Ltd, Cavaye Place, London SW10 9PG

9 8 7 6 5 4 3 2 1

© Thomas T. Noguchi, MD and Arthur Lyons 1988

ISBN 0 330 30655 3

Printed in England by Clays Ltd, St Ives plc

ACKNOWLEDGMENTS

We would like to thank the following people, whose cooperation and expertise greatly facilitated the writing of this book: Tom Ardies, Bill McMullin, Dr. Stephen Kopp, Dr. David Gura, Dr. Noel Lustig, Bob Dambacher.

To Eric Noguchi, my nephew, and to fellow members of the American Academy of Forensic Sciences, whose tireless efforts have made great contributions to criminal and civil justice.

Prologue

The thing was on him without warning. One moment, Duffy had been floating on his back beyond the surf, resting for the swim back to his Malibu beach home and dreading the thought of having to deliver the surfeit of inane one-liners the writers had managed to pack into the day's script. Then, in an instant, he was being sucked down into the dark, murky water, panic seizing him as he sank like a stone.

His hands lashed out, trying to grasp something solid, anything, but his fists closed on nothing but water. My God, he thought, I'm going to drown!

He opened his mouth to scream and his throat was stung by a flood of salt water. Choking, gagging, he scissored his legs desperately, trying to halt his descent, but the sudden weight around his waist kept taking him

9

deeper. He clawed futilely at the thing, but it refused to let him go.

The fear had used up most of the oxygen in his lungs, and his chest felt as if it were going to explode. The pain in his ears was excruciating. It's hopeless, he thought, I'm going to die, and then his foot landed on something—the sandy solidity of the bottom—and he felt a rush of hope.

Duffy bent his knees as far as he could, coiling, and pushed up with all his strength, kicking up a cloud of sand. The light of the surface was yards above him, just beyond his fingertips, but it seemed miles away. He stretched out, reaching for it, but the weight was too much, and he began to sink again.

This can't goddamn happen to me, he thought. I'm a star! That thought seemed to ignite in him one last-ditch effort. He writhed, clawed frantically at the light, then things began to dim and his thoughts became as the water, swirling, murky, without focus, before they faded into inky blackness.

His eyes were still open, but sightless. Moving with the undulating strands of kelp, his body swayed gently, gracefully, in time to the rhythmic, soothing surge of the surf.

—— **1** ——

During his six years as chief coroner for the County of Los Angeles, it had never failed to amaze Dr. Eric Parker how fast the word spread. No matter how remote the scene, they seemed to materialize out of nowhere, crystallizations of man's morbid curiosity. There must have been a hundred of them gathered outside the house already—gawkers. And, of course, the media. They especially were drawn by the smell of death.

Parker was waved to a stop by the two uniformed deputy sheriffs guarding the driveway of the house, and the crowd immediately enveloped the car like a human amoeba. He flashed his badge at one of the deputies and tried to ignore the microphones being thrust in his face and the tangled war of questions being shouted at him.

"Dr. Parker, can you tell us what's going on?"

"Is it Duffy?"

"Is he dead? What happened?"

The deputies pushed back the crowd and Parker gratefully accelerated through the gates. The brick courtyard in front of the house was clogged with black-and-whites and unmarked cars. Parker pulled the Chevy in behind the black coroner's van, and as he stepped out of the car he spied Mike Steenbargen coming out of the front doors of the flagstone-fronted house, briefcase in hand.

"Chief," Steenbargen greeted Parker. He nodded toward the street. "Looks like it's building into a real carnival."

"Yeah," Parker agreed, glancing at the gathering crowd.

Apart from the fact that both men were tall and in their middle forties, the two were a study in contrasts. Parker was still hard, the athlete who had lettered in three sports in his high-school days. Looking younger than his age, Parker had dark brown hair only lightly salted, and his face, while stamped with intelligence, had a round, soft boyishness to it. Steenbargen was beefy and overweight, his hair and mustache completely gray. Whereas Parker wore rumpled khaki slacks, was coatless and tieless, the sleeves of his pink shirt rolled up to the elbows, Steenbargen was dapperly dressed in a gray tweed jacket, crisply pressed gray slacks, a white shirt, and a gray-and-red-striped tie.

In a way, their mode of dress was reflective of their sharply differing styles. Parker was restless, in constant motion, prone to making intuitive leaps. His chief investigator was rock steady, conservative and methodical, literal in his approach.

Over their three-year association, Parker had found that their differing styles, rather than clashing, complemented each other. Steenbargen was earth to Parker's fire. At a crime scene, there was nobody as meticulously thorough as Steenbargen, and Parker was grateful that the investigator had arrived first to coordinate the show. Parker echoed the reporters' question: "Is it Duffy?"

Steenbargen nodded. "Guaranteed page one."

Parker shot an apprehensive look up the driveway. John Duffy. Multitalented comedian-actor-writer-singer who had skyrocketed to fame, first as a standup comic on late-night television interview shows, then through several roles as a crazy cutup in monstrously successful movies of the "fraternity-party" genre, and more recently as the lead in the hit TV series Life's Tough. His humor was off-the-wall, totally irreverent, and purposely or not, that image had been enhanced by his real-life exploits, such as last Halloween, when he had attended the governor's costume party dressed as a teabag (stark naked beneath a paper bag filled with real tea) and jumped into the Jacuzzi. Such stunts had made the comedian, in four short years, the hero of the under-thirty generation. His exploits would only be recounted now, and there would be a little less laughter in the world. "What does it look like?"

"Drowning."

"Accidental?"

"There's nothing I can see to contraindicate," Steenbargen said. "No external signs of violence. None that couldn't have been caused by the surf, anyway." He hesitated for a second, as if trying to figure an easy way to break the news, then said: "There's a residue of white powder on a mirror on the nightstand in the bedroom, along with an empty prescription bottle of Elavil."

If the news bothered Parker, he didn't show it. "When was the body found?"

"About nine-forty-five." Steenbargen put down his briefcase and whipped out a small spiral notebook from his inside breast pocket. He flipped it open and read: "The next-door neighbor—John Spitzer—was having coffee out on his porch and spotted it in the surf. He called the parameds. They arrived at ten-oh-two and ran an EKG strip. It was flat."

"They make an attempt to resuscitate?"

"They tried to defibrillate, but he was gone."

"Any witnesses to the drowning?"

The investigator shrugged. "Wolfe and Gunderson are checking the neighborhood now. Spitzer says that Duffy went swimming every morning, six o'clock, rain or shine, when he was staying here."

"He didn't live in the house all the time?"

The investigator shrugged. "I guess not."

"What about next of kin?"

"I'm working on it now." He put away the notebook and took out a small black address book from his jacket pocket. "I found this by the kitchen phone, but I haven't had a chance to go through it yet. Apparently the guy had a wife and kid—found some pictures in the bedroom—but it doesn't look like they've been living here. There are some women's clothes in the closet, but not enough for a full-time, live-in wife. And the place is a mess."

"Who's in charge of the investigation?"

"Kuttner."

"Kuttner? What's he doing down here?"

"Half of Metro is here, along with the entire Malibu substation."

Although possible homicides were rarely handled by local sheriff's detectives, Parker was not that surprised to hear that a captain like Kuttner had come all the way downtown to take charge. They would all turn out for one like this, especially if there was a chance of getting on the six-o'clock news.

Parker rubbed his neck, sighed, and started for the house.

The spacious living room was swarming with uniformed sheriffs and plainclothes detectives. The architect had done his best to bring the outdoors into the house, and had been fairly successful. Sunlight streamed through the vaulted skylighted ceiling and through the glass walls that looked out onto the sea. The floor was black slate, and large rocks, like the rocks on the hill running down to the beach, had been used to make bases for several of the glass-topped tables in the room. The tabletops were littered with an assortment of beer bottles, newspapers, and opened boxes of crackers. On a small space of wall between windows was a huge fireplace fronted by weathered wood and an asymmetrical heron shaped like a cresting wave. The furniture was all overstuffed rattan. "Not a bad spread," Steenbargen commented as they stepped through a set of sliding glass doors onto a split-level swimming-pooled patio glued uncertainly to the hillside.

A set of wooden stairs led down the hill to a small horseshoe-shaped cove guarded on each end by a high, rocky promontory. Because of the privacy of the beach, only the owners of the homes above would be privileged to get a glimpse of this corpse, and a handful of them were gathered behind the yellow-tape barrier the sheriffs had staked forty yards on each side of the body. Parker could hear his name being passed around the gallery as he ducked underneath the tape and trudged across the soft sand toward the cluster of uniformed deputies and his own brown-jumpsuited men. The cool breeze smelled of salt and kelp rotting in the morning sun.

Kuttner greeted Parker with a deferential nod. He was a beefy, thick-necked man with a red face and a bluing drinker's nose, like a bruised fist. Parker liked most of the police officers he had to deal with, but not Kuttner, who tended to be obtuse and who, in fact, had no real reason to be present. He was an administrator—his job back in some office—and here only because of the publicity.

Kuttner stepped out of the way, and an expectant silence fell over the group as Parker bent down on his haunches and pulled back the white plastic sheet.

The body was on its back, the mouth and eyes partially open and full of sand. The face was cyanotic, the skin bluish and goose-bumped, and the nose and mouth exuded a white, frothy foam, characteristic of drowning cases. The cheeks and dimpled chin were covered with a dark two- or three-day stubble of whiskers. In spite of the foam and the beard, and in spite of the fact that Parker didn't watch much TV—especially mindless sitcoms like the enormously popular one Duffy had starred in—he recognized the face. He lifted one eyelid, then the other. Faint signs of petechial hemorrhage.

The EKG lead pads were still attached to the chest and there were circular markings over the heart where the paramedics had tried to defibrillate.

Parker noted the small incision in the upper quadrant of the liver where the thermometer had been inserted. "What was his temperature?"

"Ninety-four point four," Steenbargen answered.

"Water?"

"Sixty-six."

He rolled the body over onto its stomach. No marked lividity patterns where the body had settled, possibly because of the churning action of the surf. The skin of the body was goose-bumped and liberally abraded from being dragged along the ocean bottom. Most of the abrasions were light pinkish to white—postmortem—but some of them showed a clear vital reaction, possibly self-inflicted, the result of the man's convulsive struggle for air. Four or five inches above the black bikini trunks, Parker also noted a straight double line of red abrasion, which meant it had been inflicted before death. He flipped the body back over. The red lines of irritated skin were on the abdomen too.

Parker picked up the right hand and inspected the fingertips. They were wrinkled, a sure sign the man had been alive when he had entered the water. Beneath the nails there was a dark substance—blood and dirt. Probably the man's own, Parker thought. The proverbial man grasping at straws, or whatever else was handy, including himself.

"Bag his hands," he said to Steenbargen, and stood up.

He looked out on the sun-dappled sea where the orange sail of a boat listed in the breeze. "What about wind and current?"

Steenbargen consulted his notebook. "Three knots, northeasterly. The surf is two feet, the wind six miles. Mild current, but nothing a halfway decent swimmer shouldn't have been able to handle." He paused. "I already did."

Parker gave him a curious look. "Did what?"

Steenbargen patted the side of his briefcase. "Took a sample of the water."

Parker smiled. Too many investigators made the mistake of paying too much attention to the body at a death scene. Steenbargen, better than anyone else Parker knew, understood the importance environment could play in providing the final, missing pieces of the puzzle. If there was a puzzle.

"What do you think?" Kuttner asked, trying not to sound anxious.

Parker looked into the captain's eyes and knew instantly what the man wanted to hear. Accidental death. No foul play, no complications, no investigation. With a celebrity like this, it would be a pressure-cooker situation, with everybody and his brother clamoring to know what was being done about it. Parker could not blame the man: that was what *he* wanted too. "There's nothing I can see that's inconsistent with accidental drowning," Parker said truthfully. "I want to look in the house."

"Sure, sure," Kuttner said, smiling relievedly.

"I'm through," Parker told the jumpsuited coroner's attendants. "You can take him in."

Kuttner followed Parker and Steenbargen up the stairs to the house. By the time they reached the top, Kuttner's face was bright red and he was breathing heavily. Coronary in about two years, Parker judged, but didn't say it; Kuttner would never listen to his advice anyway.

The bedroom was in the northwest corner of the house, and it, too, was mostly glass, which reverberated with the rhythmic pounding of the surf. Several ID techs and plainclothes detectives were going through the walk-in closet and the drawers of the rattan bureau. The king-size bed was unmade and the quilted purple spread lay in a heap at its foot. The sheets looked as if they hadn't been changed in at least three weeks.

Parker stepped over to the night table beside the bed. On it, in front of a framed color photograph, was a hand mirror dusted with a white-powder residue, a razor blade, and a short red bar straw. Next to it was an uncapped brown prescription bottle. Parker picked it up and looked at the label: "John Duffy. Elavil. 25 mg. One per day for anxiety. No refills." The prescribing doctor had been L. Somers.

"What is that?" Kuttner asked uneasily, between wheezes.

"Elavil. Amitriptyline. An antidepressant."

Parker bent down and looked at the framed eight-by-ten. In it, Duffy and a rather plain-looking black-haired woman in her middle twenties were standing next to a golden-maned Shetland pony on which was mounted a towheaded boy of perhaps four. Duffy's dark good looks were animated, his dark eyes sparkled with a boyish mischief, as if he had just thought of some new outlandish prank, and his smile was electric, wild, making the woman's smile appear washed-out, diffident.

While he was looking at the picture, Parker's eye was caught by something on the pillowcase. He reached over and picked it up carefully between two fingers. It was a human hair, about a foot long. He held it up and inspected it more closely in the light from the window.

"Maybe I was wrong about his wife not living here," Steenbargen offered.

"Not if his wife is in that photograph," Parker replied. "This hair is blond. At least most of it is. Got an envelope?"

Steenbargen pulled a small manila envelope from his briefcase and Parker dropped the hair into it. While the investigator sealed and labeled the evidence, Parker pulled open the drawer of the nightstand.

"Oops," Parker said unhappily. "Here's trouble."

Steenbargen and Kuttner moved in. Sitting out in the open, no attempt made to hide it, was a small plastic bag containing what looked like perhaps half an ounce of cocaine.

"That's show business," Steenbargen said, trying for, and falling short of, a light note.

"Put it away," Parker ordered. He looked at Kuttner. "And let's not mention it to anyone until we know what we've got here. I don't want anyone going off half-cocked."

Kuttner gave him a look but grunted assent.

The only other things in the drawer were a ball-point pen and a small yellow spiral notebook. Taking out his own pen, Parker flipped open the notebook's cover. On the first page, in a sloppy backhand scrawl, there was a short list of one-liner jokes. One seemed to jump from the page.

Suicide is a belated way of agreeing with your wife's mother.

Parker became aware of Kuttner peering over his shoulder. "What do you make of that?" the captain asked.

"I don't know," Parker answered. He flipped over more pages, but there were no more entries in the notebook. He closed the drawer and went into the bathroom, followed intently by the brigade of police.

The bathroom walls were blue tile, the mirror above the sink was large, and its border of small round lights spotlighted all the smears and specks of dried toothpaste on its dirty surface. The sink was dirty too, and the fake marble countertop on either side of it was littered with bottles of roll-on deodorant, a half-squeezed tube of toothpaste, and an electric razor.

Parker slid open the mirrored door of the medicine cabinet and inventoried the contents. The shelves would have kept a pharmacy happy for a month. Methaqualone, Xanax, Darvon, Percodet, Benzedrine, more Elavil. A pill for every mood, or lack of mood. "I want everything here taken downtown," Parker told his investigator. "And I want every doctor on these bottles called. I want to know exactly what Duffy was being treated for." He stepped back out into the bedroom and asked Kuttner: "Where's the kitchen?"

Kuttner raised a questioning eyebrow, but knew better than to voice it. He rubbed the back of his neck and told Parker to follow him.

The kitchen was on the other side of the house and it

was a mess. Dirty dishes and glasses cluttered the sink and tiled drainboards, along with an empty bottle of Stonegate Chardonnay, several empty bottles of Lite, and a half-killed fifth of Smirnoff vodka. The garbage bag in the cupboard beneath the sink was full and smelled a few days overdue for dumping.

Kuttner and two of the detectives from the bedroom watched curiously as Parker opened and closed cupboard doors. The shelves were sparsely stocked, with bags of Cheetos, Doritos, potato chips, a box of Frosted Flakes, cans of Dinty Moore beef stew and Franco-American spaghetti. He went on to the refrigerator.

"What do you expect to find in there?" Kuttner asked.

Parker didn't answer. The refrigerator, like the cupboards, was sparsely stocked. A six-pack of Lite, some Stouffer's frozen dinners, a half-used cube of butter, a pint of cottage cheese and a quart of low-fat milk, both with expired dates, a jar of Best Foods mayonnaise, and a plastic squeeze bottle of Gulden's, its nozzle crusted with dried mustard.

Parker closed the door, satisfied. "It fits."

"What fits?" Kuttner asked, perplexed.

"This kitchen. The stubble on his face. The messy state of the house. The Elavil," Parker said, as if it were self-evident. "All this guy had in the house was junk food and fast food, stuff that didn't need preparation. This is the kitchen of a depressed man."

Kuttner stiffened. "I happen to like Cheetos, and I'm not depressed."

"You may like them," Parker said, "but you don't live on them."

22

Kuttner's tone took on a combative edge. "What would a guy like Duffy be depressed about? He was on top of the world."

Parker shrugged. "I wouldn't know. But unless he flushed the contents of that Elavil bottle down the toilet, it must have been something, because according to the date, he'd taken four times the prescribed dosage. Taken in that context, that note could make sense."

"Suicide?" Kuttner asked, scowling darkly.

"Maybe he walked into the ocean," a blond, mustachioed detective built like an ad for Jack La Lanne's offered helpfully. "Like the guy in *A Star Is Born*."

"The guy in *A Star Is Born* didn't walk into the ocean, you moron," Kuttner snapped, obviously not wanting any help. "He piled up his Ferrari."

"Not *Kristofferson*," the bodybuilder replied. "James *Mason*. In the *original* version."

Kuttner scowled at the man. He had a list of personal dislikes, which included dogs and children. Cops that corrected him—especially cops ten years his junior—were right up there at the top.

"James Mason was in the remake," Parker corrected the young cop. "Fredric March was in the original."

Kuttner, partially redeemed, nodded a "So there" at the underling.

Parker left Siskel and Ebert and went out onto the patio to watch them bring up the body. "How could you get depressed with a view like that?" Steenbargen said, appearing suddenly beside him.

Billions of rays of sunlight danced on the blue surface of

the ocean as it rolled out toward infinity. If there was a God, he was a French impressionist, Parker decided.

"I think I could find happiness here," Steenbargen said.

"At least until you made the first mortgage payment."

"Right," Steenbargen agreed. "How much do you think a little bungalow like this would go for?"

Parker turned. "Here? A million and a half. Maybe two. A mile inland, maybe five hundred thou."

"Yeah, but look what you're buying *here*. You wouldn't just be buying a *house*, for Chrissakes. You'd also be getting your own luxury yacht, which, through the miracle of modern tectonics, will soon be cruising toward San Francisco."

Parker smiled mirthlessly. He and his staff often joked about "The Big One," the earthquake that all the experts said was coming, but the laughter was more nervous than genuine. The inevitability of that grim event, in fact, was Parker's one recurrent nightmare.

He had tried to share his nightmare—a city in ruins, sixteen thousand projected dead—but the political powers that be would not listen. They said such doomsday talk was just another ploy for additional funding. They would be on him fast enough for this one, though. Tell them an entire city was living on borrowed time and they were deaf and dumb, but give them one dead TV star and they would all mobilize, demanding to know what was being done.

"I just talked to Wolfe," Steenbargen said, breaking into his thoughts. "The neighbor across the street spotted a red Porsche pull into Duffy's driveway at approximately six-fifteen. Whoever was driving it stuck around about five minutes, then pulled out in one hell of a hurry."

Parker looked at him with interest. "That would have been about the time Duffy was swimming."

"Right."

For a moment, neither of them said anything, but the thought hung there silently between them. Finally Steenbargen said: "They're going to be waiting for a mistake on this one."

Parker nodded. "That's why I'm going to do the post myself. Get everything down to the lab as fast as you can, will you, Mike? Including that notebook. I want to know if that was Duffy's handwriting."

Steenbargen searched the face of his boss and friend. "You think it was a prediction?"

Parker shrugged and looked away. "If it was, he was right on the mark."

2

Parker put his key into the slot by the elevator and pressed the button for the security floor of the Forensic Science Center. Strictly monitored, the security floor was open twenty-four hours a day to handle the more than eight thousand autopsies that were performed there annually.

California's Government Code of Section 27491 made it the duty of the office of the county coroner to investigate and determine the circumstances, manner, and cause of all deaths in the county, "other than natural." In addition to deaths due to accident, suicide, and murder, that broad classification also included all nursing-home deaths and deaths by illness in which a physician had not been in attendance for at least twenty days. Of the fifty thousand deaths in L.A. County each year, the office of the medical examiner-coroner investigated approximately one in three. That usually made for a busy day for its staff of one thousand five hundred and Monday was always the busiest.

As he stepped off the elevator, Parker could see this Monday would be no exception. A procession of gurneys was lined up against the corridor wall outside the autopsy room, their sheeted loads waiting their turn with patience only the dead could practice. Parker had never believed that old myth about the full moon bringing out the loonies. Full moon, new moon, it didn't make any difference. They came to the party every Saturday night, regardless of the lunar phase.

He stopped by the assignment board and was checking the autopsies scheduled for the morning, when Dr. Jim Phillips, his chief operations officer, came up holding a clipboard. "'Morning, Chief."

"Hi, Jim. A body was just brought in—John Duffy—"

Phillips lifted a dark eyebrow. "The TV star?"

"Right. I'll be doing the autopsy myself as soon as they finish fingerprinting and X-ray. I want Petronelli to assist. Reassign his eleven o'clock, will you?"

Phillips checked the board. "Okay. I'll give it to Schaffer."

Parker looked at him doubtfully. "He's already scheduled for three today . . ."

Phillips shrugged. "He'll do it. He'd do six if you asked him."

Schaffer was one of Parker's most promising young pathologists. He had been with the department for only a year, but he had already learned more than most did in

28

three. Ambitious, bright, and eager, he reminded Parker of himself when he started out. Parker waved at the hallway. "Heavy weekend?"

Phillips nodded and consulted his clipboard. "Homicides, twenty-three. Suicides, fifteen. Accidental, twenty-nine. Probable naturals, forty-seven. Undetermined, five. Twenty-four of the naturals I've signed out to mortuaries without autopsy. Seventeen show sufficient complications to be put on the holdover list." He paused, then said, "Do me a favor—talk to Kubuchek."

"What's the problem?"

"I'm holding up death certificates on twelve cases because I can't get the lab results from toxicology. Every time I try to talk to the guy, he flips out and starts screaming about being shorthanded. Hell, we're *all* shorthanded."

All Parker could say was: "I'll talk to him." The manpower shortage had become quite acute in the past three months. They desperately needed two pathologists and three more toxicologists, but Parker's requests had fallen on deaf ears, and the extra workload had started to take its toll. Conversations had become tight-lipped and clipped. Tempers flared. Even with the adjusted work schedules, they were falling farther and farther behind. Something had to be done—fast—but Parker was stymied as to what.

He blamed himself for the situation. He had never been known for his political deftness. His intolerance for the bureaucratic mentality, plus his fierce protectiveness of the department, had partially led to the current crisis. When Harry Brewster, the county administrative officer, had dragged his feet about Parker's requests for additional funding, Parker had made the mistake of going over the man's head to the Board of Supervisors. Brewster had seen the move as a deliberate attempt to politically embarrass him and had used his longtime alliance with Supervisor Tartunian to make sure the requests were turned down. Now they were all suffering.

Before going upstairs, Parker stopped into the autopsy room. The six stainless-steel tables were all occupied and Parker experienced an intense feeling of pride as he watched his surgical-gowned staff busy at their work. To an outsider, that might have seemed strange, but to Parker this room was the reason for and the achievement of his life.

In medical school at UC San Francisco, Parker's classmates had all thought he was suffering from temporary insanity from hitting the books too hard when he announced his decision to specialize in forensic pathology. It took five years of graduate training in anatomical and clinical pathology and one more year of forensic pathology before one could qualify for the American Board of Pathology examination, and none of Parker's friends could fathom a student of his potential wasting that much time—or the rest of his life, for that matter—specializing in a field that offered so little in the way of either pay or prestige.

What they could not understand was that Parker had been drawn to it for the very reason that they were not. Because the most talented students gravitated naturally toward more lucrative medical specialties, such as psychiatry and surgery and cardiology, Parker saw in forensics a clear field for running, a field in which a man with ability, with vision, could rise rapidly to the top of his profession. And in those days, Parker was in a hurry.

The fact of the matter was, Eric Parker was a driven man. Ever since he could remember, he'd had to be the best at whatever he did, whether it had been in academics, football, or pulling his most outlandish college pranks. His ambition, which at times had caused him problems, had also been the fire that had kept him going and ignited his purpose. In forensic pathology he had seen a field in which one man might be able to make a difference.

After med school, Parker returned home to Los Angeles, and after interning for a year at the USC Medical Center, went to work for the L.A. medical examiner's office, then headed by the legendary Milton Ebenstein.

A remote and stern figure, the squat, gnomelike, cigar-chewing Ebenstein ruled his staff with an iron hand. A widower and childless, the great man had been lured from New York six years before by the promise of a new state-of-the-art Forensic Science Center, the construction of which he had supervised, and which subsequently became his baby. The chief often did not leave the center for days at a time, and his disconcerting habit of suddenly materializing at any hour of the day or night gave credence to the rumor that the man never slept and saw all—a rumor Ebenstein himself did nothing to dispel. "I'm not God," he would tell his staff members who displeased him, "but I'm close enough that you don't want to piss me off."

In those first two years Parker had thrown himself into his work with a passion, cheerfully volunteering to work nights, overtime, Sundays, and on those unpleasant decomposed cases that most pathologists abhorred. It was one of those days, after everyone else had gone home, while finishing up an autopsy on a young dope dealer who had been shot and buried in a shallow grave off Topanga Canyon, that Parker felt a presence behind him and turned to see the Great Man thoughtfully chewing his cigar stub, watching him. In spite of the extra ventilation in the room, which was designed specifically for decomposed cases, the putrid stench of the corpse was almost smothering, yet Ebenstein seemed unfazed as he waved for Parker to finish.

After Parker had showered and changed, he found Ebenstein waiting for him in the hallway. "I want to see you in my office," he said.

Ebenstein rarely received visitors in his inner sanctum, and Parker felt privileged, if a bit nervous, when he entered. It was early evening, but the large office was tightly shuttered and dark, except for the solitary bank of track lights that shone directly down on the huge sarcophaguslike desk. Ebenstein had designed the effect to give visitors the feeling they were in the presence of divinity, and the effect was not lost on Parker as he sat on a couch just outside the circle of light, watching the old man fill two Styrofoam cups with Remy Martin. Ebenstein handed Parker one of the cups and said: "Most pathologists would rush a job like you just did because they want to get it over with."

32

Parker took a stiff jolt of the brandy, trying to kill the smell and taste of the dead man that lingered in his nose and throat. "I believe you should take twice as much time with a decomposed case. Decay can cover up a lot of things."

"Obviously," Ebenstein said, smiling; and then, "You have a lot to learn, Parker."

"Yes, sir."

The old man tapped the dead ash of his cigar on the edge of the ashtray. "And I'm going to teach you."

From that day on, Parker was under the wing of the Great Man. He absorbed the man's technique, the way he thought, his passion for truth. When Shirlee Cummings, the buxom blond sex goddess of the silver screen, was found dead in the living room of her Beverly Hills mansion, surrounded by an eerie ritualistic display of votive candles and funeral flowers, Ebenstein assigned Parker to do the autopsy.

Sources claiming to have been close to the star speculated darkly in the press about murder, saying that the blond bombshell had been heavily into "black magic" and "devil worship," and when Parker's verdict was made public—"probable suicide resulting from acute intoxication due to an overdose of barbiturates and alcohol"—the cry of "cover-up" immediately erupted.

Actually, there *had* been a cover-up, but not the kind the conspiracy buffs were peddling. It seemed that the glamorous star, wanting her final scene to be her most hauntingly beautiful, had ordered flowers and the candles herself, donned a silver lamé nightgown, and after washing down fifty Seconals with half a pint of vodka, had lain down in the middle of her self-made shrine to await death.

Unfortunately, the pills and booze did not settle well. Shirlee had thrown up on herself, then run for the bathroom, vomiting all the way. From the tracks found by the police and medical examiner's investigators, it was determined that she had slipped on the vomit-slicked floor just outside the bathroom door and fallen headfirst into the toilet, where she was found the next morning by her maid.

The devoted servant, in an attempt to salvage some of her patroness's dignity, had carried the body back to its intended resting place, but had been distracted by the arrival of Miss Cummings' agent before she could clean up properly.

Because the details had no bearing on the cause of death, the coroner's office and the Beverly Hills police saw no need to go public with the information. But the persistent rash of rumors, plus vociferous charges by one of Ms. Cummings' ex-husbands, who was writing a book about the alleged cover-up, precipitated enough public pressure to reopen the case a year later. Although a board of inquiry upheld Parker's findings, it bowed to pressure from the movie colony to keep the rest of the story under wraps, and later, the cloud of mystery still hung over the death of Shirlee Cummings.

It was the Cummings case that made Parker's name nationally known. It was also the Cummings case that made Parker swear to himself that he would never try to cover up the facts in a death. After the Cummings case, Parker continued to receive national publicity. His work figured prominently in the prosecution of several sensational murder cases, the most spectacular being the stabbing death of rich industrialist Paul Cavendish. Through a new technique devised by Parker, a negative cast had been made of the knife wounds by injecting them with a mercury-laden substance called Wood's metal. When the substance had solidified, it was withdrawn, providing a three-dimensional replica of the knife blade. A tiny chip at the end of the tip of the cast, where the knife had hit bone, matched up perfectly with a knife found in the possession of Cavendish's illegitimate son, Jonathan Dodson. It secured the conviction of the disgruntled and disinherited teenager and also Parker's media label as the "Whiz Kid of Forensic Pathology."

When Ebenstein announced his retirement in 1980, it was no surprise to anyone that he recommended to the County Board of Supervisors that Parker succeed him. At the age of thirty-nine, Eric Parker became the youngest chief coroner in the history of Los Angeles, and during his six-year tenure, he had indefatigably sought out the most promising young doctors and technicians and lobbied for state-of-the-art equipment, ensuring the Forensic Science Center's reputation as one of the finest medical examiner's departments in the country.

Now a few pigheaded politicians were threatening to tear down everything Parker had worked so hard to build, all for their own personal petty motives. He wouldn't let them. He *couldn't* let them. He would get through this roadblock somehow; he always had. He'd tried to go around Brewster once; this time, if he had to, he would go through him.

Parker drifted through the room, pausing briefly to inspect each doctor's work. He stopped to watch Dwayne Brown, the newest addition to his staff, remove the heart and lungs from the body of an elderly Oriental male. The young doctor's technique was sloppy. Too much blood. Parker made a mental note to talk to him later. One thing Parker tried to inculcate in his students was the importance of neatness. Too often, the attitude of pathology students was one of carelessness—the patient was dead, so what did it matter?—but just as in surgery, too much blood could cover up crucial evidence and cause a pathologist to render a mistaken diagnosis.

Parker had often toyed with the idea of requiring his weekly medical-school class to wear tuxedos while performing an autopsy. If they had to pay for their own cleaning bills, perhaps they would be less inclined to sloppiness. Parker smiled to himself. Why not? He would talk to Tom Barnes at USC about it.

Dr. Ron Schaffer looked up from the table as Parker passed and said through his surgical mask, "Can you spare a minute, Chief? I'd like your opinion on something."

On the table was a male Caucasian of about thirty-five. The top of the skull and the brain had been removed. Parker noted the round hole in the forehead, just above the bridge of the nose. "Gunshot wound?"

Schaffer nodded. "Only, no bullet. I've cross-sectioned every inch of the brain. No fragments, nothing. And no exit wound."

Parker looked at the doctor curiously, then bent down and examined the wound in the forehead with a magnifying glass. It was identical to thousands of gunshot wounds he had seen over the span of his career, right down to the indented ring of abrasion around the wound's edges where the bullet had entered. He straightened and pointed to the bloody scratches that marked the dead man's cheeks and neck. "Looks like he struggled with his killer."

"And whoever it was had pretty good nails."

"Where was he found?"

"In his car, parked on a residential street just off Santa Monica," offered a man standing nearby. Parker did not recognize the voice, and the face was hidden behind a surgical mask.

"This is Sergeant Burke, Chief. Sheriff's Homicide. This is his case." With the AIDS scare, even police spectators were required to wear precautionary surgical garb in the autopsy room.

"When was he found?" Parker asked the detective.

"Last night, about midnight."

"I estimate the time of death to be maybe two hours before that," Schaffer said.

Parker nodded. "Who is the decedent? Know anything about him?"

"Name's Denhom," Burke said. "He was a stockbroker from Beverly Hills. Married, two kids. I figure he picked up a hooker on Santa Monica—there are a lot of them working that neighborhood—and drove down the street figuring he'd get a quick blow-job on the way home. He was sitting behind the wheel of the car with his pants down around his knees."

"There were traces of lipstick around his genitalia," Schaffer remarked.

"The broad must have waited until the guy's pants were down and he couldn't chase her so easy, then made a grab for his wallet. Only he caught her. In the struggle to get away, she must have panicked and pulled a gun from her purse and plugged him. His wallet was missing."

"Only, where is the bullet?" Schaffer piped up.

"There *has* to be a bullet," Burke told him. "You just missed it."

"I didn't," Schaffer insisted stubbornly.

The detective thought a moment, then said, "What about an ice bullet?"

"A what?" Parker asked.

Burke nodded. "I saw a TV program once, where this guy stabbed another guy with an icicle. It broke off inside him and melted and nobody could find the murder weapon."

Parker shook his head. He would have thought that the city's finest had enough real problems to face without dreaming up homicidal hookers running around the streets carrying portable ice-bullet-makers in their purses. But the image of the icicle triggered a thought. "Anybody in the neighborhood hear a gunshot?"

"No."

"Did you search the vicinity?"

"Sure." The detective nodded. "No gun."

"How about a shoe?"

38

Above the surgical mask, Burke's bushy eyebrows knitted. "Huh?"

"A woman's spike-heeled shoe."

Schaffer looked at Parker with astonished admiration. "I never thought of that."

"Wait a minute," Burke broke in. "Are you telling me that a woman would have the strength to drive a spike heel through a guy's skull like that?"

"Probably not," Parker said.

"Well, a high-heeled shoe isn't exactly a man's weapon," the detective said. Then his eyes widened as he caught on. "A transvestite!"

"Or a transsexual," Parker said. "It's just a thought."

"And a damned good one," Burke said. "I'll get right on it. Thanks, doc."

3

Cindy looked up from her Selectric as Parker came through the door, her blue eyes ludicrously enlarged behind the thick lenses of her tortoiseshell glasses. It struck Parker that something was different about her, and then he remembered. This was Monday. Cindy changed her hair color every weekend. The latest version was dark, almost black, with frosted highlights.

"Like your hair," Parker remarked, adhering to the routine. "Messages?"

"Are you kidding? The phone hasn't stopped ringing since I got in. It's terrible about John Duffy."

"He's down in X-ray now if you want one last look," Parker told her.

"I'll be seeing him enough on reruns," she said, shaking her new head. "It's a shame, though. He was so *cute*." She picked up two stacks of messages and handed one of

41

them to him. She patted the stack she had kept. "I separated out the media."

Parker nodded. "Call them down to Charles. Tell him to announce a press conference for two o'clock."

"This afternoon?" she asked, surprised.

"Yep."

"Isn't that pushing a bit?"

"It can't be helped. The public will want answers." He opened his office door. "Anybody else calls, I'm tied up until after lunch."

Parker's oak-paneled office was spacious, the shelves on the walls filled with fat medical texts. On the wall beside the oversize mahogany desk, a bank of closed-circuit TV screens monitored the activities in the nerve centers of the Science Center. Sunlight slanted through the venetian blinds behind the desk and fell in a striped rectangle on the worksheet on his desk blotter. He sat in his high-backed swivel chair and glanced through the messages.

Jan Bukowski, foreman, grand jury—courtesy call.

Miles Novak—will be by tonight at nine.

Dr. Jonas Silverman—will call back.

Alan Nakamoto—re speech, Disaster Preparedness Committee. 555-9091.

Eve. 555-7611.

Parker wondered what Eve could want—if it was about Ricky, if something was wrong, if the weekend was still on.

Please, not next weekend, Parker thought. He really wanted to see his son.

According to the divorce settlement, Parker had visitation rights every other weekend, but half a dozen times during the past year, Eve's mother had been taken mysteriously "ill," always a few days before his weekends, requiring Eve's immediate attention in Palm Springs. Invariably, she would take Ricky with her, returning to L.A. Sunday night after Mother's strange ailment cleared up.

Eve had had a rough time—emotionally and financially—during the six years since the divorce, and to a large degree she blamed Parker for it. In a way, he blamed himself as well. As a child, the traumatic divorce of her parents had left her with a deep-seated fear of abandonment which Parker's long hours at the Forensic Science Center had exacerbated. She might not have minded so much if he had been an absentee surgeon—she had always castigated him about his career decision—but she had been unable to understand how anyone could work so many hours and bring so little home.

Parker had thought that the emotional scars would heal over time, but they didn't seem to. He just hoped her resentment didn't break open this weekend. Another two weeks would be an eternity.

Another possibility crossed Parker's mind and he cringed inwardly. Maybe she had changed her mind about Boomer. Boomer was a golden Lab pup, Ricky's big birthday surprise. Ricky had been asking for a dog for a year, and Eve and Parker had debated the issue, at times hotly. She had been against it—with good reason, Parker had to admit—but had, in the end, reluctantly agreed. There was no guarantee, however, that the decision would hold, and that thought struck fear in Parker's heart. He and

Boomer had been roommates for four days now, and Parker had already cleaned up a lifetime's quota of dogshit.

He was reaching for the phone when line one flashed and Cindy buzzed him. He grabbed the phone and said, "You've got to hold the calls—"

"It's Alex Tartunian," she said apologetically. "I thought you'd want to take it."

"Okay," he said, and pressed the button. "Yes, Supervisor?"

"I hear John Duffy was found dead this morning," Tartunian said gruffly, without so much as a hello.

"That's right."

"How did he die?"

"I don't know yet. It looks like a drowning, but I won't know until I do the autopsy."

"Were drugs involved?"

"Not that I know of," Parker hedged, knowing how sensitive the man was on the subject.

"I just got a call from Byron Fenady. You know who he is?"

Parker confessed that he didn't.

"He's one of the biggest independent television producers in the business. He produces Duffy's show."

Parker remained silent, waiting.

"He wanted my assurances that the matter would be handled with discretion. He's concerned about adverse publicity. I can't blame him, considering your handling of such matters in the past."

He waited for Parker to respond to the rebuke, and

when he didn't, asked, "When do you expect to know something?"

"I've called a press conference for two this afternoon."

"I don't want a repeat of the DeWitt affair," the supervisor said sternly. "Is that clear?"

"Perfectly," Parker told him, trying to keep the bitterness he felt out of his voice.

"Call me when you get the results," Tartunian said peremptorily. "*Before* the conference." The supervisor hung up without saying good-bye.

Tartunian's imperious manner and his mention of DeWitt angered Parker and at the same time made him apprehensive. The man wielded a lot of power. More than any other single member of the board, Tartunian had been responsible for Parker's appointment as coroner. Since then, relations between the two men had deteriorated drastically.

Tartunian had always had strong ties to the movie industry—he went to the parties of stars and moguls, attended their charity functions, and gratefully accepted their generous contributions to his campaign funds—and those ties had been clearly demonstrated by his public condemnation of Parker's handling of the DeWitt case.

When Alan DeWitt, handsome lothario and romantic leading man in over fifty feature films, had been found dead on the tile floor of his living room a year and a half before, female fans the world over grieved. The cause of death had been cerebral hemorrhage, the result of his falling and hitting his head on the edge of a marble coffee table. The body had lain there for four days before being discovered by a concerned friend. At a press conference, Parker had deemed the actor's death to have been "alcohol-related" (DeWitt's blood alcohol at the time of his death had been .21), resulting in a storm of controversy as the movie colony rallied to the fallen star's cause.

At its own press conference, the Screen Actors Guild, through its president, a friend of Supervisor Tartunian, denounced Parker for "character assassination" by depicting DeWitt as a "drunken recluse." Tartunian echoed the sentiment by issuing a statement accusing Parker of misusing the tragedy for the purposes of his own self-aggrandizement, and later cited the affair to bolster support for Brewster in his budget feud with the coroner.

But there had been more behind Tartunian's support of the attack than merely his friendship with members of the movie industry. The resentment ran much deeper than that.

Four years after Parker's installation as coroner, Tartunian's sixteen-year-old son was found drowned in the family swimming pool. An autopsy revealed that the boy had ingested a large dose of LSD shortly before his death, leading Parker to the conclusion that he had fallen into the pool and in his disoriented state, drowned. When Parker had refused Tartunian's request to delete the drug references from his report, the supervisor had become enraged, and since that time, their relationship had ranged from frigid to openly hostile.

Just as Tartunian had used the DeWitt case to rally Parker's enemies, the Duffy case, too, might prove to be a political bombshell that could blow up in Parker's face if he wasn't careful.

He tried to push the thought to the back of his mind as he dialed the advertising agency and asked for Eve's extension.

"I just wanted to make sure you'd be able to take Ricky," she said, surprising him. "I'm going out of town for the weekend and won't be back until late Sunday."

"Going to Palm Springs?"

"No. I'm going to San Francisco. With Matt."

Matt was Matthew Brautigan, the fifty-two-year-old president of the advertising agency where Eve worked. They had been seeing quite a bit of each other during the past six months, according to Ricky. Why not? At thirty-eight, Eve was still a damned handsome woman, and Brautigan could offer her financial security, something Parker had never been able to do. She deserved to find security in some aspect of her life.

"You two getting serious?" Parker asked.

"That," she said icily, "is none of your business."

Parker could tell by her tone that it would be better to drop the subject. "What about the dog?"

"What about it?"

"It's still all right, isn't it?"

"Why wouldn't it be?"

They said good-bye and Parker hung up, relieved. It took about thirty seconds for his thoughts to cloud. Brautigan had begun to creep more and more into Ricky's conversation of late. Parker began to wonder how serious this thing really was. He didn't see Ricky nearly often enough, but with another man in the picture, he would in all likelihood see him even less. Parker had met the man several times and he seemed nice enough. But to be supplanted as a father figure by someone who created ad campaigns for breakfast cereals . . . Parker felt a twinge and made a mental note to find out more about the man.

Before going downstairs, Parker returned Dr. Jonas Silverman's call at Westbrook Hospital. He had an uneasy feeling what it was about, but he couldn't avoid his old friend. Might as well get it over with now.

"Jonas, how are you?" Parker asked when Silverman answered.

"To tell you the truth, Eric, I could be better. I talked to your Dr. Roberts this morning. He informed me about his findings in the McCullough autopsy. I'd like to talk to you about it."

"I don't know what there is to talk about . . ."

"I'm asking as a personal favor," Silverman said.

Parker had enough to deal with today without adding Silverman's defense plea for Westbrook to the agenda, but he had known and respected the man too long to deny his request. "Four-thirty? My office?"

Silverman said he would be there and rang off.

Parker scribbled down a note and went outside. On his way out, he handed the memo to Cindy. "Call Tom Barnes at USC and tell him this is how I would like his students to dress for next week's autopsy."

She read the note and shot him a questioning look.

"Tuxedos?"

"And make sure they know they're going to have to pay their own cleaning bills."

Cindy looked up at Parker incredulously, trying to determine if she were being put on. "Are they coming to an autopsy or the Academy Awards?"

Parker merely smiled in answer, and started out the door.

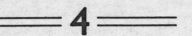

4

"The unembalmed body is that of a well-developed, well-nourished Caucasian male of the stated age of thirty-four, measuring seventy-one inches and weighing 175 pounds," Parker droned into the microphone suspended over the autopsy table. "Hair is dark brown and the eyes are brown. The face shows red-blue cyanosis, the skin has a goose-bumped appearance, especially in both extremities."

He noted the presence of lividity on the posterior aspects and light rigor mortis over the upper portion of the body. The legs showed very slight rigor. The liver temperature at 1057 hours was 92.6. He lifted the eyelids and noted a few pinpoint petechial hemorrhages on the inner surface of the eyelids, then looked into each nostril with an otoscope. The mucous membranes in the nose were severely ulcerated, possibly by irritants, such as cocaine.

Parker applied pressure on the thorax and a thick white froth exuded freely from the nostrils and mouth.

Slowly, methodically, Parker went over the body, inch by inch, with a magnifying glass, reciting identifying marks and scars. The back and posterior aspects of the shoulders showed numerous shallow linear abrasions, but their pinkish-white appearance told Parker that they were postmortem. The reddish, swollen contusion on the second knuckle of the right hand was a different story.

"This one is antemortem," Parker told Petronelli, who concurred with a nod.

He picked up the hand and inspected it carefully, noting the wrinkling of the fingertips and the dark brown material under the nails. With a pair of surgical scissors he snipped off each nail and placed it into its own evidence envelope, clearly marking the envelope with the ID number of the decedent. He signed each envelope, jotted down the time and Petronelli's name as a witness.

That done, Parker went on with his inspection at the torso, noting several other postmortem abrasions. At the right side of the mid-abdomen, he stopped. "Horizontal dark red linear abrasions with ecchymosis," he observed, "two inches above the umbilicus, extending from the right flank to the posterior axillary line to the left side of the abdomen. Lumbar region also shows similar dark red lines of abrasion with directionality left to right." He bent down for a closer look. The skin was red and swollen, definitely a type of friction burn. He looked up at Petronelli. "What do you think might have caused this?"

The short, balding pathologist hunched over the body,

squinting through the magnifying glass. Petronelli was one of the ablest forensic specialists, which was why Parker had wanted him to assist on this case. Petronelli straightened up and shook his head uncertainly. "Some of these wounds definitely look like fingernail scratches. This other, I don't know. The skin is chafed. Definite histaminic reaction. What was he wearing?"

"Just trunks," Parker said. "The abrasion lines were a good four inches above the line of his trunks."

Petronelli shook his head. "Any rocks in the area where he drowned?" he asked.

"I don't know. We don't know how far out he went, or even where."

The assistant shrugged. "Are you sure this happened while he was drowning? Maybe whatever caused it occurred before he went into the water."

"Maybe," Parker conceded. But he was still bothered.

He went on, winding up the external examination by noting an antemortem rectangular contusion, right calf. On the standard drawings of a featureless, hairless body, posterior and anterior, Parker sketched in the areas of antemortem injury, trying to approximate their shape, then with his own 35mm Nikon snapped off a couple of closeups of the abrasions on the flanks and the bruise on the calf.

He probed the ears with a scope. "Hemorrhagic edema, middle ear, left eardrum ruptured, hemorrhagic edema, petrous sinuses." He was not surprised to find water in the sphenoidal sinuses, and with a syringe drained off a sample.

"I guess we're ready to go in," Parker said, selecting a scalpel from the assortment of tools on the instrument tray.

He began the incision at the left shoulder, making a perfect arc through the pectoral muscles, and ending up in the exact same spot on the opposite shoulder. He completed the traditional Y by bisecting the arc with a deep vertical cut down to the pubic symphysis. A few more cuts exposed the neck organs and rib cage.

With a pair of rib cutters, Parker snipped through the cartilage of the sternum and lifted off the breastplate like the piece of a puzzle. The strong exhaust fans built into the table struggled against the gases that had begun to form from the very moment of the cessation of life, but the smell was still there, a smell like no other, the humid, cloying perfume of decay.

Parker surveyed the exposed organs. Fortune played no favorites here. The Lives of the Rich and Famous or the Lives of the Poor and Obscure, this was the way it all wound up, an impersonal inventory under the harsh glare of fluorescent lights.

After drawing off 200 ml. of blood from the heart with a syringe and dispatching it by toxicologist to the lab for an immediate drug-screen, Parker removed the tongue, larynx, and trachea, and inspected them for injury. He found none. Next, he removed the lungs and placed them in the stainless-steel pan attached to the scale at the foot of the table. He noted their soggy appearance and weight—the right weighed 800 grams, the left 750—then opened them up. He found the presence of acute pulmonary edema, and a great deal of water. No great surprise there.

Parker used syringes to draw off blood samples from the right and left ventricles of the heart. It was unclotted and dark red in color. He gave the samples to Petronelli and told him to have the magnesium level checked—marked difference between the ventricles could be a strong indication of sea-water drowning—then went to work with his scalpel. A few deft strokes, and the organ came out in his hands.

The right side of the heart was enlarged and it felt flabby, a fact confirmed by the scale—320 grams. He washed it off and began taking it apart, like a skillful mechanic going through a carburetor. The coronary and pulmonary arteries, ventricles, valves, and aorta all appeared normal, with little sign of atherosclerotic change.

He went on to the gastrointestinal system. The same meringuelike mucus was present in the esophagus, as well as vomitus and bits of algalike material. The stomach and duodenum were distended and contained a considerable quantity of water, but no food, which meant that Duffy had not eaten for at least two hours before he'd gone swimming.

Stomach contents were sometimes helpful in establishing the time of death, but in this case would not be needed. The absence of lividity, the onset of rigor mortis, and the temperature of the body relative to the ocean temperature all indicated that Duffy had not picked this particular morning to alter his aquatic routine. Parker took a sample of the water from the stomach, before proceeding to the small and large intestines, which were unremarkable.

The liver appeared slightly fatty, and acutely congested, as did the spleen, pancreas, kidneys, and gallbladder. Duffy still had his appendix. As Petronelli took fluid samples from those organs, Parker finished up with the central nervous system. With quick precision, he performed the bi-auricular incision, moving the scalpel across the top of the h ad from ear to ear. Several more incisions on each side of the head and the entire face came loose, enabling it to be pulled down across the front of the skull, like an elastic mask. Whatever false face a man presented to the world in life, he confronted nose-to-nose in death.

After inspecting the facial bones carefully for fractures, Parker used an electric vibrating saw to cut a line around the head, just above the earline, then lifted off the top of the skull as if it were a yarmulke. Methodically he severed the membranes and arteries holding the brain in place, then gently pried the entire organ loose with his fingers, working it until it came away in his hands. He sliced the organ—which just last week, with the aid of a few volts of electricity, had made people chuckle coast-to-coast—into sections and inspected it for hemorrhaging or lesions. The organ appeared to be perfectly normal and healthy.

Parker peeled off his surgical gloves and stated for the record: "Barring other findings, it is my preliminary finding that the subject, John Hamilton Duffy, died of asphyxia as a result of accidental drowning. There is no evidence of significant trauma or foul play. Specimens of blood, urine, bile, and stomach and lung contents have been taken for toxicological analysis. Eric C. Parker, Chief Medical Examiner, 1214 hours, April 20, 1987."

Parker turned to Petronelli, who nodded his agreement with the findings.

"Take those samples up to toxicology yourself," Parker told Petronelli. "I want to make sure we maintain the chain of evidence."

"Right."

"And tell them I want preliminary results by thirteen-thirty hours."

Petronelli raised an eyebrow. "Kubuchek isn't going to be thrilled about the rush."

"If Kubuchek gives you an argument, tell him to call me," Parker instructed.

Steenbargen was leaning against the corridor wall, waiting, as Parker emerged from the locker room adjusting the knot in his tie. "How'd it go?"

"Fine," Parker said, smoothing down the lapels of his jacket.

"Anything suspicious?"

He hesitated, pondering those curious abrasions, then shook his head. "Not unless toxicology comes up with something. How about you?"

"Zip. But Kuttner called. That was cocaine in the bag. Half an ounce, high-quality stuff."

Parker had been sure all along that it was going to be cocaine, but still he grimaced. It made the case all the more difficult. "Why don't we let toxicology decide how great it was. Maybe it killed him."

"Sure," Steenbargen said amiably. "But I don't think

so. Kuttner said there was a set of prints on the bag. The only thing—they're not Duffy's."

Parker shot him a look. "Which would indicate Duffy didn't use it?"

Steenbargen smiled and sidestepped the trap. "Not necessarily. Somebody else could have brought the bag in, laid out a few lines for him, then put the bag in the drawer. But I vote for him not having used it. A—it was exactly half an ounce. B—if it was Duffy's bag, if he bought it, then he'd normally be the one to handle it."

"What are you suggesting? That it might have been delivered after he went for a swim? That he never personally took delivery?"

Steenbargen shrugged. "What can I say?—except that his prints aren't on it."

Parker decided that was another good reason not to make public mention of the drug until they had a better idea of what all was involved. "Let's sit on it for a while."

Steenbargen nodded and the two men started walking. They seemed oblivious of the gurneys that clogged the hallway, some carrying loads preprocessed for disassembly, others, examples of the finished product, glassy-eyed, sutured, empty husks. Some of the faces were serenely peaceful; some were grotesquely contorted into expressions of pain and suffering, like the faces of martyred saints in medieval paintings.

"I got in touch with Duffy's widow," Steenbargen said. "She's in your office now."

Parker nodded. He disliked dealing with wives-turned-suddenly-widows. His inability to touch their grief, to ease it, always made him feel uncomfortably helpless, impotent. "How's she taking it?"

"All right," the investigator said. "I guess she and Duffy were separated. She's been living in their Beverly Hills home. The beach house was a rental."

"What about the doctors on those prescriptions?"

"I've gotten hold of three of them. The Quaalude prescription was four years old. The pills were bootlegged. The doctor who originally prescribed them—Kinsey—is a G.P. from Beverly Hills. Last time he saw Duffy was three years ago. He wrote him that one script for methaqualone, but refused to renew it when Duffy came back for more. Says he could tell the guy was a pillhead and was trying to run a game on him.

"The doc who prescribed the Elavil—Somers—is a shrink. He confirmed the prescription, says he was treating Duffy for acute depression. He refused to clarify at first. Invoked the good old doctor-patient privilege. But my persuasive eloquence finally won him over. I'm going over to talk to him now."

By the elevator, a young crew-cut detective from the MAGAT Squad—Mexican Afro Gang Assault Team— was trying to score points with a cute redheaded attendant, and from the fascinated look in her big green eyes and her intermittent giggling, he was succeeding. She stopped self-consciously when she saw Parker, but the cop went on with the story.

"So here I come into the room, my gun drawn," the cop was saying, "and here are these two black guys sitting at a table with hamburgers in front of them, only one of them, this one . . ." He stepped aside and waved at the black male on the gurney beside him. The right eye and part of the skull were missing and the sheets were stained with blood and gray matter. ". . . ain't eating. The other one is calmly eating, and I take one look at the magnum in front of him on the table and my partner and I jump him. The dude is yelling for us to take it easy, and after we get him cuffed and read him his rights, he says sure he knows the dead guy, it's his *brother*, and sure enough, when I look, the guys are identical *twins*. So I ask him the next logical question, why he did it, and he looks at me like I'm a total moron, and says, 'Can't you see? Look at his burger!'"

The redhead glanced at the chief nervously, but Parker just nodded.

"Now I look at the dead guy's burger and I can't see anything wrong, and the dude yells, 'Not the bun, the patty! Look at the patty!' So I pick up the bun and I still don't see anything wrong, and the guy yells, 'It's bigger than mine! He *always* got the big patty! I told him he'd better give me the big patty this time. Well, I showed him. He ain't never gonna get the big patty again!' I said, 'Pal, I don't think you're gonna be getting any patties for a long time, either.'" The cop laughed, then asked, "Can you figure it?"

Parker knew he would never figure it, the "why" part, anyway. Luckily, he didn't have to. For him, murder was usually pretty much what it looked like—death by gunshot, by blunt force, by stabbing or strangulation.

There was usually very little mystery in it. But "why" was another matter.

Life was full of big- and little-patty days, he thought, and that was about as close as anyone was ever going to come to explaining it. Why did two bright, attractive teenage couples climb into the backseat of a car with a six-pack and a hose pumping carbon monoxide, leaving only a note that said: "We couldn't go on"? Why did a straight-A student, a "quiet, well-mannered boy," according to his parents, decide during finals week to take his father's .38 to class and open up on unsuspecting classmates? Why did a mother listen to her baby cry for a year, then suddenly beat him to death with a rolling pin, saying, "I just couldn't take it anymore"? What did that mean, in the final analysis? Couldn't take *what*? The plain fact was that nobody knew why or where he or she would step over that irrevocable line and refuse to accept the little patty.

5

A frailer, red-eyed version of the woman in the photograph at Duffy's was waiting on the couch in Parker's outer office. Steenbargen introduced Parker, and Joan Duffy tried on a smile, but it fell short of her eyes and faded quickly.

She was tiny and pale, to the point of looking anemic, and her black, shoulder-length hair was brushed in that kinky, devil-may-care style that was popular these days. Her eyes were large and gray-green, her mouth was small, and her nose and chin were sharply pointed. She wore a vermilion suit over an ivory blouse and matching vermilion pumps.

Parker ushered her into the office and put her into a chair in front of the desk. "Can I offer you something? Coffee?"

"No, thank you."

Parker went behind his desk and Steenbargen took the

chair next to the window. She had a Kleenex in her hand, which she began twisting.

"I just completed the autopsy on your late husband," Parker began.

She seemed surprised. "Already?"

"Yes."

"You're absolutely sure it's John? There isn't a mistake?"

"We're sure."

"Don't I have to identify his . . . body?"

The all-pervasive influence of television, Parker thought. "That isn't necessary, Mrs. Duffy. We identified him by his fingerprints." He hoped she would not ask to see the body. Or touch it. They did that sometimes, to reassure themselves about the reality of it, like pinching oneself to make sure it wasn't just a bad dream.

"What happened?" she asked. "How did John die?"

"The official cause of death was drowning. *How* is another matter. We understand from his neighbors that your husband was a good swimmer."

"Yes. Very good."

"And that he swam every morning regularly, at six A.M.?"

"He swam before he went to the studio. That was usually around six or six-thirty."

"That's why I'm at a loss to explain why he drowned, Mrs. Duffy. The surf conditions were normal, and I couldn't find anything physically wrong with him. Of course, we won't have the complete picture until we get the toxicology results."

Joan Duffy dabbed at the tears forming in her eyes with

the mangled tissue. Her eyes were her best feature, Parker decided. They were soft and expressive and sadly beautiful. The sadness went back, beyond the events of the morning, however. It took years of conditioning to acquire that look. "We found quite an assortment of prescription drugs at the house, Mrs. Duffy. Along with some Quaaludes and a residue of cocaine."

"John was under a lot of pressure. Pressure from his work, pressure from fame, pressure from himself." She stopped there, as if that explained it.

"What kind of drugs was he into?"

Her gaze avoided Parker's. "I don't know exactly." She paused, then asked anxiously, "Did drugs have something to do with John's death?"

"We won't know until the lab tests are in."

She opened her purse. "Do you mind if I smoke?"

"No, go ahead."

She took out a package of Benson and Hedges Lights and extracted one with trembling fingers, and like a sleight-of-hand artist, Steenbargen materialized a lighter with a gracious flourish. He lit her cigarette, and she took a deep drag, then exhaled.

"Did he use cocaine quite a bit?" Parker asked.

Her tone grew defensive. "No more than anyone else in the business."

"I don't know what that means," Parker said.

"I didn't keep track of what John did," she said acidly. "Whatever he did, he kept away from me. He knew I disapproved of that sort of thing."

Parker toyed with the pen on the desk, spinning it

slowly, until it pointed at the woman. "How long have you been married, Mrs. Duffy?"

"Five years," she said, crossing her thin legs. "But we lived together for two years before that."

Parker judged the woman to be no more than twenty-eight or nine. "You must have been young when you met."

She leaned forward suddenly and mashed out the barely started cigarette in the ceramic ashtray on the arm of the chair and began stroking her brow thoughtfully. "I was a sophomore at the University of Illinois. John was performing with Second City. I went to see him once, and fell in love. He was so wild and crazy on the stage, so out of control. Some friends took me backstage and introduced us, and it was instant chemistry. After five minutes, he asked me out, and three weeks later, I moved into his apartment."

Parker tried to analyze what kind of "instant chemistry" this woman would give off. Whatever had drawn Duffy had not been physical or sexual, obviously—at least that Parker could see. She must have fulfilled deeper emotional and psychological needs in the man. Parker wondered what they were.

Her gaze grew distant, and she said in a tone that sounded bitter, "I gave up my education for John. I gave up everything."

"You two were living apart, I understand."

She nodded. "Yes."

"For how long?"

"Two months."

Parker handed her the notebook they had found at Duffy's. "Is that your husband's handwriting?"

She stared at it for a moment. "Yes."

"Did he usually jot down jokes this way?"

She nodded. "Sometimes. If he heard something he liked and wanted to remember. Why?"

"It's the first page in a fresh notebook," Parker told her. "I thought it might give some insight into his frame of mind that last night."

She was looking at him.

"It's probably nothing," Parker said. "Just another mother-in-law joke: 'Suicide is a belated way of agreeing with your wife's mother.'"

"You're right. It's probably nothing."

Parker took the notebook back. "I'm sorry. I have to ask these questions. Was he depressed—dissatisfied with his work?"

She hesitated. "John felt as if his talents were being wasted on *Life's Tough*. He wanted to do other things. Movies. The stage. Something more challenging."

Parker nodded. "When did you speak with him last?"

"The night before last."

"How did he sound?"

"Upset."

"Did he say about what?"

Her brow grew troubled. She hesitated, then said, "I intended to file for divorce. John tried to talk me out of it. He wanted us to get back together." She folded her arms protectively across her body. "I don't see how my personal affairs have anything to do with your job, Dr. Parker."

Parker offered the woman a palliative smile to soften what he was about to say. "In some cases, Mrs. Duffy, we do what is called a psychological autopsy, to determine the state of mind of the deceased prior to the time of death." He paused. "To eliminate the possibility of suicide."

The woman's back stiffened and the softness left her eyes. "John did *not* commit suicide!"

"Probably not, but considering the evidence, I'm afraid it's a possibility we have to look into."

"Evidence?" Joan Duffy blurted out. "What evidence?"

"The psychiatrist your husband was seeing says he was depressed. Deeply enough to be put on antidepressant medication. There is that note—"

She waved the notebook in the air and slammed it down on Parker's desk. "This means nothing, I told you. And I don't care what he was taking. John did not kill himself!"

"I'm sorry, Mrs. Duffy, but these are questions I have to ask. I realize this must be a rough time for you." The woman's reaction to the suggestion of suicide was strong, but not uncommonly so. With the acceptance of the possibility of suicide often came the acceptance of at least partial responsibility for that final, irrevocable act. Parker kept his voice soft, soothing. "I'm not trying to pry, believe me, and I can assure you that anything you say will be kept in the strictest confidence. May I ask what made you decide to divorce your husband?"

Her mood had somewhat ameliorated, but her tone remained wary. "John had changed. He wasn't the man I married. He used to be kind, considerate. Since he came to this town, he turned cruel."

Parker thought about the blond hair on Duffy's pillow. He didn't want to destroy whatever image she had of her late husband, but he had an unsettled feeling about this case, as if he were going to need all the help on it he could get. And the main source was sitting right across the desk. "Was there another woman?"

Her hand went to her throat. Parker was afraid she might explode, but she just asked, "Why would you ask a question like that?"

"Because there's evidence that a woman was at the beach house last night."

"The sonofabitch," she muttered, looking away quickly. Tears formed in her eyes again. She slumped back in the chair like a boxer whose fancy moves had left him too exhausted to go on. "Stardom can do things to a man. All the attention from adoring fans. Every day, he got letters in the mail, offers from women a lot prettier than I. I like to think that he tried to resist. I'm sure it was hard for him. In spite of the macho front he liked to put up, he was very insecure. He needed reassurance in that way, to feel wanted. For a long time, I pretended I didn't see. As long as it wasn't serious, as long as he came home after work, I didn't say anything. But then he started to stay out all night. And then I got that note. That was the last straw."

"What note?" Parker asked.

She took out another cigarette and Steenbargen repeated his magician's act with the lighter. Her hand trembled violently as he lit it. "It was a heart with an arrow through it. On the heart was written: 'Duffy + Mia.'"

"Mia?"

"Mia Stockton. John's costar on *Life's Tough.*"

"You ever find out who sent the note?"

She shook her head. "It was signed 'A friend.' That's all. I confronted John with it, and he tried to deny the whole thing. He said that he and Mia were just friends, but I knew he was lying. I did some checking and found out he'd been carrying on his little dressing-room romance for over a year. I was devastated. I felt totally betrayed. That was when I told him to move out."

She crossed her arms again, and slouched further down in the chair. She seemed to be shrinking, as if she felt smaller after the admission of her husband's peccadilloes.

Parker jotted down Mia Stockton's name on the pad in front of him and next to it wrote: "The other woman?" "What color hair does this Mia Stockton have?"

"Blond," she added quickly. "But it's dyed."

Parker and Steenbargen exchanged glances. "Who else was close to your husband, Mrs. Duffy? Someone he might have talked to in the past few days."

"Harvey Brock."

"Who's he?"

"John's best friend." Her tone turned coldly hostile. "At least John thought so."

"Obviously you didn't."

"No, I didn't. Whatever drugs John was taking probably came from Harvey. I tried to warn John about him, but he

70

wouldn't listen. Harvey was his good buddy. After all John had done for the guy, he couldn't see that Harvey wanted him to fall on his face."

"Why would he have wanted that?"

She took a drag off her cigarette and leaned forward to tap the ash into the ashtray on the desk. "Jealousy. John made it and Harvey never did. The two of them started out together with Second City. When John got his break on *Life's Tough*, he sent for Harvey. He even created a part-time character for him to play on the show— Kowolski, the mechanic."

"Oh, yeah," Steenbargen chimed in. "The guy with the speech impediment who always looks like he rolled in crankcase oil."

"That's him," Joan Duffy said.

Parker raised an eyebrow at his chief investigator, who shrugged, then went on: "And you say this Brock was your husband's drug connection?"

She nodded. "I caught him slipping John a gram on the set one day. I really chewed him out for it. I told him he was not doing John any favors by giving him drugs, but he knew that already. I told him to stay away from us."

"When was that?"

"About four months ago."

"Where can I find him?"

She took a last pull from her cigarette, then mashed it out. "You can probably reach him at the Comedy Store in Hollywood. I think he's playing there now, in the small room. He's a stand-up comic."

Parker nodded and scribbled it down. "Who else?"

"Sol Grossman, John's agent and business manager. He's been like a father to John for the past six years."

"Anyone else?"

She thought for a moment. "Maybe the producer of the show, Byron Fenady."

Parker tried not to react to the mention of Fenady's name. He took down the numbers she gave him for the two men, and then smiled and stood up. He apologized again for putting her through all of this, and her eyes started to blur once more. "It's funny," she said, sniffling. "Yesterday I was perfectly adjusted to the idea of John being out of my life—it was what I wanted. And now . . ."

Parker took her arm sympathetically and walked her to the door. As he opened it, she asked, "When will you know the results of the lab tests?"

"In a few hours."

"I would like to know."

Parker promised to call her as soon as he found out, and asked, "One more question, Mrs. Duffy. Who did your husband know that drives a red Porsche?"

"Harvey Brock. Why?"

"One of the neighbors saw a red Porsche in the area this morning, that's all." He told Steenbargen to escort the woman outside.

The phone buzzed and Cindy told him Kuttner was on the line. The captain could not keep the elation out of his voice when Parker filled him in on his preliminary findings. "Then there's no way it was *homicide*, right, doc? I mean, even if the guy was so fucked-up he thought the water was air, it was his own fault, right? He wasn't *murdered*."

Parker hesitated, then uttered the magic word that would make the policeman's day: "No."

Kuttner thanked him gratefully, knowing he could now face the cameras and report one more case solved.

Steenbargen came back in as Parker was hanging up. "How about lunch? I'll buy."

"Chasen's or Ma Maison?"

"I think Ma could use the business."

The rarity of the offer itself would have been enough to entice Parker, even if he hadn't been famished, which he was. The chief investigator's reputation for frugality was legendary; it was rumored that he even carried his own silver spoon, which he used to eat off other people's plates, but Parker had never seen it, nor had he asked to. He didn't want to be disappointed to find that the rumor was false.

Ma Maison was the vending-machine room at the end of the hall. The room used to be on the security floor, but had been moved upstairs when the AIDS scare started.

Steenbargen bought two plastic-wrapped tuna sandwiches and two coffees and they took a table next to two green-smocked male attendants who were swapping lascivious predictions about their upcoming dates. From the optimistic tone of the conversation, their fear of the dread disease had been successfully quarantined on the floor below.

"What do you think?" Parker asked, taking a bite of his sandwich.

"About the widow? I feel kind of sorry for her. She

sounds like Duffy gave her a hard time. But I don't know. Something is wrong."

Parker's head came up. Steenbargen's instincts were rarely wrong. The fact was, he felt that way too. He kept seeing those abdominal abrasions in his mind.

"First, she tried to play down Duffy's drug use, then she says she blows up at this Brock character for slipping the guy a gram of coke. If the guy had no big drug problem, why all the panic over a lousy gram? She also came on awfully strong to the suicide suggestion."

"That's not abnormal," Parker said.

"Maybe not. But there could be other reasons why she doesn't like the word 'suicide.'"

"Like insurance."

Steenbargen nodded. "I'd be interested to know if there's a policy somewhere with Duffy's name on it. Especially one with an accident-benefit clause."

Parker smiled. Always the cop, he thought. "Maybe you should check it out."

"Maybe I will. I'd also like to check out what Brock was doing visiting Duffy so early in the morning."

"If it was Brock. There is more than one red Porsche in L.A."

Steenbargen looked at him. "There's more than one blond in Nantucket. But that never stopped us before, did it?"

When Steenbargen left, Cindy buzzed Parker and told him Kubuchek was there, and he told her to send him in. The sleepy-eyed toxicologist entered without a word of greeting and tossed the five pages of his report on Parker's desk. "Alcohol, cocaine, Valium, and amitriptyline," he said as Parker snatched up the report. "The guy liked his drugs. But if you're looking for a reason why Duffy drowned, you're going to have to find it somewhere else. The amounts were not sufficient to cause major problems. I'd say he'd ingested the stuff a minimum of four hours prior to the time he went in the water."

Parker looked over the report. Alcohol, .02 percent. Valium, 0.1 microgram per milliliter. Amitriptyline, 0.05 microgram per milliliter. Kubuchek was right: there was no way Duffy would have experienced a combined pharmacologic effect from those amounts. "I don't see cocaine here."

"No, but I found benzoylecgonine—.01 micrograms per milliliter in the blood, .5 micrograms per milliliter in the liver." Cocaine broke down rapidly in the system, but benzoylecgonine was one of the products of that breakdown. It showed up two hours after the intake of the drug and remained in the blood for up to twelve hours.

Parker flipped through the pages. "What else did you test for?"

"Most of the common drugs and poisons. Because of the time factor, I concentrated on what was found at the house. Plus the major hypnotics, opiates, and barbiturates. *Nada.*"

"What about the water in the stomach and lungs?"

"The same chemical composition as the sample Steenbargen brought in. The particles in the stomach and esophagus are typical ocean algae. Duffy drowned in the ocean, all right."

The question is why, Parker thought.

"When is the press conference?"

"Two. In deference to the six-o'clock news back East. It's a big country and you've got to watch the time difference when you've got a dead star."

Kubuchek didn't wish him luck. Not that Parker expected him to. Relations between the two men had become strained of late, ever since the Delaney incident.

Roger Delaney had been a deputy sheriff who was shot to death in the line of duty. When the autopsy report was made public, revealing that the deputy's blood alcohol had been .15 percent at the time of his death, an outcry of protest had erupted from the sheriff's department and Delaney's relatives, who insisted that the felled officer had been a strict teetotaler. An investigation was called for, but before it could be made, Parker learned that the error was the fault of one of Kubuchek's lab assistants, who had accidentally switched the labels on two samples. Parker, realizing he was going to have to eat crow, had lost control and severely tongue-lashed the chief toxicologist in front of his lab staff. After he had cooled down, Parker realized he'd made a mistake and apologized to the man for embarrassing him publicly. But even though Kubuchek had verbally accepted the apology, he had continued to smart beneath the surface, and since that time their relationship had remained frigidly polite.

"Thanks for getting this done so quickly."

Kubuchek smiled strangely. "No problem."

"I couldn't have been so lucky," Parker murmured to himself as the toxicologist went out the door.

6

Parker was going over the toxicology report and making notes when Steenbargen unexpectedly returned. The investigator flopped on the couch and rubbed his eyes. "I thought I'd accompany you to the conference. Thought you might need the moral support. I even borrowed a pair of pom-poms from the cheerleader daughter of a friend of mine."

Parker smiled. "Thanks. I might need a cheer or two before it's over."

"I hear the tox report is in."

Parker nodded and ran a hand through his hair. He filled him in on Kubuchek's findings, and Steenbargen winced. "What are you going to do?"

"The only thing I can do," Parker answered, shrugging. "Tell it like it is."

"You're sure you want to do that?"

"What else can I do?"

"Maybe you should play down the drug angle," Steenbargen said, testing.

Parker threw up his hands. "How? I can't bury it. If I try to hedge about it, I'll be accused of trying to cover it up. It's right here in the report for whoever wants to dig it out. It's a no-win situation."

"Some people aren't going to like it," Steenbargen said.

"Don't you think I know that? I didn't accept this job to win any popularity contests. Nobody likes medical examiners. Politicians don't like us because dead people don't vote. The families of the deceased see us as ghoulish meddlers who want to mutilate their loved ones. Doctors see us as medical policemen. The police don't like us because we investigate the suspicious deaths of prisoners in their jails. Nursing-home owners don't like us because we expose the fact that their boarders are dying of malnutrition and neglect. It's too often a thankless goddamned job. But I know of only one way to do it."

Steenbargen put his hands behind his head and leaned back, smiling. "I would have been disappointed if you'd said anything else."

Parker had been agonizing over the news conference, wondering how he should handle it. Steenbargen's remark helped put him at ease. "Thanks," he said with a half-smile. "How did things go with Somers?"

"He'd been treating Duffy for depression and drug dependency for four months. The guy was addicted to cocaine and 'ludes. That compounded his depression. When he'd crash, he'd crash hard. The last time Somers saw him—two weeks ago—Duffy was on a real downer. Somers said he rambled on about how he'd made a total mess of his life." He paused significantly. "Said he talked about ending it all."

"Suicide?"

Steenbargen shrugged. "Somers said he doesn't know, that Duffy was not real clear and wouldn't be pinned down. His impression was that Duffy was speaking metaphorically—more in terms of quitting the TV show and going to live in the mountains somewhere than killing himself. He talked about that quite a bit. According to Somers, Duffy was totally burned-out on the show. But he said he wouldn't rule out the possibility that Duffy meant it literally. He said the guy sounded and looked different his last visit. 'Desperate' was the word he used."

"That was two weeks ago?"

The investigator nodded. "He had an appointment last week, but didn't show up for it. Somers thinks the reason was that he'd told Duffy the visit before that he was going to have to go into detox. He arranged to have him checked into Betty Ford, but Duffy never showed. And get this: Somers called Joan Duffy and told her about the seriousness of the situation, that Duffy was coming apart, and they had to get him off the drugs, but she washed her hands of the whole thing. She told him she'd had it, that she wouldn't play nursemaid anymore. She said her nerves were shot, and if Duffy wanted to kill himself, she couldn't stop him."

"No wonder she reacted to the suggestion of suicide."

"Right."

Parker checked his watch and said, "Time to walk the last mile."

"Maybe the governor will call with a reprieve," the investigator said hopefully.

"Wrong movie. This is the one where the executioner straps the guy into the gas-chamber chair and says, 'Count to ten and take a deep breath. It's easier that way.'"

At the elevator, they were joined by Charles Rademacher, the department's public information officer, who asked, "You're sure you don't want me to handle this?"

Parker grinned sardonically. "And disappoint all my fans? Thanks for the offer, but I'll take it. Just bail me out if I give you the signal."

"Sure," Rademacher said.

The first-floor corridor was jammed with reporters and the trio jostled their way through the crowd to the doors of the auditorium, trying to ignore the questions being shouted at them.

The room was packed and the three men had to shove their way through to the dais. Rademacher and Steenbargen took chairs on either side of the lectern. Parker arranged his notes and squinted against the harsh glare of the Minicam lights.

Half-blinded, Parker looked out over the sea of faces, waiting for the room to settle down. After a couple of minutes it did, and he read his prepared statement: "I'm afraid we haven't got much for you. As you know, John Duffy, actor and comedian, died at approximately six this morning while swimming in the surf at Point Dume. On the basis of the autopsy I completed this afternoon, the preliminary conclusion of this department is that Mr. Duffy died of asphyxia, resulting from drowning. The drowning was presumably accidental."

A flurry of questions hit him immediately. He looked at Rademacher, silently asking for help. It would be easier if they would speak one at a time. Rademacher shrugged helplessly.

"What exactly does that mean, 'presumably'?" someone shouted.

"Exactly that," Parker answered. "We are making the presumption, lacking any other suggestion to the contrary. There was no evidence of foul play."

"Do you know *why* he drowned?"

"No. That is under investigation at this time."

"Were drugs involved?"

"I don't know what you mean by 'involved,'" Parker hedged.

"Were drugs found in his bloodstream?"

There was no way around that. "Yes, but not in sufficient quantities to have caused a serious impairment of his ability to swim."

"What kind of drugs?"

"Alcohol, Valium, amitriptyline, and benzoylecgonine, which is a metabolite of cocaine."

The revelation caused a stir. The lights seemed to get brighter. Parker fielded questions about the drugs, translating the amounts into lay terms—drinks, tablets, and grams—and tried to explain that the exact amounts were difficult to assess, as they did not know when Duffy had ingested them.

Over the cacophony of questions, a woman's voice asserted itself. "Is it true that Duffy was despondent over the breakup of his marriage?"

"I wouldn't know," Parker lied.

"If he *was* despondent, might that have some bearing on his death?"

It was the same assertive voice. Parker shielded his eyes and tried to get a glimpse of its owner.

"I'm sorry," Parker told her. "I don't want to deal with conjecture. Does anyone else have a question? If not . . ."

"What was Duffy doing swimming at six in the morning?" the woman demanded. She would have made a good drill sergeant.

"According to the neighbors, he went swimming every morning at six. It was a part of his routine."

"If he swam every morning, isn't it unusual that he would drown for no apparent reason?"

Parker squinted against the lights, trying to find his tormentor. "The key word seems to be 'apparent,' Miss . . . ?"

"Saxby. L.A. *Times.*"

"Saxby," Parker repeated. "Of course there is a reason. People don't drown without a reason. A cramp, say. Or exhaustion. Or a heart attack. We just don't know at this time what the reason was in Mr. Duffy's case."

"Then you're saying it *is* unusual."

"I'm not saying anything of the kind," Parker insisted, not being able to keep the irritation out of his voice. "People drown all the time. Last year, 196 of them in Los Angeles County, to be precise. Many for reasons we have never ascertained."

"Really?" she retorted, her voice full of sarcasm. "And how many of those 196 drowned in the *ocean*, Doctor? *Swimming?*"

Oh, good, Parker thought. She had gotten hold of the biennial report and was using his own ammunition against him. Parker glanced at Rademacher, wondering exactly what he did to earn his paycheck. "Three," he said finally, trying to smile. A murmur spread through the room. "That's all for now, ladies and gentlemen. Thank you."

He stepped away from the lectern and said to Rademacher, "You were a big help."

Rademacher shrugged sheepishly. "I thought you handled it very well."

"Right," Parker said, unhappy with his performance, and then to Steenbargen: "Mike, let's get the hell out of here."

The reporters were not going to be dismissed that easily. They crowded around the dais, cutting off his escape, and continued to shout questions. Steenbargen ran interference, parting a path through the stubborn bodies, while Parker "No-commented" his way to the door. There was more of the same in the hallway, and Steenbargen had to position himself outside the elevator doors to make sure no reporters got on with Parker.

Parker breathed a sigh of relief when the doors slid shut, leaving him alone with only the whirring sound of the elevator and his own reawakened doubts as it took him up to the third floor. Why *had* Duffy drowned? Parker had the strange feeling that when they found the reason, it would be the wrong reason.

7

Parker's first thought when Jonas Silverman came into the office was "cancer." The man must have dropped twenty pounds in the year since Parker had last seen him and his gray suit hung loosely on his bony frame. His face was drawn and haggard and the skin on his cheeks had an unhealthy waxy sheen. "Eric," Silverman said, shoving out his hand.

Silverman's handshake was weak, as was his smile. "You've lost weight," Parker said.

"Sixteen pounds," he said proudly. "I've been on Pritikin for the past six months."

"Heart problem?"

"No. My blood cholesterol was running a little high. I wanted to see if I could bring it down."

"Did you?"

"Twenty milligrams. You should give it a try."

Parker nodded perfunctorily. Eating baked potatoes— dry—was not exactly his idea of enjoying life. He wanted good health, yes, but he also wanted to live life to the fullest, and there had to be a trade-off somewhere.

Parker had known Jonas Silverman since his intern days at USC, when Silverman had had one of the most lucrative cardiovascular surgery practices in Beverly Hills. Then he and a group of respected physicians had bought Westbrook, and Silverman's MBA skills began to supplant in importance his skills with a scalpel.

As the hospital's chief administrator, Silverman had been forced to cut his surgery workload down to a point where nowadays virtually all of his time was spent managing budgets, organizing fund-raisers, recruiting new doctors, and wooing community support. Parker had often thought it was a shameful waste of a man's talents, but Silverman seemed to like his new position, so who was Parker to criticize? Westbrook had a reputation for being one of the best-managed nonprofit hospitals in the city, and a lot of the credit for that had to go to Jonas Silverman.

But lately Parker had been troubled. Over the past year, his office had received several trauma cases which had died en route to County after being rejected by Westbrook's ER staff. Westbrook's administration had cited a lack of bed space as a cause of their refusal to treat, but in every case, the patient had been indigent.

When Parker had been assured by his old friend that the financial status of the cases had had nothing to do with their being turned away, Parker had to assume it was the truth. He could not believe a dedicated healer like Jonas Silverman could ever be responsible for such a policy, and he felt guilty for entertaining suspicious thoughts. Yet . . .

He watched Silverman as he picked a piece of lint from his right knee and turned in his chair to face him obliquely. Silverman draped an arm casually over the back of the chair and linked hands. "I wanted to speak with you in person about the McCullough case, Eric."

"What about it?"

"Do you intend to file Dr. Roberts' report as is?"

"Is there some reason I shouldn't?"

"As a matter of fact, there is." He thought for a moment, then said, "Roberts is a competent man, I assume?"

"Very."

"You've gone through his report?"

"Yes."

"You agree with his conclusions?"

"Yes, I do." Parker picked up the file on the desk and opened it. "The presence of crepitus resulting from the formation of gas in the subcutaneous tissue, the foul smell, dark red exudates, all indicate a massive infection. The tissue at the surgical incision, as well as the underlying subcutaneous tissue, facie, and muscle were edematous and dark red to black. The intimae of the blood vessels were stained with hemoglobin, indicating the patient's hemoglobin was falling rapidly. His urine was tinged with hemoglobin." He looked up. "I don't think there is any question—McCullough died of sepsis."

"The patient evinced no symptoms of sepsis," Silverman argued. "No pus, no fever—"

"He was on immunosuppress," Parker reminded him.

"Obviously, the steroids masked the symptoms. The question is not *if* McCullough died of sepsis, Jonas, but *how* he contracted it."

"Even if your Roberts is right, I don't see any great mystery about it," Silverman said. "We both know that renal-transplant patients are particularly susceptible to infection because of the complications of suppressive therapy."

Parker leaned back. "Microscopic and microbiological examinations of the necrotized tissue showed *Clostridium perfringens*, as well as several *Bacteroides* species. The only place the patient could have picked up those anaerobes would have been from a perforated bowel, which McCullough did not have."

All Silverman could offer to that was a worried frown.

Parker continued: "What I don't understand is how Westbrook's resident pathologist"—he paused to consult the hospital report in the file—"Dr. Yee, missed it and ruled the cause of death to have been kidney failure. The signs of infection were clearly visible."

"The patient had just had a kidney transplant," Silverman protested. "Dr. Yee's assumption was a natural one."

Parker shook his head slowly. "It would've been a good place to start looking. But there would have been clots in the kidney if McCullough had died of kidney failure. Once Yee took a look and found no clotting, he should have looked elsewhere."

"Are you trying to tell me that your people never miss things?" Silverman asked defensively.

"We miss plenty. Too damned much. But we didn't miss on this one."

"That's your opinion."

"That's right, it is."

Silverman twisted around in his chair impatiently and made a face. "Come on, Eric. We both know these things happen . . ."

Parker was becoming annoyed. He pulled the report over to him. "That's right, Jonas, we do both know that. Let's see just what happened in McCullough's case." He began to read: "Barry McCullough, a fifty-six-year-old male, was admitted to Westbrook on April 12 for a kidney transplant. The cadaveric kidney had been transported from L.A. General on 4/13, donated by the family of Juan Gutierrez, the victim of a fatal stabbing on 4/11. A successful kidney transplantation in the patient's right iliac area was performed on 4/14 by Dr. Myron Minkow. After completion of the vascular anastomoses, urinary reconstruction was performed by ureteroneocystostomy. The patient was taken to a private room. By midnight, his blood pressure began to drop and he appeared toxic. Within nine hours, he rapidly slipped into shock and expired." Parker looked into Silverman's eyes. "You tell me what happened, Jonas. And why."

"Who knows?" Silverman said, tossing up his arm like a marionette. "The fact remains that no matter what happened to him, we can't bring him back to life."

Parker stared at him for a good ten seconds before he asked: "Why exactly are you here, Jonas?"

Silverman pursed his lips and shifted uncomfortably in his chair. "I've seen families like the McCulloughs before. They can smell malpractice money. That's why they petitioned for a second autopsy. Roberts' report will be playing right into their hands."

Silverman had been one of the most precise and skillful surgeons Parker had ever had the pleasure to watch. To see what he had become—a politician—saddened Parker. Saving lives had become secondary to saving the hospital's ass. "I didn't get that impression from them, Jonas. They just want to know why their father died. They think there might be a conflict of interest, a Westbrook casualty being autopsied by a Westbrook pathologist. I'm not sure I disagree."

Silverman stiffened indignantly. "Are you suggesting that Yee's autopsy was part of some sort of cover-up?"

"No. All I'm saying is that the McCulloughs didn't strike me as mercenary people."

"You're wrong, Eric," he said firmly. "As soon as they get Roberts' report, they'll be on the phone to some shyster attorney. You can bet on it."

Parker eyed the man steadily. "Are you worried about the outcome?"

"Certainly not," Silverman said casually. "But it would be a hell of a lot simpler to avoid the situation altogether. No matter what the result, the hospital hardly needs the kind of publicity that would be generated by a malpractice suit. Malpractice suits don't get won by defendants. People always think: where there's smoke, there's fire."

Parker felt torn. He really wanted to believe Silverman. His own father, after discharge from the Army, had been charged with surgical malpractice, and it was a careful coroner—and a careful autopsy—that had saved his reputation. That crisis in his father's life, and its resolution, had first made Parker aware of forensic medicine and the good it could accomplish.

"What are you suggesting I do, Jonas? Change Roberts' report?"

Silverman squirmed and said, "There is always margin for error. I'm not disputing Roberts' competence, or even his findings, only his interpretation of those findings." He looked at Parker uncertainly. "You've been under the gun lately, Eric. The word is out that certain people—well-connected people—are out to get you. Westbrook has some friends that could be powerful allies when the showdown comes."

Parker felt his cheeks flush with anger. With great effort he managed to keep his voice even and steady. "Is that a bribe, Jonas?"

"I know better than that," Silverman said, smiling unctuously. "I'm just stating a fact, that's all."

"And all I would have to do to ensure this support would be to back up Yee's findings of kidney failure."

Silverman shrugged. "I can't tell you what to do, Eric. But that would seem to be the simplest solution."

"For you and Westbrook, maybe. Not for me."

"Then you're going to file Roberts' report?"

"Yes."

Silverman frowned. "Have the McCulloughs been notified yet?"

"No."

Silverman bit his lip thoughtfully, then said, "Do me a personal favor? Hold off for a couple of days?"

"My answer will still be the same."

"Just think about it. That's all I ask." Silverman's eyes looked sad, as if he were disappointed by the sound of his own voice. Parker didn't blame him. The doctor went on: "What is it going to hurt? In the meantime, it will give me time to look into this matter and find out where Mc-Cullough picked up gas gangrene."

Parker considered. He had calmed down enough to relent a bit. What could it hurt, after all? "All right."

Silverman's demeanor once again became amiable. "Thanks, Eric. I appreciate it." He stood and held out his hand. The palm was warm and sweaty. "I've always been on your side, Eric. I want you to know that."

"Thanks, Jonas," Parker said, smiling through clenched jaws.

Silverman went out and Parker stared thoughtfully at the closed door, trying to figure out what that conversation had been about. Silverman was worried about more than just bad publicity. A hell of a lot more. And although he didn't know it yet, by offering that poorly masked bribe, he had made sure that Parker would dig into what it was.

He went over to his video console and peered at the screen that monitored the investigator's room.

Four men sat with their feet on desks, chatting or reading magazines. Parker picked up the phone and watched as one of the men on the screen answered. He asked to speak to Jacobi, and the message was relayed to an immensely fat man, who put down the tabloid he was engrossed in and pushed his enormous hulk out of his chair with a grunt. The fat man took the phone and said, "Jacobi here."

"Interesting reading?" Parker asked.

"Yeah," the man said. "There's an amazing story in there about Elvis being seen aboard a UFO."

"How can you read that garbage?"

"Whaddya mean? They couldn't print it if it wasn't true, right?"

"That's one of the qualities I look for in an investigator—hard-nosed skepticism," Parker said. "I just had a visit from Jonas Silverman from Westbrook. He's concerned about Roberts' verdict on the McCullough case. Too concerned. Their pathologist, Yee, determined the cause of death to be kidney failure, but Roberts says sepsis. Silverman wants it to stay kidney failure."

"And you want to know why."

"That's right," Parker said. "Is your cousin—the scrub nurse—still over at Westbrook?"

"Yeah."

"I want you to talk to her. Find out if she knows anything about a kidney-transplant case they lost five days ago. McCullough. If she doesn't know anything, find somebody that does. The guy died of sepsis and I want to know where he got it."

"Right."

"Roberts did the autopsy. Talk to him before you go."

Jacobi nodded. "Right."

"Oh, and, Jacobi . . ."

"Yeah?"

"Find out," he said kiddingly. "Otherwise you might be taking a ride with Elvis."

8

On the way home, Parker, on a whim, drove down to Sunset Strip. He lucked out finding a parking space only two blocks from the Comedy Store, and walked back. Bypassing the line outside, he went in to the ticket counter and, after showing the kid there his badge, was turned over to a burly maître d' who led the way to the dressing room.

The split-level show room was about a quarter full, and even with the line outside, probably wouldn't be filled. In the glittering heyday of Hollywood, this had been Ciro's, the most elegant and chic of the Strip clubs, boasting the finest stage acts and the most glamorous star clientele, but now the dimly lit room was only a faded memory of its former glory. The patrons tonight were for the most part under twenty-five, dressed in jeans and sport shirts, the ceiling was exposed air-conditioning ducts, and the black walls were apptopriately adorned with neon caricatures of long-gone comedic giants—Laurel and Hardy, Ed Wynn, Groucho, W.C. Even the red neon scrollwork flanking either side of the stage looked tacky.

The maître d' took Parker down front to a door by the stage. They went through it and up some stairs to another door. The guide was about to knock when it opened and a tall, attractive, large-boned blond in a gray tweed suit came out. She looked vaguely familiar, but Parker couldn't place her. She obviously placed him, though. As she brushed past, she nodded, smiled, and said, "Doctor."

The guide said, "Harvey, somebody here to see you," and stepped back to let Parker in.

The dingy dressing room was small enough to be cramped by Parker and the two men getting dressed in it. One of the two asked flippantly without looking up, "Another reporter? Tell them I'll talk to them after the show—"

"Not a reporter," Parker said. "Dr. Eric Parker."

Brock looked up now. He was in his late twenties, short, with shaggy brown hair that framed his round, baby-fat face. He had on a pair of red-white-and-blue "Rocky" boxing shorts, and a white T-shirt that showed off every roll of flab on his soft body. "The coroner, right?"

"Right."

"I recognized you from the news. I saw the press conference tonight." Although he hadn't gone on the stage yet, Brock's face was already coated with a glistening layer of perspiration. His pupils were pinpricks and his eyes looked as if they were lighted from within, like a jack-o'-lantern. The man was wired. "What's this about? John?"

"Yes."

Brock nodded as if he figured as much. "That was a real shockeroo. John was the best friend I had in the world."

The man did not look shocked to Parker. Or even sad. Perhaps anticipating his thoughts, Brock added, "I was thinking of canceling tonight, but then I thought no, John would've wanted it this way. The show must go on, right?"

"Why not?"

"I'm going to dedicate my performance tonight to John's memory," the comedian said, smiling strangely.

"That's nice," Parker said, but for some reason he doubted Brock's sincerity. "How long were you friends?"

The other comedian, a young, skinny kid dressed in a plaid sport shirt and jeans, cleared his throat uncomfortably and stood up. "I'll let you two talk alone. Thanks, Harvey."

When he had gone, Brock said, "You mind if I get dressed while we talk? I'm running a little late."

"No, go ahead." Parker watched as Brock took a pair of purple shorts from the suitcase on the floor and pulled them on over the "Rocky" trunks. "I hear you and Duffy went way back. To Second City."

"That's right," he said. "Who told you that?"

"Joan Duffy."

Brock picked up a blue T-shirt with a white bull's-eye on its chest and slipped it on over the "Rocky" shirt. "Yeah?" His eyes grew furtive. "How is she holding up?"

"She seemed all right when I talked to her."

"I'm going to have to call her and offer my condolences." The announcement didn't sound very convincing.

"When did you talk to Duffy last?"

"Last night." Brock put on a long-sleeved white shirt and began buttoning it.

"What time?"

"About one."

"How did he sound?"

Brock thought about it, as if trying to find the right words. "Uptight."

"How so?"

"Just uptight," Brock said, shrugging. "You know."

"I'm afraid I don't."

The comic hesitated. "He was agitated, anxious."

"About what?"

"A lot of things. The show. His kid. His life."

"Is that what you talked about?"

Brock sniffled and wiped a hand across his nose. "Yeah. Why?"

"You didn't talk about anything else?"

Brock's eyes narrowed warily. "Like what?"

Parker shrugged. "Drugs, for instance?"

The comic tried to look surprised, but the expression was patently hollow. "Drugs? Why would we talk about drugs?"

"There were drugs found at Duffy's house," Parker said quietly.

"So what has that to do with me?"

The man was getting defensive, his tone beginning to take on a combative edge. Parker decided to push it. "Didn't you supply Duffy with drugs?"

Brock's shoulders bunched. "Who told you that?" When Parker did not answer immediately, the comic answered himself: "Joan probably."

"Why would she accuse you of such a thing?" Parker asked innocently.

"Because she needs a scapegoat, and I'm it," Brock said derisively. "John had been fucking himself up with dope and broads for a long time. Joan didn't want to blame herself, so she had to blame someone else. Since I was the closest one to him, she blamed me."

"Then she didn't catch you slipping Duffy a gram of cocaine on the set of the show one day?"

Brock smiled a sad smile and shook his head. He took a sport coat out of the suitcase and slipped it on, then picked up a squirt gun and put it in the inside pocket. "John tripped himself out into thinking he needed the stuff to perform. He came to me, begging me to score some for him. Just a gram, he said. I figured what the hell, he's going to go out and get it anyway. It's better for me to get it for him than for him to be out on the street somewhere, looking."

"That was the only time you ever got coke for him?"

"A couple of other times, when he was desperate," Brock admitted grudgingly. "Look, I tried to get the guy to go into detox, but he wouldn't. He kept saying he could handle it. I knew better. The guy would have snorted up Peru if he could have gotten it up his nose. He was out of control. Especially the last two months, since Joan left him. You'd go out with John for the evening and he wouldn't let you get off the train for two days. It was nuts." Brock stood back and waved a hand at his ensemble. "You ever see a dope dealer dress like this? I'm a comic, not a gangster."

Parker had to smile at the image. He was still smiling when he asked: "What were you doing over at Duffy's at six-fifteen this morning?"

That seemed to deflate the confidence Brock had built up. "Huh?"

"You were seen driving into Duffy's driveway." Parker said "you" instead of "your car," not wanting to give the man any leeway for denial.

Brock turned away toward the mirror and pretended to be applying some makeup. It was just a move to buy time, Parker knew. He used that moment to his advantage, picking up an empty ashtray that Brock had been fiddling with nervously. He dropped it into his coat pocket.

"I was worried about the guy," Brock said, finally responding. "I wanted to check up on him and make sure he was okay."

"Was he?"

Brock turned around and looked at Parker squarely. "I don't know. I couldn't find him. When he didn't answer the front door, I went around back. The sliding glass door was open, but he wasn't inside. I figured he was swimming—he always went around that time—but I couldn't spot him from the cliff. So I left."

"What time was that exactly? Do you know?"

"Between six and six-thirty. I don't know exactly." He paused, then said, "The cops haven't asked me about that yet."

"They will, I'm sure," Parker told him. "Where do you live?"

"Hollywood," Brock said uncertainly, obviously wondering why Parker wanted to know that.

"You must have been awfully worried about Duffy to drive all that way at that time of the morning, just to check up on him."

Brock shrugged. "I couldn't sleep. I felt as if John had needed me, and I'd let him down. I was always there for him, like he was for me."

"You weren't worried he might have intended to harm himself in some way?"

Brock seemed surprised by the suggestion. "Harm himself? You mean, like commit suicide?"

"Yes."

"That thought never entered my mind," Brock said with conviction.

"Had you ever heard him bring up the subject?"

"Sure, but not seriously."

"How did he bring it up?"

"You know, like how much easier it would be to deal with everything by ending it all, stuff like that. But he wasn't serious." Brock looked intently at Parker and asked, "Is that what you think—that John committed suicide? At the press conference you said it was an accident."

"We have to look into every possibility."

Brock shook his head, then took a tissue from the box

on the table and dabbed at the beads of perspiration that had accumulated on his face. "If John had wanted to kill himself, he wouldn't have drowned himself. He would have had to go out with a lot more fanfare. In a flaming car wreck or something."

"I understand Duffy created a character for you in his show—"

"I created Kowolski," Brock said touchily. "John sold the idea to Fenady, but I created him, just like I created half of John's routines."

"You mean he stole material from you?"

"Sure. All the time. But I let him. Half the stuff John did with Second City was stuff I wrote." He paused and smirked. "I suppose Joan told you John called me up and offered me the part on his show out of the goodness of his heart?"

Parker nodded.

"I called John," Brock said. He bent down and closed the lid on the suitcase. "I gave him the Kowolski character and told him he *owed* me."

The perspiration was back on Brock's face. A combination of anger and restless energy seemed to be boiling up through his pores—Parker wondered what else.

Brock's explanation of why he had gone to Duffy's house in the morning didn't ring true. If he was really worried about the man, why not go over immediately, when Duffy called him? Also, once he got there, why not wait, make certain everything was okay? Why rush off?

Parker's hand brushed his coat pocket, feeling the ashtray. It might hold the answer.

The dressing-room door opened and an anorexic-looking girl with red-brown hair and sallow, freckled skin entered. She stopped when she saw Parker, and Brock said, "Emily, this is Eric Parker. The coroner. This is Emily Braxton, my girlfriend."

She wore a gold cotton blouse and jeans stuffed into the tops of calf-high black leather boots. Parker took her hand, which was cold and clammy. Her green eyes were rimmed with too much eyeliner and they burned intensely from their sunken sockets, giving the face a skull-like appearance.

"We've been talking about John," Brock told her.

"Bummer," was all she said.

Parker tried to bait Brock: "That must have been frustrating, seeing Duffy's career take off on the basis of your material, while you were still playing small clubs, opening for bigger acts."

The comic's face darkened and he started to say something, then caught himself. He smiled easily and said, "I was nothing but happy for John. We were like brothers. Whatever happened to him, happened to me. His success was my success. Besides, my day is coming."

"That's right," Emily Braxton piped up enthusiastically. "Harvey has an idea for a comedy series that's sure to be a smash. Byron Fenady is going to produce it."

"Congratulations," Parker said.

"Well, actually, it isn't for sure yet," Brock said. "I'm pitching it to him tomorrow—"

"But once he hears the idea, he'll *have* to commit to it," the girl said. "He'd be stupid if he didn't."

Brock threw her a look, cutting her off. "It's unlucky to talk about these things before they happen, Em."

"You *know* he won't be able to resist it," the girl said ebulliently. "It's too good."

Brock smiled at Parker stiffly. "My girlfriend is my biggest fan, in case you hadn't noticed. What we want to do is get a pilot done. We're sure the networks will pick it up on the basis of that." He glanced at his watch and said, "I gotta go on in a second—"

"One more question," Parker said. "Did you know about Duffy's affair with Mia Stockton?"

"I knew they were seeing each other for a while."

"How would you describe the relationship?"

Brock shrugged. "Mia liked John, John liked Mia. They were friends."

Parker felt as if the man were hedging. "That's all?"

"Whatever John had going with Mia, it was his own personal business, and I really don't intend to get into it."

Parker felt Brock was hiding something. The comic's features loosened up and he smiled easily as he walked Parker to the door. "You going to stick around for the show?"

"I hadn't thought about it."

"Why don't you?" Brock suggested expansively. "Be my guest."

Parker decided to spare the time. Watching the man get dressed had aroused his curiosity. "Thanks. I might do that."

The acceptance seemed to please Brock, who signaled a

young stagehand standing in the hallway to find Parker a good table. Parker thanked him again, then asked casually, "What year is your Porsche, by the way?"

"An eighty-one," Brock said proudly.

"I'll bet it's nice," Parker said, feigning envy. "Set you back much?"

"Too much. But in this business, image is important. If they think you're down, they'll keep you down. Know what I mean?"

Parker nodded understandingly. "These gigs must pay pretty well for you to be able to afford a car like that."

Brock seemed to sense where Parker was headed. He smiled, but the smile was as counterfeit as a pair of Korean Levi's. "I got the car on a steal. It was going to be repo'd from a friend of mine. All I had to do was take over the payments." He brushed Parker off with a hurried good-bye and closed the door.

Parker followed the stagehand, who, after a brief consultation with the management, put Parker at a small table in the back of the club, behind a post—a testimonial to Brock's influence.

He ordered a Scotch and water from the waitress, paying for it in cash—he had no intention of accepting drinks from the comic—and then the announcer broke into his thoughts, welcoming patrons to the Comedy Store and entreating them to give a big hand to the first comedian of the evening, Harvey Brock!

Brock ran out onto the stage and was greeted by the enthusiastic applause of the half-empty room. He did his warm-up, telling them what a great audience they were, and then went into a running monologue about his wife, who had allegedly died.

"I had my wife cremated, blended her ashes in with my coke, and sniffed her up. That was the best she made me feel in years."

The reference to drugs brought a chuckle from the crowd.

"I'm a widower, but every once in a while I like to pretend my wife is still around. I sit back in my easy chair with my pipe and lean a vacuum cleaner against the wall and listen to it suck up money."

By the time he got into jokes about his deceased wife being an advocate of animal rights, to the point where his German shepherd had the same rights around the house as Brock had—including in bed—the crowd was going to sleep.

Brock knew he was losing them. His smile had grown strained. A couple of hecklers shouted at him. Brock shouted back: "I'll bet you drive a truck with tires too big for it, right, asshole?"

Brock threw himself into his props with desperation. He squirted the audience with his squirt gun and performed various routines, changing voices as he peeled off layers of clothing, and with each laughless layer, the strip-tease became more and more frantic. When the "Rocky" theme blared through the club's sound system, the comic was down to his last layer. He pranced around the stage like an overweight, sweat-drenched Sylvester Stallone, his arms raised in victory, but his elation was obviously sham.

The defeated look in his eyes belied the smile. The guy had been pummeled.

The music ended, and Brock's expression turned suddenly somber. He stepped up to the microphone and said quietly, "Ladies and gentlemen, I want to dedicate this show to John Duffy, who, I'm sure you've heard, died tragically this morning. The world has lost a great talent. And I've lost my best friend." Brock's voice got suddenly choked-up. "Keep 'em laughing, John. Wherever you are, I know you're playing the Big Room."

It was a cheap trick, a last-ditch effort to pull emotion—any emotion—from the crowd. And it worked. The room burst into boisterous applause as Brock backed away from the microphone, blowing kisses to the audience, and disappeared behind the stage curtains.

There was a lull as the emcee announced the next comic, and Parker, feeling disappointed, stood up to leave, almost bumping into the tall blond who had greeted him outside Brock's dressing room.

"Hello again," the woman said, smiling, as Parker excused himself. When it was apparent he still didn't recognize her, she said, "Alexis Saxby. The *Times.*"

That was where he had heard that voice. Parker looked around for an exit, but the woman was blocking his path. He had no doubts that it was intentional. He smiled diplomatically. "You didn't take enough out of my hide this afternoon, Ms. Saxby?"

The woman laughed. "I'm not hounding you, Doctor. Truly. I'm here for the same reason you are."

"Which is?"

"To interview Harvey Brock," she said. "What did you think of his act?"

"No comment."

She nodded in agreement. "Now I know why he called me. He can use any publicity edge he can get."

"Brock called you?"

"This afternoon. He wanted to know if I wanted an in-depth interview on Duffy."

Oh, Parker thought. Brock did not want to discuss any personal aspects of his dead friend's life. Not unless there was something in it for him.

"Did he tell you anything interesting?" Alexis Saxby asked.

"Nothing that would change what I said at the press conference, if that's what you mean."

"Nothing about the possibility of murder?"

The question startled Parker. "Murder? No. Why would you ask that?"

"The entertainment editor at the paper tells me Duffy was not a very well-liked man. Apparently he was a sonofabitch to work for. Extremely temperamental."

"That hardly constitutes a motive for murder—"

"He was also into cocaine. I mean *heavily*." She paused and locked stares with him. "You hedged around the dope angle at the press conference—"

"I tried to."

"—but Duffy's drug binges were common knowledge around the show-business community."

"The fact remains, drugs were not a factor in Duffy's death," Parker said. "If you'll excuse me . . ."

The woman made no move to get out of his way. Parker was trapped. He could see the headlines tomorrow if he tried to physically move her: "CORONER ASSAULTS FEMALE REPORTER."

"You haven't answered my question," she said.

"I didn't realize you'd asked one."

"Is it possible Duffy was murdered?"

"Just what are you trying to do, Ms. Saxby?" Parker asked, exasperated. "I realize you have a job to do, but what is the point of all this? To dream up another lurid scenario to sell more papers?"

"I'd like to think my motives are not that crass," she said, sounding hurt. "I'm just doing a job, like you. All I'm asking is if it's possible John Duffy was murdered."

"And I'm asking why you're asking. Do you have some information I don't?"

"I don't know what information you have."

They could go on like this all night, Parker thought.

"Off the record," the reporter said.

"Anything is possible," Parker told her. "In this case, however, it is extremely unlikely."

"Can I take that as a yes?"

Parker looked at his watch. "I have another appointment, Ms. Saxby. If you'll excuse me . . ."

She looked around, and stepped back apologetically. "I'm sorry. I didn't realize I was in your way."

I'll bet, Parker thought as he made for the exit.

9

Boomer, Ricky's birthday surprise, set up a howl as soon as Parker pulled into the driveway. What do the neighbors think? Parker wondered, wincing. For some reason, Boomer didn't sound like a dog, and certainly not like a puppy. He sounded . . . unearthly. The neighbors could be excused if they thought some weird experiments were going on in their medical examiner's modest redwood house. The wailings hinted of *The Island of Dr. Moreau*.

Parker gathered up the bag of groceries he had purchased at the Hollywood Ranch Market after leaving the Comedy Store. He didn't know his neighbors very well—he left for work early and usually came home late—and he imagined that they perhaps viewed him with some apprehension. His line of work didn't help. He'd noticed that they'd warmed up quicker to that new fellow across the street—what was his name, Gianella?

Gianella sold ice-cream treats from a rainbow-colored truck.

Parker let himself in, then moved around the easel standing in the middle of the living room on which was his current work-in-progress—a pastoral landscape—and deposited the bags in the kitchen. That made the golden Lab howl even louder.

Parker opened the door of the guest bedroom and was immediately set upon by the animal, who proceeded to slaver all over his slacks. Parker petted the dog, then inspected the newspapers on the bathroom floor. They were, of course, unsoiled. He found what he was looking for on the bedroom floor by the bed. Twice. Luckily, the floor was wood. It was only until Saturday, he reminded himself as he cleaned up the dog's messes. After that, it was Rick's problem.

A quick walk down the hill confirmed Boomer's total indifference to trees, shrubs, hydrants, and other usual canine turn-ons, and Parker's incipient thought that he was definitely a cat-person. He and Boomer returned to find Pat Clemens lounging on the front steps in a red Fila jogging suit.

It was an effort for Parker not to laugh at the sight. He hadn't realized they made designer clothes in "Big Man" sizes. Clemens cut a John Candy figure and his new Fila investment made him look like a red blimp. The appearance, the rotund attorney claimed, worked to his advantage in court, where many an adversary was surprised to find himself confronting a sleek, heavily armed F-14.

Clemens had handled Parker's divorce for him six years

before, and since then, had become one of Parker's closest friends. Three months ago, after resolving to get his corporal image more in tune with his courtroom image, the rotund attorney had vowed to shed forty pounds, and to help him along, Parker had agreed to run with him four nights a week. Since the inception of the program, Clemens claimed to have dropped twelve pounds, although you couldn't tell by Parker. The attorney looked the same to him, and as long as Parker was in the room, the man would not step on a scale. Parker had the feeling that the only way he would find out for sure whether Clemens was telling the truth would be to serve him with a writ of discovery.

"I forgot to call—" Parker started to apologize.

"That's okay," Clemens said, pretending to be bowled over by Boomer. "I realize you were probably busy. I saw you on the six-o'clock news. I only stopped to rest a minute."

Parker looked around. "Where's your car?"

"Up the hill." He exchanged wet kisses with the dog and pushed it away. "I was making the grand circle."

Parker laughed. In three months, he had never known Clemens to complete one of his so-called "grand circles." He usually finished only half—the downhill half—which was why, Parker suspected, he always insisted on running around Parker's neighborhood. Parker, always left to finish the uphill portion alone, was rapidly becoming a hill runner. "Does that suit make you run faster?"

"When you *look* good, you *feel* good," Clemens grunted as he pushed himself to his feet.

113

"Next, you'll be showing up with a sweatband on."

Clemens dug into the pocket of his jogging pants and came up with a yellow sweatband. Parker laughed again. "You have to work up a sweat first."

The attorney nodded, then glanced worriedly up the hill. "How about giving me a lift to the car later?"

"Sure."

Clemens pointed at the dog, who was still running around the big man in half-crazed glee. "He go?"

"No."

"Maybe he's anal-retentive."

"Not if you saw the guest bedroom."

"Maybe he has agoraphobia."

"Spoken like a true attorney. What are you working for, a plea of diminished capacity?"

"Don't worry," Clemens told Boomer. "I'll get you off yet."

They went into the house. Parker had bought the tiny two-bedroom house shortly after his divorce, and according to his calculations, he would still be paying for it well into the twenty-first century, should he make it that far. It hadn't mattered that it had been overpriced or that its grip on the side of the hill overlooking Hollywood was tenuous at best. He had bought it for the view.

The entire back of the house was glass, and through it the lights of the city pulsed and shimmered in a myriad of intensities and colors. But there was a contradiction. While the windows caught and brought indoors the immensity of the city, the house itself was so small that there often seemed to be barely enough room to move. A contributing factor, of course, was the constant state of clutter in which Parker kept the place. Every available surface was covered with medical texts, technical journals, and research papers.

Without waiting for an invitation, Clemens went to the refrigerator and helped himself to a twenty-five-ounce can of Foster's. Parker got down the Cutty and made himself a stiff one, and the two of them took their drinks into the living room.

"How is that Duffy thing, anyway?" Clemens asked after a moment.

"Over, I hope."

The attorney looked around in disgust. "You need a maid. No, I take it back. You need two maids."

Parker made a quick check of his telephone messages. The Police Benevolent League (wanting a donation). The Regents Fund (also wanting a donation). The L.A. *Times* (wanting a subscription). Ricky.

Parker wished that he had initiated the call to Ricky. The boy was always on his mind, but it was as a kind of sweet memory, a happy time now past, rather than as an immediate presence. The terms of the custody agreement dictated that.

Parker started dialing and yelled to Clemens: "Keep the dog quiet, huh? I'm calling Ricky."

Clemens leashed the puppy and took it out on the front step.

"Hi!" As always, Ricky's voice carried an enthusiasm only a twelve-year-old boy could muster, still a child but with the sure knowledge, brought by surging changes, that he'd soon be a man. This always left Parker just a little saddened. The fact of his own mortality as well as the boy's loss of innocence. "You finally got home, huh?"

"Yeah."

"So how's it going?"

"Great. You?"

"Okay."

"School?"

"Ehhh."

"A typical day in the life of Rick Parker," Parker said, laughing. "'Okay' and 'ehhh.' Listen, you all set for Saturday?"

"That's why I called. To make sure *you're* set."

"I'll be there," Parker said. He paused, wanting to say something more, to hint at the surprise, but restrained himself. The boy was very quick to pick up on things. Show him a hat and he saw a rabbit.

"Mom's going away with Matt this weekend," he said.

"I know," Parker said. "She told me." He hesitated, then asked: "How do you get along with him?"

"He's a pretty good guy. He's better-looking than you."

That was not the answer Parker had been waiting for.

"Haven't you learned anything? Nobody is supposed to be better-looking or stronger than your old man."

"Sorry. He's better-looking than Mom. And rich. He's promised to buy me my own city."

"I don't want to hear about the rich part."

"I'm kidding. It's just a baseball team. Is she going to marry him?"

"You're going to have to ask your mom that."

"I have to go, Dad," Ricky said. "Timmy's here."

"I'll see you Saturday. I love you."

"Love you too. 'Bye."

Parker hung up and shouted to Clemens: "Okay!"

"You look depressed," Clemens said immediately, coming back in. "Something happen?"

"Eve has a new boyfriend. He's richer and better-looking than I am."

"So keep your fingers crossed. This could save you two hundred a month spousal support."

Parker took his drink to the window and surveyed the glittering slice-of-pie view of Hollywood.

"Who is he?"

"Her boss."

"Tacky," Clemens said, shaking his head. "You worried about Ricky liking him too much?"

"Maybe."

"Don't. In-house romances never work out. Too bad. You know what you need?" Clemens asked rhetorically. "A woman."

"To have and to hold?"

"Why not?"

Parker shrugged. "You should know. You deal with the shredded remnants every day."

"I'm serious," Clemens said, regarding the half-finished oil halfheartedly. "You're lonely. This is no life for a man."

"I have my work—"

"That's all you have. What kind of life is that?"

"My life," Parker told him firmly.

"You need a woman's steadying hand."

"I tried that. Remember?"

Clemens threw up his arms. Parker expected the beer to slosh out of the Foster's can onto the floor, but apparently there was none left to slosh. "Just because it didn't work out the first time, that doesn't mean it won't the second. Or the third."

Parker had heard all this before. Actually, he had seen pictures of Clemens' ex-wives. Oddly enough, they were all strikingly beautiful. "The eternal optimist."

"Damn straight," Clemens exclaimed. "And as soon as I get some of this weight off, I'm going for four."

"Another Foster's?"

Clemens slapped his inflated midsection and said, "I do believe I might."

10

Parker couldn't sleep. The strange abrasions on Duffy's body kept surfacing in his mind. He couldn't explain them—and that made them a mystery that had to be solved.

Maybe he should go down to the beach, look around more carefully, try to find a witness, he thought. Perhaps someone saw Duffy setting out on his swim.

Parker smiled to himself. Here he was, usurping the police function, but what the hell, no harm done. It would just be . . . a little fishing expedition. You could never tell. It was better than staring at the ceiling.

At six-fourteen Parker was driving down the Coast Highway, through a gray fog that misted on the windshield, when he saw the Point Dume cutoff loom up through the metronome-beating of the wipers. Point

Dume. At least it was phonetically correct, he thought as he turned on his blinker.

The narrow ribbon of road wound through a thick stand of tall eucalyptus, through hillsides of tiny yellow flowers and big rambling houses with tennis courts, until it dead-ended at the street fronting the beach. Parker turned right. The yellow crime-scene tape was still across the front of Duffy's driveway as he cruised by slowly. Half a mile up, the houses ended, and fifty yards beyond that, so did the street where it connected with a short, unfinished length of road running up from the beach into an undeveloped cul-de-sac. There was a bent, rusted street sign. Nautilus.

Parker pulled over and killed his engine and stepped out into the soupy fog. He stood on the mud cliff overlooking the beach. Beyond the breaker-line, in the slate-colored sea, half a dozen diehard, wetsuited surfers sat on boards and waited for a decent wave. From the look of things, they would be waiting a long time. The ocean was gray and flat, the surf listless.

A narrow dirt footpath led precariously down the face of the cliff and Parker went down it carefully. As he got down to the sand, a bleached-blond surfer wearing a sleeveless wetsuit top was emerging from the waves, carrying his board. "Pardon me . . ." Parker called to him, and started over.

The boy stopped, his eyes narrowing suspiciously. He was in his early twenties. His arms were tanned and very muscular.

"Waves aren't very good today," Parker remarked, making an attempt at casual conversation.

The boy shrugged indifferently, but said nothing.

"You come here often?"

"Every day I can," the boy said.

Parker looked around. On his left, the beach ended in a high rocky promontory that jutted out into the sea, blocking out any view of the horseshoe cove overlooked by Duffy's house.

"Were you here yesterday?"

The surfer gave it some thought. "Yesterday? Monday. Yeah. Why?"

Parker took out his wallet and showed the kid his badge. "I'd like to ask you some questions. I'm with the coroner's office."

"Coroner?" The boy's blue eyes widened a bit.

Parker nodded. "What time do you usually get here?"

"Around six. I try to get in a couple of hours before I go to work."

Parker put away his identification. "Where do you work?"

"Over at the Sand Castle. I'm a waiter."

"What's your name?"

"Steve Patton."

Parker smiled, trying to take some of the wariness out of the boy's eyes. "You ever see any scuba divers in this area, Steve?"

"Once in a while."

"How about yesterday?"

The kid searched his memory, and his head bobbed affirmatively. "As a matter of fact, yeah. At least I think it was yesterday. Or a couple of days ago, maybe."

"Where was the diver?" Parker asked.

"Right here. He came out of the water and went up there." He motioned to the cliff face Parker had just come down.

"Did you get a look at the person?"

"No, man. I was busy. Besides, I don't think the dude even took off his hood or mask. Just his fins and tank. I remember, because the guy was having a little trouble getting up the trail and I thought, 'That's stupid. The guy might have an easier time of it if he could see.'"

"If the diver didn't remove his hood and mask, how do you know it was a man?"

"I don't know," Patton said, shrugging. "It was just the impression I got. If it was a woman, it was a big woman."

"How big?"

"Over six feet."

"What did the diver do when he got to the top? Was there a car parked up there?"

"I don't know. We don't park up there. Anyway, like I say, I was busy." The surfer squinted. "What is this about, anyway?"

"We're investigating a drowning that happened down the beach."

"You mean that Duffy dude?"

"Uh-huh."

The young man's face screwed up. "That scuba diver had something to do with that?"

"Not that I know of," Parker replied vaguely. He took down Patton's address and phone number and hiked back up the cliff.

When he reached the top, the bent street sign was the first thing to catch his eye. The foot of Nautilus.

The spiral shell with its pearly interior had numerous chambers. Like this case, Parker mused. He had a queer feeling about the diver. When his investigation was complete—when he had made his way through all the complex chambers—would the solution lie back here at the foot of Nautilus?

Some men are greeted at work by the smell of fresh-perked coffee. Parker's welcome at eight in the morning was the pungent stench of burned flesh and hair. It was like running into a wall with your face.

From the looks of things, he'd have to pitch in and help, Parker decided. He called to a young investigator, Madden, who was hurrying for the elevator, a hand over his nose and mouth.

"Take this to the police science lab," Parker instructed, giving him the ashtray he had picked up in Harvey Brock's dressing room. It was encased in a plastic bag within a sealed manila envelope. "Careful with it. Tell them it's got to do with the Duffy case. I want to know if the prints on this—it's an ashtray—match the prints from the bag of cocaine found in Duffy's bedroom. Got that?"

Madden removed his hand just enough to mumble, "Got it, Chief," and then grabbed the envelope and rushed away.

The hallway of the security floor was a logjam of gurneys, their cargo covered with plastic sheets. Parker pulled back the corner of one. The charred, twisted thing bore little resemblance to anything human.

Maurie Abramson, Parker's chief of forensic medicine, came out of the door of the main storage room and Parker asked him, "What do we have here?"

"Flophouse fire," Abramson said. The man's voice had always reminded Parker of a violin string that was keyed too tight; right now, it sounded tighter than usual. "Started about three this morning. Typical Main Street firetrap. The whole place went up. Nine dead so far, but the count is supposed to go higher than that."

Parker frowned. "Arson?"

"They don't know yet." Abramson waved a small pale hand at the hallway and whined, "What am I supposed to do here? We're out of space, we're out of men. The situation is ridiculous."

"I agree," was all Parker could say.

"Something has to be done," the paunchy, bespectacled doctor said.

Abramson was extremely capable, but high-strung, and Parker had had to talk him down from the edge of hysteria more than once. Parker peered into the huge refrigerated storeroom, where an attendant was skillfully maneuvering a forklift to hoist a fiberglass tray containing a plastic-bagged corpse onto a shelf. Loaded trays were stacked five high, from the floor to the ceiling, a veritable warehouse of the dead.

"How many John Does do we have?" Parker asked.

"Thirty-two," Abramson said.

"Have them packed and put on hold."

"Body packing" was a procedure in which bodies were doused with a strong formalin solution, then covered with a gravellike hardening compound, preserving them until they could be gotten to. "I'll give you a hand with the fire victims."

By ten-thirty Parker had completed two autopsies, both victims of smoke inhalation, and most of the gurneys had been cleared out of the hallway. He showered, trying to scrub off as much of the smell that clung to him as he could, but a residue remained in his nostrils when he walked into his office.

"You're a very popular man this morning," Cindy told him, handing him a thick stack of messages. He started to look through them, when he caught her signal behind him with her eyes, and Parker turned to see a tall, well-dressed middle-aged man standing there.

"Dr. Parker," the man began, "my name is Ashcroft. My son was murdered two weeks ago in Westwood. Benjamin Ashcroft."

"I remember the case," Parker said. A nineteen-year-old art student at UCLA, the boy had been shot and killed for no apparent reason while walking to his car after a night class. Parker had issued the death certificate, and to his knowledge, the body had been released for burial last week. "What can I do for you, Mr. Ashcroft?"

"I would like my son's possessions."

"Haven't they been released?" Parker asked, confused. Ashcroft shook his head. "There seems to be some foul-up. Your people downstairs say there is some sort of 'hold' on them pending an investigation." The man's voice was choked off and tears formed in his eyes. "There was a St. Christopher medal. It was a gift on his fourteenth birthday. My wife and I—" Sorrow choked off the man's words again.

Parker led the man sympathetically over to a chair and told him to sit down, then picked up Cindy's phone. He might not be able to do anything about the manpower shortage, but he could sure as hell do something about this. If he could not ease the man's burden, at least he did not have to be responsible for adding to it.

He called down to the investigations division and it took about four minutes to determine that the "hold" order was the result of an error of omission—the LAPD investigator on the case had failed to sign the release order—and get the problem corrected.

Parker apologized to the grieving father for the mix-up and walked him to the door, feeling an upwelling of empathy for the man. He tried to imagine how he would feel if his own son, Ricky, were felled by some senseless sniper's bullet, how he would cope.

On the bad days, confronting the seemingly ever-spiraling madness, Parker often pondered whether, given it to do over again, he would choose to bring an innocent child into this world. Then he would see Ricky's smile in his mind's eye, and any doubts would instantly melt away. That smile enabled him to get through the horror, one of the few things that made any sense amid all the lunacy.

Cindy could hardly wait for Parker to close the outer door before asking, "Is it true?"

"Is what true?"

"About Duffy. Was he really murdered?"

Parker was jarred by the question. "What are you talking about? Where did you hear that?"

She picked up a copy of the *Times* from her desk and handed it to him. As he unfolded it, the front-page headline jumped out at him: "CORONER SAYS MURDER A POSSIBILITY IN STAR'S DEATH." A knot instantly formed in his stomach.

"Well?" she asked expectantly.

"No."

"You didn't say that?"

"I told the reporter that murder was highly unlikely," Parker said weakly.

"The article doesn't sound like that's what you said," Cindy pointed out.

"No. I didn't think it would."

He took the paper and his messages into his office and sat down at his desk to read. He had to hand it to Alexis Saxby—she did an impressive high-wire act, walking between fact and fiction with the consummate skill that only a master of innuendo could exhibit. She had used his "off-the-record" admission with excerpts from the press conference and quotes from "anonymous sources close to the deceased star" about Duffy's heavy use of cocaine and other recreational drugs to make it sound as if some conspiratorial cover-up were taking place and that the circumstances of the star's death were in fact much more suspicious than were being made public. Even Parker's "no comments" had been artfully put in a context that made them sound nefarious. Brock's PR coup was limited to a quote denying allegations about Duffy's drug use, labeling such accusations "cheap shots born out of personal malice." He had obviously not been one of Saxby's "anonymous sources." Parker wondered who they were.

Parker put down the paper, thinking that he should have gone with his first instincts; the "ASSAULT" headline could not have been any worse for him than this. He considered calling up the woman and telling her what he thought of her, but nixed that idea. She would just twist that around to make it sound as if he were trying to keep the truth from coming out.

He felt queasy as he glanced at his messages. Mayor Fiore. State Assemblyman Smrek. Kuttner. Joan Duffy. Two dozen reporters. They would all want to know about the story. More significant than who had called was who had not—Tartunian. After their conversation yesterday, Parker would have expected at least his call by now, threatening castration. Something was up. Parker felt like a soldier during that tense silence after a firefight, out of ammunition and waiting for the big assault.

The phone flashed and Cindy buzzed him that the mayor was on the line.

"Eric," Frank Fiore said gruffly, "what in the hell is going on over there?"

"With what?" Parker replied, trying to act innocent.

"You know goddamned well with what. The Duffy case.

My phone hasn't stopped ringing all morning. State senators, television executives, producers, everybody wants to know what's going on."

"I told everybody what was going on at the press conference yesterday—"

"Then what's this story in the *Times*?"

"A misquote."

"You didn't say it?"

"Not exactly."

"What do you mean, 'not exactly'?"

"The reporter asked me if murder was a possibility. I said yes, but a remote one. Besides, it was supposed to be off the record."

"That helps," Fiore scoffed. "You can tell everybody not to pay any attention to the story, that it was supposed to be off the record. You already look like enough of a *schmuck*, Eric. At the press conference you say it was an accident. Bad enough you bring up that dope business, but at least it's an accident. Then you say it's murder—"

"I never said it was murder," Parker cut in.

"Whatever you said, you're going to have to make a statement to the press denying the *Times* story," Fiore said irritably. "This thing has to be defused. I hear Ed Sarandon, the president of SAG, is planning to issue a statement calling for your removal."

"He's done that before," Parker remarked. "He's a close friend of Tartunian's. As far as a statement goes, I plan to make one this morning."

Fiore grunted. "Have you issued a death certificate yet?"

"No."

129

"Why not?"

"I haven't completed the psychological autopsy."

"Psychological autopsy!" Fiore bellowed. "Why in the hell are you bothering with that?"

"Duffy made a reference to suicide in some one-liner jokes we found at his bedside. He was suffering from acute depression. It's remotely possible he committed suicide—"

"Remotely possible! If *that* hits the papers, you're finished, Eric. Why do you insist on complicating things?"

"I don't," Parker said defensively. "I'm just trying to get at the truth."

"You want the truth?" the mayor snapped impatiently. "I'll tell you the truth. The truth is that the best thing you can possibly do—for yourself and your department—is to clean this thing up as quickly as you can, in the simplest possible way. Forget about any bullshit psychological autopsy. Right now, you have a nice clean accident. Why muck it up? Why do you want to make people unhappy?"

"I want to do my job," Parker said. "What I haven't mentioned yet is that we found half an ounce of cocaine in Duffy's bedside table, as well as half a dozen other drugs. What I haven't mentioned yet is that Duffy's fingerprints were *not* on the bag, indicating that it was put there *after* he went for his swim."

"What does that mean?"

"I don't know what it means," Parker admitted. "I just know that it's another complication. We haven't got—as you would put it—a nice clean accident. We've got a lot of unanswered questions, which I don't intend to bury."

The bluster left Fiore's voice and he said with concern, "You know what I think of you, Eric, as a person and a professional. I think I've proven that more than once. But this time, things are out of my hands. I can't help you. All I can do is give you my advice. Clean it up. Now. And in the meantime, stay unavailable for comment. There are people around who have been waiting for this opportunity. Anything you say, they're going to use against you."

"I appreciate that, Frank. Thanks."

Parker hung up, deeply troubled by Fiore's remarks. Although Parker worked for the county and not the city, Fiore had always been one of Parker's strongest supporters, as well as a personal friend. During his first year as coroner, when he had come under fire from several powerful black civil-rights groups for backing up the LAPD version of the shooting of an unarmed black youth who had been on PCP, the mayor, an outspoken civil-rights liberal, had vociferously rallied to Parker's defense. And despite being heavily backed by the show-business community in his last two campaigns, Fiore had been a staunch supporter for Parker during the DeWitt affair. The fact that he seemed to be disengaging himself now, Parker did not take lightly.

He immediately called Rademacher and instructed him to issue a statement to the press denying the Saxby story, then called Joan Duffy.

"Is it true what the papers said about John being murdered?" she asked in a distressed voice.

"No," Parker told her. "That story was inaccurate, as well as a complete surprise. I'm issuing a statement to that effect this morning. A death certificate will be issued stating the cause of death to have been 'Drowning, presumably accidental.'"

"Presumably?" she asked sharply. "They'll just use that

to make it sound as if there is some doubt. With your help, that vicious reporter already made it sound as if John was some terrible dope addict."

"I can't control the press, Mrs. Duffy—"

"But you can control the statements you make," she said, the bitterness thick in her voice. "You didn't have to say all that about drugs."

"I only stated the facts—"

"You said yourself that drugs played no part in John's death," she interrupted. "So why did you have to bring up the subject at all? What purpose did it serve except to slander John's memory for the glorification of your own ego?"

The woman was becoming overwrought; her voice quivered with emotion. Parker tried to calm her. "That was not my intention, I assure you, Mrs. Duffy. I didn't bring up the matter of drugs. The reporters did. I'm sorry for any misunderstandings that have arisen from any statements I've made."

There was a silent pause; then she said in a cool tone, "John's father called me last night. He wants John buried in Chicago, and I've consented. It's what John would have wanted. This place ruined him. Scribner's Mortuary will be handling the details."

"I'll order the body released to their care," Parker assured her, and managed to disengage himself after muttering a few more clumsy platitudes.

Parker called downstairs and was completing arrangements for the release of Duffy's body when Kuttner called. After the captain's fears that he had a case to solve had been put to rest, he turned his attention to the death certificate.

He was not sure why—maybe it was just because his ego was bruised or because he felt as if he were knuckling under to pressure—but Parker was nagged by doubts as he signed the document. He kept telling himself that Frank Fiore was right, that he had to do it, for the good of the department, not just himself, but he still didn't like it.

He started going through the business on his desk. Requests for six new binocular microscopes for histology. A request by dental team for a new X-ray unit. A reminder from Kubuchek that one of the gas chromatography machines was down and needed repair . . .

It never stopped, Parker thought. Always something. He was tempted to push the papers aside in frustration, but then he remembered that a day lost on his desk could translate into a week up the line. He reviewed the requests, approving them all, scribbled a brief covering memo to the CAO, and handed the batch to Cindy. With a furor raging over Duffy's death, it would be even more difficult to get budgetary requests approved, but he couldn't back off, give up. He had to keep pushing.

"Did Brewster ever get back to me?" he asked.

Cindy shook her head.

"Let's try again," Parker suggested. He stood waiting while she dialed the CAO's office and got shunted around, finally ending up with an aide, Cortez.

"Joe, this is Dr. Parker. I keep sending budgetary requests over there and nothing happens. I keep calling your boss and he won't return my calls."

Cortez's reply was like a recording. "He's not here."

"Put him on anyway."

"Honest, he's not in," Cortez said, more friendly. "The best I can do—tell him you called."

"How about the funds I need?"

"The best I can do—ask him."

"And get an answer when?"

"I don't know."

"Jesus Christ, Joe," Parker cried. "You ever heard of a guy up to his ass in alligators? I'm up to my ass in corpses. I don't know where to put them anymore. I've got to have more people, more equipment. *More money*, understand?"

"I'll tell him."

"Thanks, Joe. And while you're telling him, tell him we're running a health risk here. Tell him that if he wants to be responsible for an outbreak of plague in this city, that's his business, but I don't think it will do his political career any good once the fact gets out to the public."

"Plague?"

"As in 'bubonic.'"

"Jesus," the aide gasped. "There's really a chance that could happen?"

"'Brewster's plague.' Has a catchy ring to it."

"I'll tell him," Cortez said hastily, and hung up.

It was all garbage, of course, but if Brewster couldn't take a little joke . . .

The office walls seemed to be closing in on him and he felt as if he had to get out. He told Cindy he would be in the library and took the elevator down to the second floor.

The library was empty. Parker closed the door and stood in the middle of the room, soaking up the silence. Around the Center, this room was jokingly referred to as the

Chamber of Horrors, for the reason that besides reference books, it contained exhibits from some challenging forensics cases that Parker and his staff had solved.

There was the knife and Wood's metal from the Dodson case that had launched Parker's career. There was the skull of Rupert the Doberman pinscher, its canines embedded in a reconstruction of the head of the Jackson baby. The dog, disturbed by the child's crying, had picked up the infant by the head and carried it to its mother, accidentally killing it by puncturing the skull. The mother had been arrested for murder, but matching the puncture marks to the Doberman's canines, Parker had proven the woman innocent and saved her life. There were the vise grips that Volker had used to torture the little six-year-old Amy Bender before brutally raping and strangling her.

Crimes against children particularly incensed Parker. Over all the years of witnessing man's barbaric cruelty, crimes against children were something to which Parker had never become desensitized. There was something so inherently evil in that assault on innocence that he could never come to terms with it. The Volker case had been a particularly emotional one, and after doing the autopsy on the girl, Parker had sworn to himself that the monster who had ravaged that little body would not escape punishment.

Through exhaustive photographic comparisons with the Scanning Electron Microscope, Parker's people had matched the pattern of the wounds in the little girl's flesh to the teeth on a pair of vise grips found in Volker's toolbox. Their determination that every tool has its own distinct patterns stamped into it when forged—like a human fingerprint—had not only secured Volker's conviction but also provided forensic science with a new weapon to fight others like him.

Parker stood in the shaft of sunlight from the window, surveying the exhibits, at once symbols of the intellectual heights and depraved depths of the human soul. Sometimes, as now, he came here when he was down, just to remind himself what he was trying to do and why he stuck with it. Why couldn't they just let him do his job? What did they want from him?

He put his hand on the case that held the vise grips and seemed to derive energy from it. If he had helped to get one depraved beast like Volker off the streets, he had done something he could be proud of, he told himself. They couldn't take that away from him.

Cindy was on the phone when Parker stepped back into the office. She pushed the hold button and told him: "Councilwoman Moreno. I think it's about Duffy."

It was clear to Parker that he was not going to be getting anything done today except play "Answer Man" to a bunch of bureaucrats. It was also clear that this would not be the best place to remain "unavailable for comment."

"Tell her I'm out for the rest of the day," Parker said.

Cindy frowned confusedly. "Where are you going?"

"I'm taking some sage political advice," he told her. "I'm going to clean up a mess."

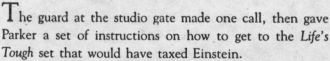

The guard at the studio gate made one call, then gave Parker a set of instructions on how to get to the *Life's Tough* set that would have taxed Einstein.

For a moment Parker thought of asking the man to repeat his directions from the beginning, but that was somehow unbecoming. What would a *real* detective do? Parker mused, very much aware that he was playing policeman again, and that he was not strictly justified in doing so. Yet he couldn't let the Duffy case be mishandled just because everyone else was afraid of rocking the boat. He had to press ahead independently—do his own digging, if necessary—to satisfy his own code of ethics. And if his code was stricter than most, so be it.

Parker left his car in the lot and set out on foot. He went between two huge hangarlike soundstages, down the deserted street of a false-front city, complete with row after row of false tenements. He rounded the corner of the city street and found himself in a dusty western town. Another hundred yards, and he was strolling down the tree-lined sidewalk of a quiet suburban neighborhood. The sound of screams made him turn. It was the studio tour, vocalizing its collective delight at being terrorized by a thirty-foot great white shark. Parker walked on.

Five minutes later, he knew he was lost. On the hill above him, looking foreboding even in the daylight, was a creepy old Victorian house complete with garret and parapets. Parker was not about to ask directions there. Janet Leigh had done that, and look what had happened to her. He turned around and went back to the western town and asked a cowboy who was loading his six-shooter in preparation for the tour's gunfight for directions to soundstage six. Parker found it without much more trouble, but too late. A stagehand informed him that *Life's Tough* had broken for lunch but that he could probably find Mia Stockton in the studio commissary.

This time he didn't get lost. The commissary was crowded, and the young hostess at the front desk looked at Parker as if he were a complete dummy when he asked if she could point out Mia Stockton. She indicated a blond in a blue turtleneck sweater sitting by herself at a table, talking to a couple of hovering star-struck Japanese businessmen. The men beamed as they were introduced by a studio PR man. He *had* to be a PR man, Parker decided, because he bowed lower than the Japanese.

Parker hung back until the courtesies were completed, then stepped forward hesitantly, feeling, for some strange reason, slightly nervous. Normally he took show-business personalities in stride; he knew better than anyone that they would all be the same when they stopped breathing. But something in this woman made him react. The mysterious chemicals again.

Although amply breasted, she was small, petite. She was not beautiful, or even very pretty, really. Attractive, yes, but not pretty. She had good high cheekbones and large, extremely blue eyes, but her nose was large and she had a rather prominent overbite. Those flaws, however, made her face somehow more interesting than it would have been without them. She started to take a bite out of her tunafish sandwich, but stopped when she looked up and saw Parker.

"Yes?"

"I don't want to disturb your lunch, Miss Stockton—"

"That's all right," she said, and put the sandwich down. She pulled a paper napkin from the place setting next to her and held out a hand. "Pen?"

Parker gave her his.

She poised it on the napkin and said, "Who to?"

"Eric Parker."

She wrote, "To Eric, Mia Stockton," and handed it to him.

Parker looked at it and decided to take a gamble. He handed it back. "Could you do me a big favor? Could you write down on here what you were doing at John Duffy's the night before last?"

Her eyes widened. They were too blue to be real, Parker decided. Contacts, probably. "Who are you?" she asked.

"Eric Parker. Dr. Eric Parker. Chief medical examiner with the County of Los Angeles."

If she was flustered, she didn't show it. There was curiosity in her eyes, nothing more. "What makes you think I was at John's?"

"You left some of yourself behind," Parker told her. "A hair."

"There are a lot of blonds around. How can you be sure it was my hair you found?"

"I can pull one out now and match them," Parker offered.

She smiled bemusedly. "Say I save you the trouble and myself the pain and concede ownership. Duffy was a lousy housekeeper. That hair could have been there for months."

Parker shook his head and tried to sound serious. "We carbon-dated it. It was left there Sunday night. Scientific fact."

She shrugged. "Well, who am I to argue with science?" Her blue eyes made a quick appraisal and she motioned to a chair. "Well, Mr. Coroner, are you going to stand there all day or sit down? Would you like some lunch?" She did not wait for an answer, but signaled the waiter. Parker didn't protest. He had not eaten breakfast and his stomach was beginning to voice complaints. She picked up her tuna sandwich and took a bite. "I don't mean to be rude and eat in front of you, but I have to be back on the set in twenty minutes. We're going kind of nuts. Rewrites."

A waiter brought a menu and Parker glanced at it. All

the sandwiches were named after movie and television stars that had graced the lot. "What are you having?"

"A Lloyd Bridges."

It figured. Parker ordered a John Wayne (rare roast beef) on rye, and coffee.

"They're changing the last two episodes," Mia went on, "trying to create a spin-off. I'd be a . . ." She paused and shrugged stoically. "It's not going to work, so why talk about it?"

Parker did not comment, more intent on a matter of true import—a speck of tuna salad had lighted, inexplicably, on the woman's nose.

"What's wrong?" she asked, noticing that he was staring.

"Nothing." He decided to let it stay. It made her somehow easier to deal with.

The waiter returned with Parker's coffee and he used the interruption to formulate his line of questioning. "You and Duffy were friends?" he asked, taking a tentative sip. It was, as expected, not very good.

Mia Stockton took another bite of sandwich. "That's the question?"

"No. The question is, how good?"

Her stare was challenging. "As good as you can get." She considered going back to her sandwich, then decided to set the record straight. "You're going to get this in bits and pieces from everybody else, so you might as well get it all at once from me. When the show first went on the air, John and I had an affair. It was what a vulgarian would

141

have called 'hot and heavy.' It might have gone the route."

"And?"

"It didn't."

"Why not?"

"You probably know by now. Duffy had a drug problem. Coke. You're the doctor. I don't have to tell you what that does to a man's sex drive. That can get hard on a romance. After things cooled down, we became friends." She paused thoughtfully. "I felt sorry for John. I'm the mothering kind. Which, when I think about it, might have been what he wanted all along."

Parker continued to stare at the speck of tuna on her nose.

"You have a problem with that?" she asked, her voice picking up a tone of annoyance.

"I have a problem with that hair. It was on Duffy's pillow. What did you do, tuck him in?"

"As a matter of fact, I did," she said, her tone almost snide. "John called me around nine Sunday night. Asked me to come over. He sounded like he was in a bad way, so I went."

"As a mother," Parker said skeptically.

"And for self-survival," she replied unabashedly. "My career was linked with his. I have talent, sure, but John was the show. I wanted to make sure he was happy."

Parker didn't believe her motivations were that simple or that selfish. Maybe he just didn't want to believe. "But you couldn't manage it?"

"Nobody could. He'd been acting crazy for a long time.

The coke and all the drugs. And he was really shook-up by his wife leaving him and taking the kid. That was what we talked about mostly."

"You mean Sunday night?"

"Yes. He said he wanted his family more than anything and he knew he was destroying it. One minute, he was going to clean himself up, get straight. The next, he was tooting, saying he was going to quit the show, the hell with everybody. He wasn't rational. That was why I stayed with him. I had a funny feeling about him. Like he was going to do something weird. I'd seen him go up and down before, but never so drastically."

"Did you think he might harm himself?"

"I'm not sure. I guess that's what I thought. He kept saying that he was no good for anybody, even himself. Then he ran out of coke and started to get really crazy."

"What did he do?"

"Started phoning around, trying to find some more."

Parker's sandwich arrived. He took one bite and immediately knew how it had gotten its John Wayne tag. The meat was tougher than hell.

"That was when he called Harvey Brock?"

Her eyes grew curious. "How did you know that?"

"Harvey told me."

"Oh."

"Do you want to tell me what happened?"

She tilted her head and looked at him circumspectly. "I thought you talked to Harvey?"

"I did. I'd like to hear your version of it."

"Harvey told John he didn't have anything, and John

went nuts. He called Harvey a fucking asshole—pardon my French. He said he'd carried him all these years and that Harvey had *better* find something for him if he wanted the relationship to continue."

"Rough talk."

Mia shrugged. "Nothing out of the ordinary. John was always doing that to Harvey—humiliating him in front of other people, using him as a gofer. Especially when he was coked up."

Parker's mind was working. "Why did Harvey take it?"

"He had no other choice. John controlled his life. If John wanted to, he could snap his fingers and Harvey would be through. Harvey hated that—he hated knowing it—but there was nothing he could do about that."

"He could try."

"I don't know. I guess that at some deep psychological level, Harvey knew that the closest he was ever going to come to making it was vicariously, through John."

"Standing in Duffy's shadow was better than not being able to stand?"

"Something like that."

She returned to her sandwich. Parker waited for her to look at him again. "What do you think of Brock?" he asked.

She stared at him levelly. "Not much."

"Why not?"

"John was ruining himself, and Harvey was just helping out the process."

"Consciously?"

She shrugged. "I wouldn't know about that." She

added, "Anyway, I don't like drug dealers, no matter what their rationale."

"Brock was dealing to other people than Duffy?"

She looked away, as if she had already said too much. "Byron had him kicked off the set for dealing."

"Fenady?"

She nodded.

"When was that?"

"A while ago. You'll have to ask Byron about that."

Parker could tell she did not want to talk about it. He decided he would pursue it later, if necessary. "How did the conversation with Brock wind up?"

"I guess Harvey told John he'd be making a score later and that he'd bring it by before he went to the studio in the morning."

That would be the reason for Brock's early-morning trip to the beach, not any vague feelings of concern. "What time was that call?"

"About eleven, I guess."

"What time did you leave?"

"I'm not sure. Close to two. I finally managed to talk John into taking a Valium about one. He mellowed out after that and I put him to bed."

Parker ruminated on it over a forkful of potato salad. It was a familiar story. A man of small consequence could achieve everything—fame, fortune, loving family, dedicated mistress (if wanted)—and then sacrifice it all for a drug he knew was going to bring him down. It wasn't as if it was an unknown. It brought everybody down, no exceptions. Some farther than others, admittedly, but the difference wasn't worth gambling upon, the difference between being screwed up and dead.

"I don't know what got into him," Mia said. "Maybe it was the show. We were at a watershed. They put another hit up against us, and where we usually could be assured of a thirty-four share, we got as low as twenty-seven."

"Did the network intend to pull the plug?"

"There was talk, but I don't know. That's a moot question now."

Parker took another bite of his John Wayne and decided it wasn't one of the Duke's steers—it had to be his chaps. "I hear Duffy was thinking of quitting the show."

"He'd talked about it."

"What was his problem? Just the drugs?"

"That was part of it. Part of it was . . . You ever see the show?"

"I must confess I haven't."

She nodded knowingly. "Don't tell me. You only watch educational TV."

"Actually, I don't watch much television at all."

"You're probably better off," she said. "Duffy played a stage mentalist who used his phony psychic act to deal with his wife—me—and our two adopted kids, one a Mexican, the other a Chinese. Sounds kind of dumb, huh?"

She was the mentalist, Parker thought. "I have to admit, it does."

"That's what Duffy thought. Especially after trying to pretend it wasn't for two seasons. He'd had it. For three or four months he'd taken to delivering long harangues on the set about the idiocy of the scripts. The past few episodes, he'd even started to play it that way. He'd recite his lines in a way that made his contempt obvious."

"That must have made the producer happy."

"John wanted to do his own show, one in which he'd have complete artistic control. He had this idea for a comedy series—it was wonderful—about a writer who's committed by his wife to a mental institution after a bout of depression and winds up being the father-confessor and chief therapist for the ward. Sort of comedic *Cuckoo's Nest*."

Parker nodded. It seemed as if everyone had a surefire idea for a hit TV show. He wondered if they were the same idea. He moved on: "Did you know about the note Joan Duffy received about you two?"

Her sandwich stopped on the way to her mouth and she put it down as if she had suddenly lost her appetite. "Yes."

"Any idea who sent it?"

"No."

The uncertainty of the response made Parker think she was lying, but he did not push the point. For now. "Who, besides Brock, did Duffy talk to that night while you were there?"

She thought about it. "Sol Grossman."

"His agent?"

She nodded. "Yes."

"What did they talk about?"

Again she wavered. "John's treatment idea."

"What about it?"

"John thought it was finished, but Sol thought it needed more work."

"That's all?"

She touched the side of her nose, missing the tuna. "Yes."

Again, Parker thought she was lying, but decided not to pursue it. "While I'm here, I'd like to talk to Fenady. Is he around?"

"I think he's supervising a shoot on the other side of the lot. For *Street Angels*. That's his other series."

"Sounds like he keeps busy."

She shrugged. Her mouth remained tight-lipped.

In an attempt to lighten the mood, Parker asked, "Did you know you have tuna salad on your nose?"

She looked at him, but her expression did not change. "How long has it been there?"

"Fifteen minutes." He waited for her to laugh, smile, do anything, at least remove the speck, but she simply looked at him. For some reason, it made Parker feel like an idiot. "If I seem to be wandering all over the place, it's because I don't know where I'm going."

"Where is there to go?"

"I'm not sure. Maybe nowhere."

She tossed up a hand. "So why are you doing this? If he drowned, he drowned. Do we have to carry on about it forever? Why can't we just have the service?"

"I'm not sure he 'just drowned.'"

That stopped her. "What do you mean? You said at the news conference—"

"That Duffy drowned. He did drown. I'm just not sure how."

Her brow wrinkled, perplexed. "How does one drown?"

"In several ways," Parker told her. "Accidentally. On purpose. With help."

Her mouth dropped open in disbelief. "What are you saying? That he committed suicide, or was murdered?"

"No," he assured her. "But there are some puzzling aspects that haven't been explained to my satisfaction, so I must look into every possibility. And please, don't be perturbed, if you happen to read today's L.A. *Times*, at how badly I've been misquoted on precisely this subject."

She wasn't sure what he meant and Parker didn't bother elaborating. "Did you ever hear Duffy express a fear of anybody? Anything?"

"No," she said immediately. "He wasn't the type to be afraid of something physical. When he got scared, it was in the head, emotional. Like the fear of success."

"Or the fear of losing his wife and kid."

Her stare was cool. "Yes."

"If you know that, how come you got involved?" Parker asked, to satisfy his own curiosity more than anything else.

"He didn't feel that way until he had the kid. I'm not really sure when he changed. About a year ago, maybe. When the bloom wore off. Us *and* the show. When he realized it wasn't heaven." She smiled wanly. "When he realized it was shit, everything was shit."

Parker studied her for a moment. This was the first indication that she might be under stress.

"There's something else," he said then. "We found a notebook in Duffy's beside table. He'd made a list of one-liners, one of which was: 'Suicide is a belated way of agreeing with your wife's mother.' Should I be concerned about that?"

"Of course. One should always be concerned about bad jokes."

All right, Parker thought, deciding that he liked her directness, and her precise manner too. No wasted words or motions. Despite her problems, she seemed sure and confident, traits he found attractive in a woman. Maybe it was just an actor's mask, and then again, maybe it wasn't. It would be interesting to find out.

Then, as always, he thought about Eve, and where that had led. He quickly shrugged. You fall off a horse and you have to get right back on. Otherwise you'll always be afraid to ride. "If I have some more questions, can I reach you at home?"

She smiled, seeing through the transparency of the ruse. "Do you still have that pen?"

He gave it to her and she jotted down her number on a paper napkin. "I'm usually home after seven."

He nodded and tucked the napkin into his breast pocket, then started to reach for her check, but she snatched it away before he could get to it. "Not on this occasion," she said, her voice conveying that she meant it. She stood abruptly.

"One more question," Parker said. "If it was chicken salad, would you still leave it there?"

She smiled and walked away, leaving him alone at the table with the remnants of John Wayne and Lloyd Bridges. Stubborn, he thought, staring after her. He tried to remember if he liked stubborn women, but it had been so long, he wasn't sure.

12

Parker found Fenady's production company on an isolated section of the huge studio lot, in front of a block of fake slums. They appeared to be almost ready to wrap, the action confined to a ramp and a couple of parked cars. Equipment trucks blocked off both ends of the streets, and two camera crews on gigantic mobile dollies maneuvered for the best angles.

Parker used his ID to get past the security guard and made his way toward a group of men huddled around a shocking-pink Maserati. There were four of them and they all looked worried and harassed, a seemingly ubiquitous look in the television business. Maybe they felt that look somehow justified their salaries.

Parker excused himself, and the athlete of the group, a tall, tanned, well-muscled man in his mid-forties, looked up in annoyance. "What is it?"

Parker displayed his identification again. "Dr. Eric Parker, county medical examiner. I'm looking for Byron Fenady."

"You just found him," the man said coldly. He had black hair, combed straight back from his forehead, and that made his features, which were too close together, look even more bunched on his face. His eyes were dark and intense, covered by dark brows, and his thin-lipped mouth looked like a knife wound. He was dressed in khaki pants with an elastic-band waist, and a blue-and-green-checked short-sleeved sport shirt. "Well?"

Parker looked at the others. "I'd like to ask you a few questions—"

"That's right, a star expired," the man said sarcastically. "You guys just can't bury someone, can you? You have to screw with the corpse, get your name in the papers."

Parker ignored the outburst and said amiably, "Here or downtown. Whichever is more convenient."

"Here is fine," Fenady said grudgingly. He glanced at his watch, so quickly the time could hardly have registered. "Just let me get this meeting over. Five minutes, tops." He motioned to a row of canvas chairs set facing the Maserati. "Find a seat. Enjoy the show."

Parker looked at his own watch and settled into one of the chairs while Fenady's group moved off out of earshot. They seemed to be arguing now. Fenady was gesturing angrily.

"Hello, hotshot," a woman's voice said, seemingly emanating from under the Maserati's hood.

Parker stood up and stepped over to the car. The dashboard looked like the controls in the cockpit of a 747, complete with dials and gauges and flashing lights. The only thing it didn't have was a pilot or a copilot. Parker glanced around.

"Yes, you," the woman's voice confirmed, oozing sex appeal.

Parker turned back around.

"Like to take a little spin?"

The green lights on the dash flashed in sync with the voice. Parker looked around, trying to spot the woman, who had to be broadcasting from somewhere nearby. Though there were no other witnesses to his discomfiture, he was starting to get embarrassed.

"What's the matter?" the Maserati cooed. "Don't you think I'm cute?"

Parker sat back down and closed his eyes, trying to ignore it. He was damned if he was going to start talking to a car.

"I could come back," the Maserati said, its engine roaring to life. Parker looked inside again. There had to be a driver. Cars didn't start themselves. The cockpit was still empty.

"Meet you here, what, ten o'clock? You bring a six-pack and a couple of joints and I'll bring some ethyl. We'll do it in the back seat. Whoo! Whoo!"

"There is no back seat," Parker found himself saying, immediately regretting it.

"Then we'll do it in the front!" the voice said breathlessly. "Just watch the gearshift!" The engine suddenly quit. "Oh, oh, here comes dickhead. Don't tell him I was talking to you, okay?"

Parker looked up to see Fenady returning. "Okay," Parker answered, finally seeing the humor in the situation. "But I have to warn you—I'm in love with a Chevrolet."

"What's a Chevy got that I haven't?" the Maserati whispered. "Haven't you heard? Latins are the best lovers. . . . Until tonight, *amore mio*. . . ."

Fenady came up looking more relaxed, as if he had won whatever argument he might have had. Again he flicked a glance at his black sport watch, not so much to check the time as to show that he was a very busy man, his every minute valuable. "Sorry I jumped on you," he said, smiling ingratiatingly. "I've been under a lot of pressure lately. Sweeps week."

Parker nodded as if he understood what that meant, and Fenady asked, "The car wasn't talking to you, was she?"

"No," Parker said, immediately feeling foolish for lying.

Fenady produced the stump of a pack of Rolaids and popped one into his mouth. "Mona the Mouthy Maserati. The old days, the stars used to be the celebrities. Now it's machines. It's the times we live in. You ever see the show?"

Parker admitted that he hadn't.

"What do you think of the concept?"

Parker hesitated, trying not to hurt the man's feelings. "Don't you think it's a bit . . ."

The producer's eyes narrowed. "A bit what?"

"Well, a bit derivative. I recall seeing something vaguely similar."

"The *other* show," Fenady said derisively. "That's a *boy* car, this is a *girl* car. That's why she's pink, get it? And she is always flubbing her lines. That's the gimmick. We didn't plan it that way, but the space cadet who does the voice, she kept fucking up so much, we decided to write it into the script."

"And that's enough difference?"

"Let 'em sue," Fenady said, closing the subject. He turned and waved to a group of men standing beside a bakery truck parked across the street, then pointed. One of the men went around, hopped into the back of the truck, and the Maserati's engine cranked over with a roar. Parker watched in fascination as the machine made a U-turn and parallel-parked at the curb in front of the truck.

"Pretty nifty," Parker commented. "That car may be the solution to the drunk-driving problem."

Fenady grinned sardonically. "That'd be bad for business, wouldn't it?"

"My business will always be good," Parker assured him.

Fenady dug out another Rolaid. The man's face turned serious, signaling the end of the good-natured show-business patter. "So what's this about, anyway?"

"Some questions have come up about Duffy's death—"

"What? That crap in the *Times*? 'Murder Possible'? What was that garbage?"

"A misquote."

"If you don't talk to them, they can't misquote you." Fenady frowned, thinking about it. "That kind of yellow journalism is just the kind of thing I wanted to avoid. For everybody's sake. I was assured that the investigation would be handled with discretion—"

"By whom? Alex Tartunian?"

"I talked to Alex," Fenady admitted.

"Tartunian a close friend of yours?"

"Not close, but we know each other. Anyway, Alex isn't the only one who wants to keep this thing from getting out of hand."

Parker had intended to apologize for the story, but the man's overbearing manner made him dig in. He had had enough people try to push his buttons today. "I know. The movie colony wields a lot of influence in this town. But as long as I'm coroner, I don't intend to compromise the truth, no matter what kind of pressure is brought to bear."

"Truth?" Fenady said angrily, tossing a hand in the air. "Is that what you call that bullshit this morning?"

"There might be more truth in it than you know," Parker retaliated.

That stopped the man. "Huh?"

"There is evidence that Duffy experienced trauma that may not have been caused by drowning. And a witness near the scene saw a scuba diver coming out of the water about the time Duffy drowned."

"A scuba diver?" Fenady asked, his tone blatantly skeptical. "Are you saying someone drowned Duffy?"

"I'm not saying anything at the moment," Parker said, regretting that he had let himself get carried away. "Just that there are unanswered questions that need answering. For example, the man apparently had a serious cocaine problem—"

"I thought you said on the news last night that cocaine didn't kill him."

"It didn't."

"Then why bring it up?" Fenady asked, turning up his

palms. "As far as I was concerned, as long as the guy performed on the set, I could care less what he did when he got home."

"From what I hear, it wasn't just at home. I hear it was starting to interfere with your production."

Fenady looked at him suspiciously. "Yeah? Where did you hear that?"

"Mia Stockton."

Fenady rubbed his chin thoughtfully. "We had a few problems. The main one was that little no-talent gofer buddy of John's. But I got things under control."

"You're talking about Harvey Brock?"

He nodded and pursed his lips. "I worked him into a few shows as a favor to Duffy. Then I found out the little creep was muling drugs into Duffy right here on the set. Not only Duffy. Hell, the sonofabitch was supplying half the crew."

"You mean he was selling the stuff?"

"That's exactly what I mean."

"What did you do?"

"Had security ban him from the set. John raised holy hell about it, but I stood firm. I couldn't get it through his skull that the little prick—his bosom buddy—was trying to kill him."

"You mean that literally?"

"Kill his career, kill him. Same difference. Duffy was his career. The man was ego-deficient. His definition of himself was wrapped up in his work. It's not uncommon in this business. Brock wanted to see Duffy crumble. He was jealous. He saw Duffy making it and it ate him up."

"Brock told you that?"

"He didn't have to. I've seen it before."

"I talked to Brock. He says he's coming over to pitch you an idea he has for a new show."

"He won't get through the gates," the producer growled. "He tried to pitch me one of his ideas while he was on the show. Bionic drapes. Brilliant, huh?"

Parker glanced across the street at the pink car and held his tongue. Still, a little baiting might shake up the man's smug manner. "I understand Duffy was making noises about quitting *Life's Tough*—that he thought the show was stupid."

That got a rise out of Fenady. He raised two fingers to emphasize the points he wanted to make, folding them as he did so, and said in an irritated tone, "One, he couldn't quit. He had a contract. Two, the show is not stupid. If it's what the people want, how can it be stupid?"

That struck Parker as a doubtful premise, but the more he thought about it, the more uncertain he became. If he could only adopt that philosophy—give people what they want—he might yet find his own salvation.

"I could care less what the critics think," Fenady went on. "They don't buy airtime. I give the audience what they want, because if I didn't, *I'd* be stupid."

Parker glanced down the street at the Maserati. They were setting up some sort of stunt. Behind a row of nondescript cars, an engine roared roughly, readying for a ramp run. This was what the audience wanted, Parker mused. "But *Life's Tough* was slipping, wasn't it? Aren't the ratings down?"

"They did drop," Fenady admitted. "But they were

coming back. And either way, the question still is: What the hell's that got to do with Duffy's death?"

"I'll never know unless I ask."

"Brilliant."

Parker backed off, wishing he had more to go on, some excuse for sweeping the myth aside and confronting the man. The myth was his power. It kept him safe.

"How about the Mia Stockton spin-off?"

"What about how about it?"

"Do you think it will work?"

Fenady sighed tiredly. "What am I? An oracle? How should I know if it's going to work? The only thing I know—the only thing I *can* know—is that it's a natural. There's a big audience out there that knows and loves Mia Stockton. So why not give it a try?"

"Sure, but by the same token, why take the chance?"

"I didn't get where I am by passing on a good thing," Fenady said after a while. "In this business, once you start resting on your so-called laurels, you're not in the business. You may think you are, but you're not. In this business, you gotta be a shark, always moving, always looking."

"For what?"

Now there was no hesitation. Fenady bared his teeth in a hungry grin. "The next meal."

Parker was distracted by the squeal of tires. A moment later, a stunt car came off the ramp and hurtled over the parked cars, barely missing the Maserati. It hit the street with a sickening thud, rolled over several times, then landed upside down. The director yelled, "Cut!" and the crew ran over to the demolished auto, where the driver was slithering out of a window, smiling.

"You know what that little stunt just cost me?" Fenady asked. "Three grand. One for the driver, two for the car. This kind of high-concept show is a money-eating machine. You can't even make back the licensing fees. *Street Angels* has been on for two seasons now, and I'm still in the red."

Despite himself, Parker was still engrossed with the wrecked car, wondering how the driver could have escaped completely unscathed. "So why bother?"

"You haven't been listening," Fenady complained. "To stay on top, you've got to keep a lot of balls in the air, and this is one of the balls, okay? I've got other balls supporting this ball, and one day this ball—I trust—will be supporting other balls. Around and around they go, and when they stop, nobody knows. Meantime, enough of them make it to syndication to keep me on top."

"And that's what it's about?"

"*Part* of what it's about," Fenady corrected. "How big a part? You have to get there to find out." The smile flashed again.

"So that's the magic word for you? Syndication?"

"The magic word," Fenady repeated. "You hope to keep a show on long enough so that it starts bringing in residual money. But even that's changing. The whole business is changing. It used to be, three seasons, and a show like this was over the hump, but no more. Cable and direct-for-syndication series have screwed everything up. Hour-long, high-concept adventure series are hard to sell. Now, the syndication market is for half-hour sitcoms. That's where the money is. One set, a cast of seven. No car wrecks, no stuntmen, no outdoor shoots. I'm regearing my development of new series in that direction."

"I understand Duffy had an idea for his own comedy series."

Fenady shrugged.

"He ever discuss it with you?"

"No," Fenady said. He took out another Rolaid and pushed it into his mouth. On the outside, the man seemed to be very much in control, but inside, things were apparently different, boiling, ready to spill over. That's show biz, Parker thought.

Fenady looked at his watch again, and said impatiently, "Look, if that's all . . ."

Parker nodded. "Thanks for your time, Mr. Fenady. I know you're busy." He looked out at the crew, which was busy setting up another shot, and said, "You know, I never really thought about it before, but what I do as a coroner is a lot like the making of a TV show, except in reverse. We start at the end and run the film backward, frame by frame, until we get to the title. Just like in your business, we're interested in the credits. The name of the star."

"Yeah, well, that's fascinating," Fenady said as if it were anything but. "Excuse me."

Parker watched him go and thought that, all things considered, it had been more enjoyable talking to the car. The difference between making out and making an enemy.

161

13

Sol Grossman's office was a small one-story Tudor stucco building on La Cienega across from a Fat Boy's hamburger stand. The sign on the door said "Grossman Management" and the welcoming message on the doormat said "Wipe Ur Feet."

Inside, almost lost in a jubilation of silk flowers, a small, intent, almond-eyed receptionist viewed Parker with studied indifference. If she had any idea that he was expected, she wasn't going to admit it.

"I'm Dr. Parker," Parker said after a while. "To see Mr. Grossman."

"You'll have to wait," the girl said. "Boodry is running late."

The way she said the name, Boodry apparently was somebody important, expected and allowed to run late, perhaps quite late, but Parker didn't recognize the name.

Probably a rock star, he thought. He was particularly bad on rock stars. His interest had waned with the demise of the Beatles.

"Can I get you something?"

"No, thank you."

Parker sat down and picked up a copy of *People* magazine. He flipped through, experiencing a kind of popular-press déjà vu, and then checked the date and discovered it was almost two years old. A good sign, he decided grudgingly. Tight management. No frills.

Down the hall, a man yelled, and then another man yelled, even louder. Although muffled by a door, they still could be heard quite clearly, each making X-rated observations about the other's origin.

"You're a *pussy*, Grossman! A pussy!"

Parker got the *People* magazine again—something to hide behind—and then the screaming match broke out into the open. A huge bear of a man with a shaved head that looked like a dinosaur egg came striding down the hall, his purple cape wreaking havoc with a row of silk fig trees. The giant stopped when he saw Parker and pointed a menacing finger at him. "And *you're* a pussy too!"

Parker stared at him without comprehension. Beneath the cape, the man's muscular body threatened to burst his purple-sequined body stocking, and his head, when lowered, displayed a colorful bull's-eye.

Parker didn't move, and the giant, apparently satisfied he had made his point, whatever it was, went slamming out. Through the closed door, the man could still be heard as he repeated his accusations of feminine gender at the traffic outside.

The girl at the desk waited until the building stopped shuddering to tell Parker that Mr. Grossman would see him now.

Parker stood to discover a man approaching him from the direction of the fig trees. He was going to duck, but the outstretched manicured hand looked friendly enough. "Dr. Parker! I'm sorry. That must have sounded awful. The A Team in heat."

Grossman was fifty-odd, heavyset, with a pink complexion set off by dark hair and an immaculately trimmed chinstrap beard. If it hadn't been for the five-hundred-dollar blue silk suit, Parker would have taken him more for an Amish farmer than a high-powered Hollywood business manager. He told Parker to come on back, then turned to the girl. "I don't want to be disturbed. By anybody."

"How about Boodry?"

"Especially by Boodry."

Parker followed Grossman down a narrow glass-walled hall. Behind the glass, several women were at work, bent over calculating machines. None of them had a typewriter.

"Boodry is a pain in the ass," Grossman said matter-of-factly. "I think he's been body-slammed too many times. It must have shaken something loose."

"What is he, a wrestler?"

Grossman nodded and sighed. "Amazing, isn't it? A

man can become a public figure just because he's as big as a truck—and can talk. He has his own cartoon show on Saturday mornings. I just got him a featured part in *Superman VIII* and we just signed a high-six-figure deal with Mattel for a line of 'Boodry the Beast' toys."

"And he's unhappy?"

"Boodry is *always* unhappy. He's starting to live his ring role—a giant relegated to live in a world of wimps and pussies." He stopped in front of a door. "Here we are."

Grossman's office was as Spartan as the rest of the place. On the wall, one framed diploma, saying he was a CPA. On his desk, one calculator, the tool of his trade. In the corner, one silk fig tree, which required no plant food, no water—a good sign, Parker mused. Tight management. *Really* tight management.

Parker took one of the two chairs.

"We get all kinds," Grossman said, apropos of nothing, but an apparent reference to Boodry. "How can I help you?"

Parker thought that Grossman didn't seem particularly distressed by the death of one of his major clients.

"We have to check everything, you understand?" Parker said. "When we get this kind of death, involving someone . . ."

"A star," Grossman said, waiting. For the first time, he appeared impatient.

"I understand Duffy called you the night before he died," Parker said.

There was a subtle shift in the man's expression as his eyes took on a hooded look. "Where did you hear that?"

"Phone records," Parker lied. "Malibu is a toll call."

Grossman pursed his lips thoughtfully and nodded. "That's right."

"Was he alone?"

"As far as I know."

"What did you talk about?"

Grossman shrugged. "What we usually talked about—money. John wanted some and I wouldn't give him any."

"Why not? It was his, wasn't it?"

"It wouldn't have been for long if he had easy access to it. John's cash withdrawals lately had been excessive and he'd been lying about what they were for. I knew what they were for. We all knew."

"Cocaine."

Grossman nodded, and for the first time his brown eyes looked sad. "He was killing himself with that crap. I told him he had to get off it, get himself some help, and time after time he promised he would, but we both knew he was just bullshitting."

"So you cut him off?"

"For his own good," the man explained. "I instructed the accountant that John would get no cash, except for his immediate needs. Everything else—household expenses, car payments, medical insurance, the wife and kid, checks to his parents—went through me."

"He agreed to that arrangement?"

Grossman shrugged. "He knew I was doing it for him."

"How much money did he want on Sunday?"

"Twenty-five hundred."

Mia Stockton hadn't mentioned that. Parker wondered why.

"What did he say when you wouldn't give it to him?"

"He blew up," Grossman said. "I told him I couldn't help it, that there was no money available, and there wasn't."

"Where was it?"

Grossman leaned back, in control, seemingly relaxed. "All of John's money is tied up in high-end, low-liquidity investments that require continuing payments. I made sure of that. Shopping centers, real estate. I spread it around that way, complicated, all being bought on time and not easy to get rid of—not on the spur of the moment, at least—so he would be stuck with them. When he asked for cash, I could legitimately tell him he couldn't have it because he was on the line for whatever."

"Wasn't that kind of dangerous?" Parker asked. "Considering Duffy's drug problem and the fickle nature of the television business? If I get the picture right, everything the guy made went into a sort of blind pot where it stirred around uncertainly, always needing more and more to stay viable. What if the show had folded? How would the payments get made?"

The man put out his hands. "There was no other way. If John had been allowed free access to his funds, he would have gone belly-up in a year. Everything would have been up his nose. Sure, it was a gamble, but if he'd been given free rein, it would have been a sure thing."

"What happens now?" Parker asked. "Without Duffy's salary, how do the payments get made?"

"The same thing that would have happened if the series got canceled. Something gets sold."

The pot continues to stir, Parker thought.

"There was no choice," Grossman repeated sadly, as if trying to convince himself. Or maybe Parker. "Sure, the kid got mad. You just saw Boodry. The same kind of mad. The exact same problem. Well, not exactly the same— Boodry's just an asshole. But he won't stay mad, any more than John ever stayed mad. Deep down, John knew I was doing it for him. I managed that kid for six years. I loved him like a son."

Somehow, Parker doubted that. More likely, he'd loved him like a money machine.

"Duffy's psychiatrist says Duffy was despondent, especially since his wife had left him. Had you noticed?"

"Nothing I hadn't seen before. John talked about Joan, sure. He missed his kid. But he was confident he could get them back."

"Then he didn't strike you as being inordinately depressed of late?"

Grossman stroked his beard thoughtfully. "Not inordinately, no. John had been up and down, but he'd been up and down since I first met him. He was a manic-depressive. I'm really going to miss him." He smiled. "Funny, but I never thought I'd be saying that."

"Why not?"

"Because John could be a royal pain in the ass. At least once a week I'd tell myself the money wasn't worth the aggravation, that the best thing I could do for myself would be to get the hell away from the guy, just walk away."

"But you didn't."

"No," Grossman said, looking at Parker earnestly. "Because for all the aggravation he caused me, John had something—a lovable, childlike quality—that prevented me from staying mad at him. Like I said, I loved him like a son."

The man sounded convincing enough—Parker wondered, then, why he wasn't convinced. Maybe because he was used to everyone in Hollywood trying to protect an image. If Grossman had purposely adopted the image of an Amish farmer—the very picture of ascetic honesty—perhaps it was to convince his clients he was something he was not.

"The analyst also says Duffy talked about quitting his TV show."

Grossman laughed. "Duffy talked about a lot of things. Starting a rock band. Starring in his own movie. Sailing around the world. Becoming a lumberjack in the Northwest woods. It changed from day to day, always something else, but he never did anything about it, and nobody took him seriously."

Maybe that was the problem, Parker thought. "Then it was just talk?"

"About quitting the series? He couldn't have quit *Life's Tough*, no matter how badly he wanted to. It would have meant throwing a ton of money away to walk before the show went into residuals, not to mention the possibility of a lawsuit. But what it would have done to his reputation—that would have been worse. In this business, key performers don't break contracts, and they especially don't break them in the middle of a hit. That's professional suicide. Nobody's ever going to take a chance on you again."

"Yes, I suppose not," Parker decided.

"Not *suppose*," Grossman said quickly. "*For sure.* We're talking about many millions of dollars being invested in a guy—that's what it takes to get something on the air—and if he's gonna walk for no good reason, dragging everything down with him . . ." Grossman made an exaggerated gesture of helplessness. "Well, it's nothing I'd want to do and then hang around town, let alone expect other offers."

"Okay," Parker said. "I'll put it down as just talk. Perhaps he was a little overanxious about doing something bigger and better?"

"Who isn't?" Grossman demanded. "Tell me someone who isn't. But you must proceed wisely, not impetuously. Sure, Duffy wanted to do more movies, and he could have done movies. Nothing stopped him except timing. The offers were coming in hot and heavy, and as soon as we got a good one that didn't interfere with the television show, we'd have done it. Preferably *without* annoying Fenady."

"Fenady packs that much clout?"

Grossman smiled leniently, as if he were a missionary trying to teach an aborigine how to use a knife and fork. "Anybody who can get several hit television shows going is a power in this town. Fenady has had more than several. He's one of the mini-majors."

"Mini-major?" Parker asked.

Grossman sighed heavily. "A few major production companies dominate network programming. At the top are the television departments of what were once the major movie studios—Universal, Warners, Paramount. At the bottom are the small independent producers who constantly pitch the networks, trying to get an idea to pilot. In between are the mini-majors, independent suppliers who have pyramided their successes into big production companies with their own staffs and studio equipment. Aaron Spelling, Glen Larson, Steven Cannell, Byron Fenady—those are the mini-majors."

"Duffy had an idea for a new series—"

Grossman grunted.

"You didn't think much of it?"

"Not in the state it was in."

"Did you talk about it that night?"

"I believe so, yes."

"What was said?"

"John wanted me to farm it out. I told him he'd been listening to Mia Stockton too much."

"You don't like Mia Stockton?"

"I don't have anything against her as a person," Grossman said. "I just objected to her relationship with John. Not only was their little affair harmful to John's marriage, it also wasn't doing John's career any good. She encouraged his ideas about the series treatment. God knows why. If John had tried to quit *Life's Tough*, his chances of getting a pilot done for that show would have been zero, no matter how good it was."

"From what I hear, the affair between Duffy and Mia Stockton was over a while ago."

"That's what John claimed."

"You didn't believe it?"

Grossman shook his head sadly. "Poor Joan. She deserved better than John gave her. He dished it out and she hung around taking it. The drugs, the women. She kept hoping. We both did."

The agent shifted uncomfortably, remembering. "Don't get me wrong. Duffy really loved her. That's the tragedy. He just couldn't help himself. When they had the kid, I thought he might change, and he did for a while—he really loved that kid—but then . . ."

"The Wannabees and the Cuddabins," Parker said. "They spend so long wanting it, and when they get it, they don't know how to keep it. It's too bad."

"A tragedy," Grossman agreed.

Parker decided he wasn't getting anywhere. Grossman was like a slug. Step on him, and he could go any way. He stood up and thanked Grossman for his time.

Grossman's song and dance about having to "protect" his clients' money hadn't been too convincing. In Duffy's case, with his mind blurred by drugs, some of that money might get diverted, not find its way back home.

Grossman's methods warranted a closer look.

14

Parker was not really in the mood to cope with Boomer's ebullience this evening as he deposited the groceries in the kitchen and went to the bedroom door, but at least he would not have to clean up any of the puppy's mistakes, having covered the entire bedroom floor with newspapers before he left that morning.

The dog jumped all over him as he opened the door, and after calming down the ecstatic pooch, Parker inspected the room. The newspapers were shredded, but unsoiled, and Parker was about to tell the dog how good he was when he glanced in the bathroom. He had neglected to put papers down in there. At least the floor was tile.

After cleaning up the mess and completing Boomer's nightly unsuccessful walk, Parker opened all the windows in the house, and listened to Earl Wild playing Rachmaninoff's second piano concerto as he prepared the vegetables.

Usually, cooking helped him unwind. He liked the ceremony, the meditative aspects of it. He enjoyed washing the crisp vegetables, the gentle sounds of popping oil and the lid dancing on the pot, but tonight he derived little pleasure from the process.

He felt restless, bothered, but the source of the feeling was vague, nebulous. He went through his pockets and came up with the number. She said to call anytime, he told himself, as he dialed.

Mia Stockton sounded sleepy when she answered. Her voice was husky and sensual.

"This is Dr. Parker, Miss Stockton. Did I wake you?"

"I was just taking a nap. What time is it?"

"A little after six."

"Ummmmmm," she said groggily.

"I have a couple more questions I'd like to ask."

"I figured you might."

"Really?"

"I play the wife of a psychic, remember? Some of it has to wear off. For instance, I'll bet you're going to suggest that you ask them in person."

He suddenly felt like a jerk. "If another time——"

"That's okay," she said. "I have to study some lines anyway. You want to come over here?" She gave him an address and directions. Parker put the vegetables in water and got there in twenty-five minutes.

The address was a two-story château-style house on a

side street near UCLA, fronted by lavish plantings of colorful flowers. Mia Stockton answered the door in black pedal pushers and a loose-fitting white cotton blouse. She was barefoot. She looked better without her makeup, a rarity in her business, from what Parker had seen. He had been right about her contacts; her eyes were brown now. He liked them better brown, he decided. They were softer, more vulnerable.

She showed him into a living room furnished with French antiques. Not exactly Parker's style—especially the flowery prints on the fabrics—but he admired the old English-style landscapes on the walls.

She told Parker she had just made a fresh pot of coffee, indicating a tray on the coffee table, and asked if he would like some. He said yes, and she went through a swinging door into the kitchen. When she came back out, Parker was looking at the landscapes.

"You like those?"

"Very much," he said.

She sat on the couch and poured two cups of coffee. "Turner is my favorite. Who knows? Maybe one day I'll get a series that runs long enough so that I can afford one. Ooops. There go those dreams again."

An extremely attractive, smart, talented Turner fan. Some package. "Don't sell yourself short."

She smiled. "I don't, Doctor, believe me. It's just the nature of the business."

"Call me Eric."

"Okay, Eric," she said obligingly.

He sat down in a chair opposite her and creamed and

sugared his coffee. He took a sip and said, "You should teach them how to make coffee in that commissary."

"I've championed enough lost causes," she said, smiling good-naturedly.

"I talked to Sol Grossman this afternoon," Parker said after a beat.

One of her eyebrows became a question mark. "And?"

"He said Duffy called him demanding money. For cocaine. He said Duffy became infuriated when he wouldn't give it to him."

The news did not seem to faze her. "What's your point?"

"You didn't mention that this afternoon."

"No, I didn't."

"Why not?"

She shrugged. "Because I didn't think it was any of your business. I still don't think it's any of your business."

Parker stared at her face, and after a moment she asked, "Why are you staring? Do I have tuna on my nose again?"

He shook his head. "I was just admiring your frankness. And thinking that I like your eyes better brown than blue."

She smiled crookedly. "A little flattery to loosen the tongue?" She sighed and crossed her legs. "Okay. I guess we might as well get this over with. I didn't mention it because I thought it would sound like sour grapes. Sol and I have had our differences in the past, but I bear him no malice. I didn't want to make it sound like . . ."

"Like?"

She hesitated. "John was half-crazy on toot. I told you that. I'm sure he didn't mean what he said."

"What did he say?"

"When Sol wouldn't give John the money, John threatened to fire him. He said some pretty nasty things."

"Like what?"

"He accused Sol of being a thief," she said. "He said he had evidence that Sol had been stealing from him for some time and that he was going to get an auditor in to prove it."

A minor detail Grossman had left out of his account. "Did he say what kind of evidence he had?"

"No." She sat forward and tried to erase what she had said by waving a hand in the air. "I'm sure there was no evidence. John was just talking. I told you, he was all worked-up."

Parker nodded. "You say you've had differences with Grossman. Over your affair with Duffy?"

She nodded. "Sol didn't approve of John and me. I could understand that. He wouldn't believe that we were just friends, that the romantic part of the relationship was dead a long time ago."

"Do you think that Grossman could have sent that note to Joan Duffy?"

Her eyes widened a bit. "Why should he?"

"To try to break you two up."

She shook her head. "I don't know."

"Who did *Duffy* think sent it?"

She raked her lower lip with her teeth pensively, and

was about to answer, when Parker's beeper sounded. He asked if he could use a phone and she pointed out a French phone on an ornate Louis XVI desk in the corner.

The message center referred him to a West Hollywood number and said Steenbargen was waiting for his call. An L.A. sheriff's deputy answered, and Parker identified himself and asked for Steenbargen.

Cradling the receiver between his shoulder and his ear, Parker jotted down the directions Steenbargen dictated, said he would be there in twenty minutes, and hung up. He looked at Mia and asked, "Perhaps we can continue this another time? There are still some questions I'd like to ask you."

"Of course." She caught the troubled look on Parker's face and asked, "A problem?"

He nodded. "It doesn't look like Harvey Brock is going to have to worry about being barred from any more sets. He's dead."

The actress was not acting as her hand flew to her throat. "How?"

"That's what I'm on my way to find out. Thank you for seeing me. I'll find my way out."

15

The Cheops Apartments were in West Hollywood at the end of a narrow street off Vine. Parker identified himself to a uniformed patrolman out front and was directed to a parking space ahead of a couple of black-and-whites.

The place was a piece of whimsy from the twenties, a parody of a bazaar scene from a movie set of *The Egyptian*. It was a one-story stucco bungalow court with a red tile roof and striped canvas awnings covering the windows. A cusped archway, flanked by seated plaster Egyptian guards, opened into a courtyard in which an algae-clogged fountain gurgled and hissed.

A few of the building's inhabitants stood in front of their doorways watching the police production, but for the most part curtains were drawn across lightless windows, and doors were tightly shut. It was the kind of place where the sight of a police uniform would send the sniffling, watery-eyed tenants scurrying into their holes to wait in the dark until the danger passed.

Number eight was at the end of the courtyard. Parker nodded at the deputy at the door and went inside.

The living room was stuffy and small enough to be cramped with the four plainclothes detectives and SID men who were dusting the place for prints. The walls were rough plaster, the furniture cheap and nondescript. There were evidences of habitation around—an ashtray full of cigarette butts on the Formica coffee table, a sport jacket thrown casually over the back of a fraying chair, an open box of Ho-Hos on the flimsy-looking dining table. A Formica counter separated the living room from the kitchen, and on it was a potbellied, glass water pipe. A stereo setup and a dozen or so paperbacks occupied the shelving built into one wall, and a nineteen-inch Zenith television on rollers sat in front of that.

A tall red-haired sheriff's detective Parker recognized from Duffy's house came through the arched hallway by the kitchen. He greeted Parker with a battle-weary expression and introduced himself as Wolfe. He had on dark brown slacks and a tan corduroy coat with a tiny gold "187" stickpin in the lapel—the California Penal Code number for murder.

Wolfe ran a hand over the back of this thickly pomaded hair and said, "Gunderson and I dropped by to ask Brock why his prints happened to be all over that plastic bag full of coke we found at Duffy's place. Looks like he'd been dead a couple of hours before we got here."

"When was that?"

"About an hour ago. We knocked, but got no answer. We thought that was kind of funny, 'cause Brock's car was out back and we could hear music playing inside the place, so Gunderson went down and got the manager and he let us in. We found him in the bedroom. OD, I'd say. We called the parameds, but they didn't even try to defibrillate." He paused and eyed Parker curiously. "That was a pretty good call about those prints. How did you know?"

"I didn't for sure," Parker said. "It was just a shot. I talked to Brock last night and he said a couple of things that made me wonder."

Parker followed him back to the apartment's only bedroom. As they stepped into the small room, a photographer was popping off pictures of Brock, who was lying on the bed on his right side, with his back to the door. He was clothed in a pair of faded blue jeans and a flower-print sport shirt; no shoes. The seat of the jeans was dark where death had relaxed his sphincter.

Steenbargen emerged from the adjoining bathroom. "Hi, Chief."

Parker returned the greeting and stood very still in the middle of the room, taking everything in.

Wolfe started to say something, but Parker silenced him with a wave of his hand, as his eyes roamed over the walls, the floor, the ceiling. The detective seemed confused that the coroner was making no move toward the body, but Parker knew that the body wasn't going anywhere. It was a lesson he tried to drill into his students—the scene and the corpse could often tell differing stories, and if you were too anxious, you could miss important details. In this case, there didn't seem to be anything—no blood splatters, no bullet holes, no chipped plaster.

The worn carpet, as in the living room, was the color of dirt, and as in the living room, it was hard to tell if that was intentional. Brock's "Rocky" outfit lay on the seat of a brown easy chair by the bed, and next to it a steam iron sat upright on a frayed ironing board. A guitar leaned against one wall, its strings broken. On the cheap Formica bureau against the wall was a large plastic zip-lock bag full of white powder, a box of Johnson and Johnson cotton balls, and a small plastic bag containing a minute quantity of what looked like marijuana.

"It looks like Brock was dealing," Steenbargen remarked. "There must be close to two ounces there, and there's packaging paraphernalia in the closet."

On the nightstand was a teaspoon containing a small wad of cotton, a quart bottle of distilled water, a surgical syringe, and a red plastic balloon, out of the end of which spilled more white powder. Parker guessed the powder was heroin. Plastic balloons or prophylactics were often used to package large amounts of that drug. He inspected the end of the needle on the syringe. It was small-gauge, and the tip was crusted with blood.

Everything indicated that Brock had been into "speed-balling," injecting himself with a mixture of heroin and cocaine. Depending on the purity of the heroin, the mixture would not have to be heated. A small amount of each drug could be mixed in the teaspoon and made into a solution with the addition of distilled water. A small wad of cotton was then dropped into the spoon and the solution was drawn into the syringe through the cotton, which filtered out most of the impurities. Drug users claimed the ensuing high was like winning the hundred-yard dash at the Summer Olympics—the ones that were still alive to talk about it.

Parker moved around to the other side of the bed. Brock's eyes were half-open and glazed and his face was dark blue. The tip of his tongue poked out from between his parted lips and a stalactite of brownish dried saliva ran from the corner of his mouth and stained the pillow beneath his head.

Parker waited until the photographer finished, then rolled Brock over on his back. The lividity was marked on the right side of his face and body. Parker pushed a finger against the purple skin. The blanching effect was minimal, which meant that the blood had already started to clot. He touched the face and neck. The skin was still warm and there were no signs of rigor. He looked up at Steenbargen. "You get a temperature?"

"Ninety-seven-point-five."

Parker nodded. "I'd say he's been dead at least two, three hours."

He picked up each of Brock's hands and inspected the veins on the backs, and the veins on the inside of each arm. He could detect no marks, but that didn't mean much. The needle on that syringe was a "skinny," and any puncture it made would heal rapidly. "His girlfriend been around?"

"Nobody has been around," Wolfe said.

"She was at the Comedy Store with Brock last night. Emily-something. She might know what happened here, or at least help us to pin down an exact time of death." It came to him then. "Braxton."

"I'll check it out," Steenbargen said, and went out.

Parker asked for a chair and stepped inside the tiny walk-in closet, which was bathed in the glare of a naked twenty-five-watt bulb in a wall socket above the door. A chair was brought and Parker stood on it.

The ceiling was too low for him to stand upright and he had to bend his knees and crane his neck sideways to keep from punching out the acoustic tiles with his head. On the shelf that ran above the clothes pole was a Triple-beam Dial-a-gram scale and a shallow desk drawer filled with paraphernalia—plastic bags, paper bindles, a strainer, playing cards, razor blades, a large jar of Manitol, and a bottle of ether. Manitol was a powdered baby laxative often used by cocaine dealers to cut the purity—and increase the profitability—of their product, and ether was used in the process of "freebasing" the drug. It appeared that Fenady had been right: along with his unfunny act, Brock had had an unfunny sideline.

Parker braced himself against the shelf and looked up at the ceiling. The ceiling in the bedroom was of rough plaster, just like the walls, and at least two feet higher than this. He began pushing gently on the two-foot-square tiles. Most of them did not budge, but one gave way easily and lifted out. A flashlight was provided by an obliging patrolman and Parker poked it and his head up through the hole.

As he had suspected, it was a fake ceiling—suspended from the original plaster. The space was about four feet square by two and a half feet high, a nice cozy little hiding place to store goodies away from prying eyes. The only prize the space held, however, was a foil-backed roll of fiberglass insulation.

"Anything up there?" Wolfe called to him.

"Only a roll of fiberglass insulation," he said, stepping down again. "You might want to check it out, though."

Parker began sorting through the clothes hanging on the pole beneath the shelf. Most of Brock's changes from his act were there, as well as his regular street clothes. What Parker found more interesting was the black neoprene wetsuit sandwiched between two garment bags.

He pushed the clothing aside. On the floor, partially obscured behind a brown canvas duffel bag, was a compressed-air tank with a diver's backpack still attached. "Has this been dusted for prints?" Parker asked Wolfe.

"Not yet," the detective said.

"I need a pair of gloves." One of the evidence men brought him a pair of white cotton gloves and he slipped them on and pulled open the drawstring on the top of the bag.

The bag contained basic scuba equipment—regulator, mask, fins, knife, inflatable life vest, a weight belt to compensate for buoyancy. Basic, except for one item. At the bottom of the bag was a second weight belt. It looked like the other weight belt except for two features—it had thirty pounds of weight attached instead of the other belt's fifteen, and its buckle was of a specialized design Parker had never seen before. Instead of the standard quick-release buckle, which could be operated easily with one hand in case of an emergency, this one had a clip-type arrangement that was released by a short wire trigger-ring.

Parker was stuffing everything back into the bag when Steenbargen came into the bedroom holding a piece of paper. "There's an Emily B. in the address finder by the telephone in the living room. I tried the number, but it's busy."

Parker nodded and stood up. "I want this duffel bag taken down to the Center after it's dusted for prints, along with the wetsuit hanging here."

"Wetsuit?" Steenbargen asked, picking up on the significance of that.

"What's with this diving stuff?" Wolfe asked, his eyes narrowing. "Has it got something to do with Duffy?"

Parker told them about his conversation that morning with Steve Patton, the surfing waiter. Wolfe jotted down the name and phone number in his notebook and asked, "Are you saying that Brock drowned Duffy?"

"No. I'm saying that there is a witness that says he saw a scuba diver coming out of the water on the day and approximate time that Duffy drowned. There were some contusions on Duffy's body that bothered me when I did the autopsy. At the time, I dismissed them as inconsequential. Now I'm not so sure."

Wolfe's look grew troubled. "But we also have a neighbor who saw Brock drive into Duffy's driveway and leave five minutes later. The guy would have to be a quick-change artist to be able to pull on all that gear, get in the water, drown Duffy, and get out of there."

"Patton says that the diver got out of the water at the foot of the cliff where Nautilus Street ends. Brock knew Duffy swam every morning. He could have parked at the end of Nautilus, gone into the water, drowned Duffy, then driven to Duffy's *afterward.*"

"What for, if the guy was dead?"

Parker shrugged.

"Maybe Duffy had something that Brock wanted," Steenbargen offered. "Maybe Brock went back to get it."

"Like what?" Wolfe asked.

Parker glanced at Steenbargen. "Brock told me he had a dynamite idea for a TV series that he was sure to sell to Byron Fenady, Duffy's producer. According to Duffy's widow and his business agent, Duffy had finished work on a series treatment. Was anything that looked like a series treatment found at the house?"

Wolfe shook his head. "Not that I know of." He paused and said doubtfully, "You telling me that this Brock murdered his best friend for an idea for a TV show?"

"I'm not saying anybody murdered anybody," Parker insisted. "But Byron Fenady, Mia Stockton, and Joan Duffy all attest to the fact that Brock was jealous of Duffy's success, to the point that he kept him well-supplied with dope, hoping Duffy would destroy his own career. And Duffy apparently went out of his way to humiliate Brock. He embarrassed him by treating him like an errand boy. All that can eat at a man. Maybe Brock saw Duffy as standing in the way of his own success. Brock told me last night that Duffy had gotten to where he was because he had stolen all of his material. Maybe he decided to get even."

Steenbargen frowned. "If Brock went back to the house to pick up the treatment, why would he leave a half-ounce of coke lying around with his prints all over it, knowing Duffy's death would bring half of LASO sniffing around?"

Parker had no answer for that.

"So what do we have here?" Wolfe asked. "Brock got an attack of remorse and overdosed himself?"

"I'll let you know what we have here when I do the autopsy," Parker said.

Steenbargen chimed in: "I was paid a visit this afternoon by a claims adjuster from Aetna. There was a life-insurance policy on Duffy, all right. Half a mil, with an ADB clause. That would make it a million for accidental death."

"Who is the beneficiary?"

"Joan Duffy. And get this: the adjuster says that the amount of the policy was doubled only two months ago. At the insistence of Mrs. Duffy."

"No wonder 'suicide' was a dirty word to her."

Steenbargen nodded. "All that beautiful double-indemnity money would blow right out the window." He lifted a speculative eyebrow. "Maybe she and Brock had a little plot going to split the money?"

"Fred MacMurray and Barbara Stanwyck in *Double Indemnity*?" Parker asked, trying to superimpose the roles onto Brock and Joan Duffy in his mind. No matter how hard he tried, he couldn't get the images to stay in focus. "I can't see them together, but I don't know."

"She sees a way to get rich and recruits Brock to take care of the deed, promising to split the proceeds—"

"If she was going to divorce Duffy, she'd get more than half a million just for alimony and child support."

Steenbargen shrugged. "Maybe she thought the guy was a rotten investment for the future. Maybe she saw him pissing away his career with the drugs and all. There's also the jealousy motive."

"Jealousy?" Wolfe asked. "What are you guys talking about?"

"There is evidence that Duffy was somewhat of a womanizer," Parker said, without getting specific. "I'm not dismissing the possibility altogether, I'm just saying it's unlikely. You might try checking into the affairs of Sol Grossman also. Duffy's business manager."

Wolfe rubbed the back of his neck as if he had a sudden pain there. "What's with him?"

"Duffy called him the night before he died and threatened to fire him. Accused him of impropriety and theft."

"Where did you get that information?" Wolfe asked.

"Mia Stockton," Parker said. "She was at Duffy's house that night."

Wolfe made a face. "Captain Kuttner isn't going to like this. He was real happy with the Duffy thing like it was, wrapped up all nice and neat. He isn't gonna like it when he hears the ribbon is coming off the package."

Parker could believe that. Suicide would have been all right as far as Kuttner was concerned, but murder was another matter. An LAPD lieutenant had once told Parker that the main function of a homicide detective was to find believable ways to turn homicides into suicides, and Kuttner, during his career as a detective, had tried admirably to fill that job description.

One case Parker remembered years ago that Kuttner had investigated and decided had been "suicide" was that of a thirty-seven-year-old dockworker who had been stabbed seventeen times with a boning knife. Kuttner had tried to dispute Parker's conclusion of murder by contending that the man had killed himself because only the final stab wound, which had punctured the heart and nearly severed the spine, had been fatal, and that the "defense cuts" on the man's wrists where he had tried to defend himself, were really false starts while the man had tried to work up enough nerve to slash his wrists.

"It might still be a nice neat package," Parker said. "Duffy's death might very well have been an accident and have no connection with this equipment or Brock's death. And until a connection is proven, the best thing we can all do is keep a tight lid on things."

"As far as I'm concerned," Wolfe said, "this is just another junkie overdose."

Parker nodded. "Anybody from the media wants to know about any diving equipment found here, let them dig it out of your report."

Parker and Steenbargen went outside into the courtyard, and the investigator asked, "What do you think?"

Parker shrugged. "We might have twenty-four hours before news of the diving equipment gets leaked to the media. I think we'd better have some goddamned solid information before then. And I don't think Wolfe or Gunderson is going to be real anxious to dig for it, not with Kuttner sounding the retreat."

Steenbargen nodded. "I might check on a few things myself tomorrow."

"It might not be a bad idea," Parker agreed. "You have the Braxton woman's address?"

Steenbargen dug out the slip of paper and handed it over. "What are you going to do?"

"Talk to the lady."

"*Now?*"

Parker nodded and glanced at his watch. "She's home now. If Brock was responsible for Duffy's death and she knows about it, she might not be tomorrow."

"Want me to go along?"

"No. I need you to personally make sure that diving equipment gets down to the lab. Take it yourself if you have to."

Parker walked out of the courtyard, past the two Egyptian guards, feeling strangely like a pharaoh who had just heard augured the doom of his kingdom.

16

Cole Street was just off the freeway on the edge of Inglewood, about a quarter of a mile from LAX. The neighborhood had a blue-collar feel to it. Its sidewalks were lined with stunted elm trees and modest stucco-box houses. The only thing that set it apart from the others on the block was its urgent need of paint and a gardener. The patch out front that had presumably once been lawn looked as if it had been sprayed with Agent Orange. A brown Hyundai sedan sat in the driveway alongside the house. Light bled faintly through the curtains drawn across the front windows. There were very few cars parked on the street.

As Parker killed his engine, the car windows were shaken by the scream of a 747 as it took off from a runway somewhere nearby. No wonder the trees on the block were stunted, he thought.

From the volume of the rock music blaring inside the house, living in an LAX flight pattern must have impaired Emily Braxton's hearing. Parker got out of the car and was heading up the front walk, when he was frozen by another scream. This one was not a jet engine. It was the steady, shrill, terror-filled scream of a woman and it was coming from inside the house.

The front door burst open suddenly and Emily Braxton staggered out, twisting and flailing spastically, trying to beat at the fire that enveloped her from the waist up. She was a human torch. Her hair and clothing were burning, her agonized face was sheathed in eerie blue flame.

She held out her arms to Parker imploringly and then the nerve-shredding scream was choked off as she pirouetted and collapsed on the sidewalk.

Parker ripped off his jacket and ran to her. He worked frantically, trying to hold down her writhing body while he smothered the flames, and then she finally lost consciousness and became still. In what seemed like an eternity, but was in reality probably no more than ten seconds, he managed to extinguish the fire. Suddenly he heard the sound of a car ignition. An engine roared to life, and across the street a red Corvette peeled away from the curb, its lights out.

Not thinking, Parker ran into the street, trying to get a look at the car's license number, and had to make a running dive for the opposite curb to avoid being hit by the car, which was fishtailing, almost out of control. He turned his shoulder as he landed, and rolled, making it to all fours in time to see the Corvette's taillights wink on and disappear around the corner.

He ran to his car, and snatching up the car radio, instructed the Command Watch to call the paramedics, then turned his attention back to Emily.

She lay in an unmoving heap, her legs tucked up in a fetal position. Her clothing had burned away, revealing blackened, blistered skin, and her hair and eyebrows were completely gone. As he bent down to feel for a pulse, his nose picked up a smell beneath the stench of burned flesh and hair, faint but unmistakable—ether. That would explain the blue color of the flames that engulfed her.

He put his fingers on her throat. She was in shock, but alive. Parker stood up and for the first time noticed the people staring at him from the open doorways of their homes.

A small terrier ran across the street at him, yapping, and Parker stamped his foot to ward it off. The dog put on the brakes, but continued its taunting from a safe distance. The canine's black female owner shouted from the house across the street for the dog to return, but it paid no attention.

A rough-looking pale man in a summer undershirt trotted up the sidewalk, glanced down at the twisted thing on the pavement, and gasped, "Jesus."

"It's all right," Parker assured him. "I'm with the county coroner's office."

The man's eyes narrowed, then widened in recognition. "Hey. You're what's-his-name. I've seen you on TV—the coroner?"

There was a loud popping sound and the tinkling of shattering glass from inside the house. Smoke poured through the open front door. Parker glanced down at Emily. He spread his coat over her, which was about all that could be done for her until the paramedics arrived. "Have you got a hose?" he asked urgently.

"Yeah, sure," the heavyset man said, still uncertain.

"Then get it, quick!" Parker ordered.

Parker left Emily and ran up the front walk, scanning the yard for a water spigot. He spied one half-hidden in the bushes by the front door. He turned it on full and soaked himself down. Shivering from the shock of the cold water, he wet his handkerchief, put it over his nose and mouth, and plunged into the house.

The fire was just beginning to take hold, but the smoke was thick. The flames seemed to be concentrated in the center of the room, where a couch and two overstuffed chairs blazed intensely. Parker hunched low, hurrying from room to room, checking for other possible victims, but could find none.

By the time he got back out into the living room, the fire had spread, lapping at the walls and threatening to cut off his escape. He was dizzy and disoriented, and the smoke was so thick that he couldn't see the door. He knew he had to move now or be quickly overwhelmed by the toxic fumes given off by the burning furniture. He made a guess and charged. The night air was cool, clear spring water to his raw throat as he staggered, coughing and gagging, out onto the lawn. Strong hands braced him up and a voice asked, "You okay?"

Parker tried to blink away the tears from his stinging eyes. It was the heavyset man from down the street "Yeah, I'm fine."

The man nodded and let him go as two neighbors ran up carrying coiled garden hoses. "Anybody else in there?"

"I don't think so," Parker managed to get out between fits of coughing. He pointed out the spigot and told the man to hose down the walls first, to try to keep the flames from reaching the roof. The man hooked up his hose while the other two ran around the side of the house looking for other water outlets.

Parker turned and staggered back to Emily, sucking down deep breaths. He knelt beside her and took another pulse. He stood up dizzily as the sirens screamed around the corner and the front yard became full of pounding feet. He struggled up just as two young paramedics reached him.

"You all right?"

Parker nodded and indicated that they should attend to Emily. They quickly did so, checking for vital signs, covering her with a sheet and blanket, starting an IV. Parker moved off to the side to make way for the firemen who were now arriving. The heavyset man had his garden hose taken away from him and was told to clear the area.

It was tough being a hero, Parker thought wryly, watching the man return to his own yard. There was no room for amateurs anymore. Too many professionals. He stood taking deep breaths and waiting for his head to clear. Then he went over to talk to the paramedics.

"How is she?"

"Would you please clear the area?" one of them began brusquely, and then he glanced up and recognized Parker. "Oh, hello, Dr. Parker." He got to his feet. "What are you doing here, sir?" The man did not say it, but the rest was implicit in the question: she isn't dead yet.

"I put her out."

The medic nodded. "Her vitals aren't good. I don't know if she's going to make it. Her pulse is one-thirty. BP is seventy and dropping fast."

"Respiration?"

"Thirty-eight and shallow."

"Where are you taking her?"

"Westbrook ER is the closest. We've already called. They're standing by."

Emily's eyes opened suddenly and her mouth began to move like a fish's, gasping for air. She seemed to be trying to say something. Parker bent down and got his ear close to the blistered mouth, getting a good whiff of burned hair, which was a stubble of brittle, blackened wire. The sound that came out of her throat was something between a squeak and a wheeze, and then she lost consciousness again.

Parker stood and watched them load her gently onto a gurney and into the back of the ambulance.

Sirens moaned and died as a white fire-department Chevy with its running lights on pulled up behind the fire truck, followed by two LAPD black-and-whites. A pair of men dressed in dark suits stepped out of the Chevy. One of them, a tall Hispanic with a pockmarked face, walked back to the LAPD officers and instructed them to seal off the scene. The other—a no-nonsense Clint Eastwood type—sought out the fire captain, who was talking to his crew inside the house through his HT. The two men nodded to each other and began conversing. The fire captain gestured toward Parker and the two men came over.

"Dr. Parker?" Eastwood said. "Terry Heisman, Arson. I understand you saw what happened?"

"I didn't see how the fire started," Parker said. "I pulled up as the woman came out of the house."

The Hispanic drifted over and Heisman introduced him as his partner, George Gonzales. Parker recounted for them what he had seen.

"What year was this Corvette?"

"Late model, I'd say. The last three digits of the license number were 381."

"Did you get a look at the driver?" Heisman asked.

"No."

"Think whoever it was had something to do with this?"

"I don't know," Parker told them. "Nobody came out of the house but the girl. But whoever was driving was in one hell of a hurry to get out of here."

"How did you happen to be at the scene?" Gonzales asked.

"I was coming over to talk to the woman about her boyfriend. He was found dead in his apartment earlier this evening."

Heisman looked up from his notebook. "Dead? How?"

"I don't know yet for sure, but it looks like a drug overdose."

The captain's HT spit and a voice announced through the static that the fire was out. The water was cut off and three firemen emerged from the house wearing gas masks and carrying axes. "Let's see what we have," Heisman said, walking to the back of the Chevy.

The two investigators peeled off their sport jackets and from the trunk of the car pulled out two canvas jackets and two pairs of rubber boots, which they proceeded to slip on. They picked up two nine-cell flashlights and started for the house, trailed by the fire captain and Parker.

The fire had blown out the breakers in the house and the interior was dark. Heisman stepped through the door and swept his flash around the room. From the center of the room to the far wall was blackened, and holes had been chopped in the wall. Parker's feet made squishing noises on the sodden carpet. There was broken glass everywhere. The atmosphere was thick, humid, almost suffocating with the smell of charcoal.

Heisman fixed his flash on the cluster of gutted, burned furniture in the center of the room and walked over there. He bent down and took out a pencil and began poking around the debris on the floor. He put the pencil through the neck of a brown bottle and held it up. "You have a hell of a nose, Doctor," Heisman said. "Ether."

He put the bottle back on the floor and poked around some more. The light struck something blindingly bright. A broken piece of mirror. Heisman glanced up knowingly at his partner. "This is where it started, all right," he said, training his light on the blackened metal belly of a water pipe.

Parker glanced at it and surveyed the rest of the room. His eyes landed on a flimsy straight-backed chair with metal legs, toppled in a corner. Something about the chair's presence in the room bothered him. It was the kind of chair that more properly belonged in a kitchen. He went over to it and took a closer look.

The chair lay on its side, and the heat had bubbled its once brown plastic seat and back. Next to it, smashed on the floor, was a scorched ceramic lamp, the kind ground out by the thousands and sold at places like K-Mart for twelve dollars. He was still staring at the chair when he was distracted by Gonzales nudging him. "Smell that?"

Parker sniffed the air. Along with the ether, there was another smell, sharp and distinct. "Ammonia."

"It's used in freebasing," Gonzales said. "First, the cocaine is dissolved in distilled water and mixed with ether. Then, a few drops of ammonia are added. That separates out the impurities. The top part is drawn off and dried on some surface—in this case, probably the mirror there. The residue is scraped off and smoked, usually in a water pipe with a little grass."

Heisman stood up. "The girl's hand must have shaken a little too much. Either she spilled the ether or got it too close to one of those candles, and went up like flash paper. It doesn't take a lot with that stuff."

"How could somebody be stupid enough to handle ether around an open flame?" Parker asked.

Gonzales shrugged. "If these people had any brains, they wouldn't be doing this shit, would they?"

Parker silently conceded the point.

"Better notify Narcotics," Heisman told the fire captain, who transmitted the message through his HT.

While the two arson investigators sifted through the living-room rubble, Parker borrowed a flashlight from the captain and went through a door into the kitchen.

The fire had not reached here, but it probably would have been an improvement. Serious drug users were generally not the best housekeepers, and Emily Braxton was no exception. Dirty dishes and glasses, opened boxes of crackers and cookies, empty wine bottles, a jar of Skippy peanut butter, stood all over the sideboards and in the sink. Several pots, the contents of which had boiled over and dried, sat on the grease-caked top of the stove. The main attraction, however, was the battered brown suitcase that lay open on the top of the breakfast table in the corner of the room.

Parker went to it and shone his light inside. It was empty. He ran an index finger across the brown nylon lining. A distinct trail was left in the thin, almost invisible layer of dust that covered the surface. Parker held up his finger in the light. White.

Both locks on the suitcase were broken—jimmied, from the look of the bent clasps and the scratch marks on the metal. Parker inspected one of the locks closely and noticed several tiny yellow strands of some synthetic material adhering to one. The luggage had no ownership tags.

There were three brown plastic chairs pushed in around the table, cousins of the fire victim in the living room. One chair had been taken from the kitchen into the living room. Why?

He stepped back into the living room and trained his flashlight on the ceiling above the toppled chair. It was solid plaster. No acoustic tiles there. He shook his head. She needed another chair in the living room, so she brought one in from the kitchen, so what? His mind was beginning to find something suspicious in everything.

He went back into the kitchen and swept the room again with his flash. There was a door by the sink, partially ajar. He went to it and pulled it open and stepped outside into the cool night air.

A small concrete porch looked out onto a weed-choked postage stamp of a backyard surrounded by a high wooden fence. Parker went to the latched gate in the fence and opened it. A huge gray cat, surprised by the human intrusion, bounded noisily off the lid of a garbage can and took off down the alley. The surprise had been mutual. Parker stood for a moment waiting for his heartbeat to slow down, then went back through the gate. On his way into the house, his light caught something on the concrete porch he hadn't noticed on his way out, and he went down on his haunches for a closer look.

It was a small circular patch of white powder laced with tiny chunks of white rock. Parker went back out to the alley slowly, scanning the yard for more of the powder, but could see none.

Heisman had worked his way into the kitchen and was moving the beam of his flashlight over the walls as Parker came back in. "There's a powder residue in that suitcase in there that might be cocaine."

Heisman shrugged indifferently. "That's for the Narcotics boys. I'm an arson investigator, and I can't see any evidence of criminal arson here."

They went back into the living room. A hawk-faced man in a dark suit and tie appeared in the front doorway and looked around guardedly. A voice behind him said, "C'mon, Sam, let's move. I wanna be home by midnight."

The hawk-faced man took a step onto the sodden carpet, looked down in disgust at his dark blue patent-leather, imitation-alligator shoes, and swore. "Shit. These shoes cost me ninety-five bucks. On sale."

An older, paunchy man came in on the hawk-faced man's heels. "I keep tellinya, Sam," the man remarked gaily, "you should shop at Kinney's like me. Then you wouldn't give a shit."

The man didn't look as if he cared much about the rest of his ensemble, either. He wore a red-and-blue-plaid jacket, khaki slacks, and a green alpine climber's hat, the kind with a brush stuck on the side of the band.

"You guys from Narcotics?" Heisman asked.

"That's right," the older one said, coming over. "I'm Stroud. The ad for *Gentleman's Quarterly* over there is Holmes." His expression noted Parker's presence, and he asked, "Anybody hurt?"

"The occupant of the house is in bad shape. Dr. Parker happened to be at the scene when the fire broke out. That's probably the only reason she's alive."

Holmes had hold of his neatly pressed pant legs and was stepping gingerly over the carpet. Stroud watched him with some amusement and asked, "What happened?"

"Looks like the girl was freebasing and spilled some ether," Heisman said.

They went into the kitchen and inspected the suitcase.

Stroud took the plastic end of a Tiparillo out of his pocket, inserted it into the corner of his mouth, and began chewing on it. The jocular boredom was gone from his eyes and his face took on an intent look. "If there was a stash in here, where did it go? The girl couldn't have freebased it all."

Holmes shrugged. "How do we know how much was in there? We don't even know for sure it's coke. It might be powdered sugar."

"And those might be real alligator skin," Stroud said, pointing at his partner's shoes. He looked at the locks. "They've been jimmied, all right."

Parker told them about Harvey Brock's death and about the hidden compartment in his closet ceiling.

"The guy was dealing, huh?" Stroud asked, interested.

"That's what it looks like."

The detective pushed up the brim of his hat with a forefinger. "You think this suitcase was his?"

Parker pointed at the latch on the suitcase. "I don't know, but the fibers in that lock might tell you. They look like fiberglass and there was a roll of fiberglass insulation in Brock's ceiling."

Parker told them about the Corvette and Stroud exchanged glances with his partner. "You think the girl was torched?"

Parker shrugged. "I don't know. As I was telling the arson investigators, nobody came out the front door besides the girl."

The quartet went onto the porch, where Parker pointed out the patch of white powder. After examining it, Stroud

207

stood up and said, "Could be coke. We'll get an analysis, along with the residue in that suitcase." To Holmes: "Call SID and get some evidence men down here before we start tearing this place apart."

Stroud tugged on his lower lip. "If this was a drug ripoff, somebody might have tried to get cute and make it look like a freebasing accident. The asshole could have grabbed the dope, torched the girl, split out the back door and down the alley, then come up the other side of the street to the Corvette as you pulled out—"

"Why would someone that smart risk being seen?" Parker argued. "Why not just park in the alley in the first place?"

Stroud made a face and nodded at the logic of that. "I'll get someone over to Westbrook, just in case the woman regains consciousness and starts talking. In the meantime, I'll run possibles on that plate and see what we come up with."

Parker gave them Wolfe's name so that they could interface with him on the case, then asked, "You need me anymore?"

"If the arson guys are through with you, we are," Stroud said. "We'll have to get a statement from you, but we can do that later. I guess we know where to find you."

17

The Westbrook ER looked like a battle zone. Every bed was in use and the overflow was being treated on gurneys set up in the corridor. Several accident victims, all apparently from the same crash, were just being brought in, moaning and begging for painkiller. Sometimes, Parker thought grimly, the law of averages didn't hold, and that's when everything happened at the same time.

The ER staff was too frantically busy to help him. Parker could see Emily on a bed behind a partially closed curtain. She was very still and appeared to be unconscious. Parker went over to the bed and stood beside her, trying to evaluate her condition, which seemed to have worsened.

"Emily," he said softly, but there was no indication that she heard him.

Parker stood staring down at the wasted girl. In his

work, he considered himself, first and foremost, a medical detective, but now a subtle change had taken place, and he was starting to view himself as a homicide detective.

A hand was placed on his shoulder. Parker wasn't sure whether it was gentle or simply tired. "I'm sorry—no visitors," a man's voice said.

Parker turned to find a young white-jacketed doctor with thick steel-rimmed glasses and a droopy mustache. He'd be thirty at most, but right now he looked a lot older, probably because he'd been working for sixteen hours straight, with only an occasional catnap as a refresher. His name tag said he was Dr. Franklin.

Automatically Parker showed his own ID, not bothering to speak, and Franklin accepted it without comment. If he wondered why the county's medical examiner had suddenly ventured into his emergency room without announcement, that wasn't apparent in his dull, let's-not-argue look. Two tired people, Parker thought.

"Her condition is critical," Franklin said, moving in to check on Emily. "She sustained full-thickness burns over eighty percent of her upper body and she is still in a coma. All we can do is try to stabilize her, then move her to a burn center."

"How are you treating her?" Parker asked.

Franklin gave a kind of helpless shrug. "There isn't much we can do. Try to replace the fluids she's lost. Keep her temperature down."

Parker nodded. "Has she said anything?"

"No. She hasn't regained consciousness. And even if

she did, I doubt she'd be able to speak. Her larynx and trachea are severely burned."

Inhalation injury. Parker had been afraid of that. In a great many cases, it proved fatal.

Franklin hesitated. "Is this official," he asked finally, then quickly added, "or are you a relative, friend?"

"It's official."

"Oh," Franklin said, his attitude changing subtly. The care and friendliness left his voice. "The next twenty-four hours are the watershed period for her. Frankly, I wouldn't get my hopes up."

"Thanks."

Parker turned away abruptly and went out into the corridor, headed for the exit, but an angry shout—"Eric!"—made him swing around. Dr. Jonas Silverman was coming down the hallway, fixing him with a gaze that could equate with the guidance system of a heat-seeking missile.

"What are *you* doing here?" Silverman demanded shrilly. "Coming to do some spying yourself? Your fat snoop detective didn't gather enough dirt to please you?"

"Jonas—"

"Don't try to defend your actions, Eric," Silverman cut him off sharply. "I don't want to hear it. You betrayed my trust. You lied to me."

Parker looked around. Even in the ER's bedlam, people had paused, staring.

"You're a liar!"

"Hey, hold on, Jonas," Parker said, trying to keep his own temper. It had been a long, hard day, and he didn't need another diatribe. "I promised to hold off filing the report for a couple of days. I didn't make any sort of promise not to investigate."

Silverman continued to shout at him. "You've gone too far this time! I was always your defender, but now I understand what you've turned into. Power has gone to your head. You've not only betrayed our friendship, you've betrayed our profession."

"Actually, I was defending our profession," Parker said mildly. "And, as a friend—an old and good friend—I had hoped you would understand my position. I can't let friendship—or anything else—interfere with the job I have to do."

"You damned fool!" Silverman shouted, enraged. "The system doesn't operate that way. If it did, we'd be working with our backs to the wall, always watching for the next attack, and nothing would get done! Mistakes are made and they are corrected. No system is perfect. But this sort of back-stabbing only tears it apart."

Parker felt a pang of guilt about going behind Silverman's back, but not enough to accept this kind of public abuse. He turned to leave, but Silverman restrained him, and grabbed his arm. "I'm not finished, but you are. You just continue to isolate yourself from the rest of the medical community. You'll find it's pretty lonely playing by yourself on the other side of the net." The older man barely stopped for breath before continuing with his harangue. "You know what your problem is, Eric? You have no loyalty to anyone but yourself. You want to be a big man, no matter what the cost to others, and you've become your own worst enemy. You've already alienated most of this town with your superior, high-handed attitude. You're finished as a coroner!"

Parker politely but firmly freed himself. He couldn't imagine what had set off the man. "What did Jacobi find?"

"Nothing," Silverman said, smiling smugly. "Not a damn thing."

"Then why are you so upset about this, Jonas?"

The man's face reddened. He looked apoplectic.

"Why?" he sputtered. "Why? If you can't see it, I can't tell you. There are certain unwritten rules in this profession, Eric. How can you turn on your own? You know how things are today. You know how hard it is to provide quality health care in the conditions we're forced to operate under. Yet, despite all the flak, we carry on, we manage, and we succeed. We survive because we stand and work together. So it's particularly hurtful when one of our own turns Judas and sets out to destroy us from within."

"*Destroy?*" Parker couldn't believe what he was hearing. "If we don't clean our own house, nobody else will. They don't know how—"

Silverman shook his head. "You aren't trying to clean house, Eric. You're feeding your overblown ego. You didn't come to me like a man, never mind a friend, and ask me for my cooperation in this matter. If you had, I would have gladly given it to you. Instead, you sent your snoop over here to sneak around behind my back. You *wanted* to find something wrong here, Eric, so you could

213

make a few more headlines and present yourself to the public as some sort of crusading champion of truth."

"That's not true, Jonas—"

"No? They why didn't you tell me when I came to your office what you intended to do?"

Parker didn't know what to say. That after all these years of friendship and respect, he didn't trust the man anymore? That the duties of his profession required him to sacrifice all personal relationships to the pursuit of truth? Silverman's words stung, and for the first time Parker felt uncertain about his own motives. Perhaps there was some truth in what the man said: perhaps he was trying to feed his own ego.

"You put yourself out on a limb this time," Silverman said. "And I'm going to saw it off."

Silverman turned abruptly and walked away and Parker looked around, embarrassed by the openmouthed stares of the hospital staff, who had stopped to watch the tirade. He exited quickly, pondering the meaning of Silverman's last remark. It had sounded distinctly like a threat, but Parker dismissed it as a meaningless statement tossed off in a moment of anger.

Parker was heading across the parking lot lost in thought when he was alerted by the sound of squealing tires. A black coroner's Chevy pulled into the driveway and screeched to a stop beside him. Steenbargen stuck his head out of the window and said, "I heard about your call when I got down to headquarters. What happened?"

Parker told him about it and the investigator rubbed his graying mustache dubiously. "This is getting a little too coincidental for me. First Duffy, then Brock and Braxton. All 'accidental' deaths. Two of them drug-related, on the same day? Sorry. Something is rotten in Denmark."

Parker concurred, then asked, "You seal Brock's apartment?"

"Yeah. The key is at the Center."

"What about the diving gear?"

"It's in your office." He looked at Parker with concern. "It's almost eleven-thirty, Chief. Why don't you call it a night? You look all-in."

Parker nodded noncommittally. As weary as he was, he knew that if he went home, he would never be able to sleep. He would just sit there staring out at the lights. That idea was intolerable to him at this moment. Not just because of the events of the evening, but because he felt like a man running on doomsday time. "You're right, Mike," Parker said, running a hand through his hair. "It has been a long day. I'll see you tomorrow."

Steenbargen continued to look concerned. "You all right? You want to get a drink somewhere?"

Parker shook his head wearily. "No. I think I'll head on home."

Steenbargen nodded and drove out of the lot. Parker watched him go, then got into his own car and took off.

He waited until he was almost downtown, when Steenbargen would be out of transmitting range, then picked up the radio and advised Center security that he was coming in.

18

Parker sat alone in the silence of his office, staring at the photographs and the weight belt on his desk. He examined the brass clasp and ring that had been sewn onto the belt. He snapped it shut, then pulled the small ring on the side, releasing the clasp. No knowledgeable diver would ever replace the normal quick-release buckle with such a dangerous arrangement. Unless he didn't want it to open.

Parker looked closely at the contusions in the photographs and the shape and size of the five-pound lead weights on the belt. They were approximately the same.

He stood up, slipped the belt around his waist, and fastened it. The thirty pounds dragged the belt heavily around his hips. He was a bit thinner than Duffy had been, so the actor would have carried the weights higher, which was borne out in the photographs. Parker adjusted the weights to approximate the position of the markings in the pictures. That would have put the release clip over his left kidney. Operating the release would have been difficult under the best of conditions—even if Duffy had known exactly where it was and how it worked. With it back there, panicked and drowning, he would have found it impossible.

Parker visualized the scene in his mind. Brock knew about Duffy's morning swim. He would have been waiting and ready. The diver's wetsuit and life vest would have compensated for the extra weight the man had been carrying. He had followed Duffy, keeping behind him to make sure his trail of bubbles was not detected, stalking his prey from the dark depths like some predator shark, waiting for the right moment to strike. Then, perhaps when Duffy had paused to rest from his exercise, Brock had come up fast from below, wrapping the death belt around the actor's waist and fastening it before he had a chance to react.

Panicked, Duffy must have torn at the belt, which would have been the reason for the abrasions on the abdomen and back. Parker picked up the photograph of the bruise and hematoma on Duffy's right calf. He took off the belt and went to the diver's bag and began rummaging through the equipment. His hand came out with a diver's knife holstered in a black ankle sheath. The butt of the handle was a round stainless-steel knob about the size and shape of the bruise in the picture. Perhaps Duffy had struggled briefly with his assailant, the bruise resulting from kicking the knife.

The struggle must have been brief, however. In his

panic, Duffy's primary goal would have been to get to the surface. He would have let Brock go, and the man could have just swum away and watched his friend drown. It wouldn't have taken long. Even the strongest swimmer could not have stayed afloat long with thirty pounds on him. After the deed was done, Brock could have just disengaged the belt and swum to shore, probably exiting the water somewhere down the coast, in case anyone had witnessed the drowning from the beach. But why would he bother lugging the belt with him? Why not just drop it somewhere along the way? It wouldn't be likely to be found, and even if it was, it wasn't likely that it would be connected with Duffy's death. A souvenir, a reminder so that he might keep his jealous hatred alive? Or had the belt had another effect? Had the reminder of his act of murderous betrayal wrought such remorse in Brock that he had decided to take his own life with an overdose of drugs?

Speculation of that sort was useless at this stage of the game, Parker knew. First, he had to prove that Duffy had been murdered, and to do that, he had to get the body back. If his critics had howled before, they would be snapping at his jugular with that request. His only chance was to get Joan Duffy on his side, and considering her mood this morning, he doubted there was much chance of that. He picked up the wetsuit and headed down to the security floor.

It was after midnight and an eerie hush had settled over the place, the quiet interrupted only occasionally by the muted voices of the few investigators or attendants unfortunate enough to pull the graveyard shift. Parker smiled sardonically at the irony of that term as he walked down the brightly lighted corridor. They were *all* graveyard shifts here.

The body of Harvey Brock lay on the table in the autopsy room, washed in the harsh glare of the lights. Parker had decided to perform the autopsy unassisted. There was no need to roust any of his staff out of bed for this. Besides, what could he tell them? He wanted them to help him do an autopsy in the middle of the night because he could hear the political hounds behind him, snapping at his heels? Anyone would have thought he was losing it. Except Schaffer, perhaps. That young buck would have come in gladly, even if it had been three in the morning. After considering, Parker decided against it. Let the kid sleep. The way things were going around here, he was going to need all he could get just to make it through the day. He would do this one alone.

After five minutes of arduous struggling to tug and pull the top of the wetsuit onto Brock's torso, Parker began to regret his decision. He left the body and stepped out into the hall. A young black attendant with corn-rowed hair stepped out of the refrigerated storage room and Parker called to him, "Come here a minute, will you?"

The young man complied and Parker asked, "What's your name?"

"Emmett Jackson, sir." The young man was tall and big, built like a football player.

"How long have you worked here, Emmett?"

"About a year, I guess," he said, shrugging his large shoulders.

"You like it?"

"It's nothing I want to do permanently, if that's what you mean," the green-frocked attendant said, wondering where this was all going.

"What do you want to do permanently?"

"I'm studying to be a dentist, sir."

The kid was respectful. Parker liked that. "Where?"

"USC."

Parker nodded. "You squeamish, Emmett?"

The attendant smiled broadly. "It's about a year too late to be asking that question."

"I need an assistant. How would you like to help me?"

That took the young man by surprise. "*Me?*"

"Yeah, you."

"Assist you? Doing an autopsy?"

"That's right."

"*Now?*"

Parker nodded.

"But . . . I wouldn't know what to do—"

"I'll tell you what to do," Parker said.

Emmett shrugged doubtfully. "All right, Doctor. If you say so."

Parker showed Emmett into the autopsy room and pointed out the wetsuit. "First, we have to get him dressed."

Emmett's look said that he was wondering if the cheese had slipped off Parker's cracker. "I don't mean to sound

221

stupid, sir," he said uncertainly, "but isn't it kind of unusual to dress up a cadaver *before* performing an autopsy?"

"I don't intend to perform the autopsy with the body dressed," Parker assured him, smiling.

Emmett's eyes grew wary. "You mean, you're going to dress the body up, then undress it again?"

"Precisely. Now, give me a hand."

The dental student set to work, and Parker could imagine what he was thinking—what kind of fetishistic ritual had he wandered into?—yet he couldn't very well refuse to help. Parker knew it was mean not to explain, but it was also amusing, and so he kept his counsel, thinking that the opportunities for amusement were rare enough these days.

Even with Emmett's strength assisting him, it took Parker a good ten minutes of strenuous struggle to zipper Brock's body into the wetsuit. He stood back, wiped the perspiration from his brow, and surveyed the fit. "Strange."

Emmett still had that look. Everything here was strange. "What?"

"These suits are supposed to fit snug—that's the principle behind them—but this is ridiculous."

"Maybe he bought it a long time ago and gained some weight," Emmett offered, trying to be helpful.

"Maybe," Parker said. "But that doesn't explain why the arms are too long."

"You're sure it's his?"

"It was hanging in his closet, but to answer your question—no, I'm not sure." Parker smiled. "You just hit on a cardinal rule of forensic pathology," Parker told him. "Preconceived ideas can lead to wrong conclusions. A good forensic pathologist questions *everything.*"

Steve Patton had described the diver he had seen as being over six feet. That had not particularly bothered Parker at first; eyewitness testimony was notoriously fallible. But now he was not so sure. The wetsuit would have fit a man of that height a lot better than it fit Brock.

They pulled off the suit, and after Parker completed his examination of the external surface of the body, describing scars, moles, and other identifying marks, he directed his attention through a magnifying glass to the left arm. He started with the hand and stated to the dictating microphone: "There is no evidence of trauma in the left hand, knuckles, or nails. The left forearm shows no abnormal skin surface. No swelling or blue ecchymosis is noted."

He moved his hand up to the crook of the elbow and squeezed the inside of the arm, noting no recognizable hardness. He examined the veins around the inside of the elbow carefully. The puncture mark was so clean, he nearly missed it, even with magnification. That stimulated his curiosity. When a person gave himself an injection, it was rarely so neat. There was usually more bleeding and tearing of the skin. This looked almost as if it had been done in a doctor's office.

Parker asked his draftee assistant for a black felt-tip marker he had laid out with the other instruments, and with it drew a grid on the skin over the puncture, about fifteen centimeters by eight centimeters, marking the direction and outline of the veins. Emmett watched fascinated as the chief medical examiner selected a scalpel and began cutting out an ellipsoid of skin around the grid, about one centimeter deep. With surgical precision Parker removed the patch of skin, along with the subcutaneous tissue and portions of the antecubital veins which drained into the cephalic and brachial veins, and placed it on a slide.

Emmett followed Parker to the dissecting microscope, where the forensic scientist prepared the specimen for examination. Parker put his eyes on the binocular lens and first examined the veins. There was little detectable scarring, which indicated that if Brock shot up drugs, he hadn't done it often. Parker stepped back and asked his new assistant if he wanted to take a look. Emmett bent over the microscope and Parker slipped automatically into his tutorial voice.

"As you can see, a hypodermic needle leaves a track in the flesh much like a fork leaves in a piece of raw meat, except, of course, its size. Fortunately, the track fills with blood, which makes it fairly easy to trace. What we have to do now is determine the direction of that track in relation to the grid we have drawn, as well as the downward angle it followed, through the subcutaneous tissue and the vein."

"Fascinating," Emmett said sincerely.

Parker smiled, pleased. "Isn't it?" He resumed his place at the microscope and within minutes had made his calculations. On an axis running straight down Brock's arm, the needle had entered the skin at a forty-five-degree angle upward, on the inner left side of the elbow.

Parker went back to the autopsy table and picked up the syringe he had placed there. He put it in Brock's right hand, between the thumb and the middle finger, with the forefinger on the plunger, and brought the arm across the abdomen to the left arm, trying to position the needle so that it would enter the arm at the calculated angle.

"I have a theory, Emmett," Parker explained as he worked. "I look at the human body as a skeleton with hinges. The arm is hinged at the elbow and the wrist, the leg at the knee and ankle, et cetera. Now, those hinges can only move in certain directions. Thus, when you consider a man's hand—like this man's hands—the length of his fingers, the flexibility of the joints, the length of his arms, you should be able to determine, by the angle and location of a puncture mark, if he injected himself."

"Makes sense," Emmett said.

Parker nodded. "Every puncture mark, in effect, would be like the person's signature, unique to his skeletal and muscular joints. For example, as you can see, with this man's arm at his side, the normal position a junkie would inject himself, there is no way we can get the track to match the angle of the needle." He looked up. "Pick up his arm there and see if we can get a match in another position."

The black man moved the arm around until Parker had achieved his angle.

"For this man to have injected himself," Parker concluded, "he would have had to be holding his left arm at a ninety-degree angle out from his body. Even then, it would have been difficult."

"There's no way someone would shoot himself up that way."

"Precisely," Parker agreed. "Which means that unless my geometry is wrong, someone else must have administered this injection." He went back to the microscope and reworked his calculations. They came out the same.

All of the tiredness had left Parker's body, replaced by a feeling of exhilaration. Although his "signature" theory was just that—a theory—and would in all likelihood be dismissed by his critics as highly speculative, he was sure he was onto something, and plunged eagerly into the job ahead.

He worked quickly, all the while avidly pointing out the telltale signs to his curious pupil—the abundant gray shaving-cream-like froth in the trachea and bronchi; the severe edema and congestion of the lungs, the heaviness of the heart; the brain, which was swollen and weighed 1,630 grams—200 grams more than normal; the distended bladder, which contained 450 cc. of urine. He drew off the standard samples of blood, urine, and bile, removed intact the stomach, gallbladder, and one kidney, and set aside significant portions of lung, liver, and brain, but he did not have to wait for the results of the toxicological analysis to know that Harvey Brock had died suddenly of an overdose of drugs.

Emmett watched the chief sew up the gaping Y incision and said, "I'd never really watched an autopsy before.

Working this shift, I've only gotten to see the end product."

"Did you find it interesting?"

"Very."

Parker finished up suturing, then told Emmett to store the body and meet him in his office. Parker left the office door open, and twenty minutes later the young black man stepped in tentatively. "Sit down," Parker told him, and motioned him into the VIP visitor's chair, the one that was soft. The rest were hard, which made for brief stays.

"I was watching you down there," Parker said, falling into his own chair. "You started out thinking: 'Who the hell would want to do this?' Then you changed your mind."

Emmett didn't answer. His face remained implacable as Parker continued.

"Most people never get by that first cut. Because it's a cadaver, they're turned off, disgusted, and they're lost forever." Parker saw Emmett's eyes move unbidden to his watch. It was almost three o'clock in the morning and Parker's argument was going to self-destruct on his own contrary compulsions.

"The sad truth is, not very many medical students are anxious to be pathologists. All the bright medical students want to be heart surgeons, or oncologists, or endocrinologists, or shrinks with fat practices in Beverly Hills.

"What most people don't realize is that forensic science can be a tool to aid the living. By studying the pathology of a disease, we can aid in finding a cure. Studies of wounds and injuries have pioneered new technologies invaluable in preventing lethal injuries."

Emmett looked on politely, his face expressing a mild degree of curiosity.

"And the frontiers are just opening up. In the next few decades developments in forensics are going to revolutionize the entire medico-legal system. Through DNA research, we'll be able to identify a criminal by protein-enzyme analyses of the secretions left at the scene of the crime. Within a decade or two we'll be able to put together complete psychological profiles of the deceased through neurochemical studies. We'll be able to tell what kind of temperment the person had and whether he or she was depressed or angry, homicidal or suicidal at the time of death. As the technology advances, the applications of science are going to be limitless."

"You sound excited," Emmett said, smiling slightly.

"These are exciting times." Parker could see the young attendant was wondering where he was leading. "Are you serious about being a dentist?"

"Yes," Emmett said, but a bit uncertainly, it struck Parker.

"Forensics offers special opportunities and satisfactions. The opportunity to achieve something, to be unique. Watching you tonight, I thought you'd be good at it. I hope you'll think about it."

Emmett looked at his watch. "Well, I better get back to work, sir. But thank you. It was very . . . enlightening."

Parker laughed. "No doubt." As he watched Emmett leave, he wondered if his speech had made any impression. It was hard to tell. Emmett Jackson was a man who kept his own counsel. Unlike himself.

He rubbed his tired eyes and rose. He was tired enough now that he figured he would be able to sleep, even if just for a few hours. He contemplated sacking out on the office couch, but decided to drive home. Even when he was young, his body had complained about nights on couches. Besides, he found he was looking forward to being greeted by at least one face today that would be happy to see him, even if he did step in something.

19

Parker was awakened at six by Boomer, who had jumped up on the bed and was licking his face. He swung his legs over the edge of the bed groggily and tried to focus his vision. The Lab jumped off the bed and ran to the bedroom door, doubled back, then ran to the door again, checking to see if Parker was following. The significance of the gesture finally dawned on Parker and he threw on a robe hastily and took the dog outside.

Half a block down, the puppy stopped and performed his morning duties like a seasoned trooper and responded gleefully to the praise being heaped on him. This could be an omen, Parker decided as he walked Boomer back to the house, a positive sign for the future. He sealed off the bathroom, left food and water for the dog, and drove downtown.

It was a few minutes before 0700 hours when he stepped

onto the security floor and checked the day's schedule with Dr. Phillips. The night had been relatively quiet, which would give them a chance to catch up on some of the backlogged cases. Cindy was not in yet when Parker entered the office. He put on a pot of coffee, and while it brewed, looked up the number of Scribner's Mortuary.

They started work early at Scribner's, but it was too late for Parker. He was told by the chief embalmer that John Duffy's body had been embalmed and shipped to Chicago late last night. Interment was to be handled there by Wiebel Brothers and was set for the day after tomorrow at one.

Parker checked his watch. It was early to be calling someone in L.A., but he dared not wait. The time difference to Chicago was two hours and it was imperative to get in touch with the Cook County medical examiner before he went to lunch. Joan Duffy's voice was thick with sleep when she answered.

"I'm sorry to disturb you so early, Mrs. Duffy," Parker apologized, "but something urgent has come up—"

"Urgent? What is it?"

"Some new evidence that your husband's death might not have been an accident, that he might have been murdered."

It took her a few seconds to absorb that. "I thought you said the story in the papers was false?"

"This has nothing to do with that story."

"What does it have to do with?"

"Harvey Brock died last night from a drug overdose. Evidence found at the scene indicates that he might have been involved in some way in the death of your husband."

"How? What evidence?"

"I'm afraid I can't go into that."

"John was my husband. If he was murdered, I have a right to know."

"And you will know, as soon as I'm sure."

"When will that be?" Her voice was turning sibilant.

"As soon as I make another examination of the body."

"Another examination?"

"That's why I'm calling," Parker explained. "I would like your permission to have the body brought back to Los Angeles."

"The service is set for the day after tomorrow," she said uncertainly.

"I realize that—"

"First you imply John committed suicide, then you say it was an accident. Now it's murder. Yet you won't even tell me what this new evidence is."

Parker was in a corner. He wanted her cooperation, and to get it he was going to have to lay out for her the basis of his suspicions. He sighed. She was right in one respect: she had a right to know.

He told her about the discovery of the scuba gear at Brock's and the marks on Duffy's body, and she said, "That's all?"

"Yes," Parker said, a little surprised by her reaction.

"That seems . . . rather fantastic."

"The only way to find out if it is is to bring your husband's body back."

She wavered. "I don't know. I'll have to think about it. Can I call you back?"

"Certainly. But time is of the essence, Mrs. Duffy."

When she called back ten minutes later, her voice was stronger. "I just talked to Sol Grossman, Dr. Parker. He and I have agreed. I will not give you permission to bring John's body back."

"May I ask the reason for your decision?"

"To do what you propose would only provide more mud for the scandal sheets to dig up." Her tone became vituperative: "Or is that what you want?"

The question took Parker aback. "Pardon me?"

"Frankly, Dr. Parker, both Sol and I have doubts about the sincerity of your motives, after the press conference and that story in the papers. You seem more interested in your own press clippings than the truth." She took a breath.

"Sol is right. John is dead. Nothing is going to bring him back. I have to bury him and get on with my life."

Parker was beginning to wonder if Grossman's interference and his interest in seeing his former client buried two thousand miles away could be rooted in something other than his concern for Joan Duffy's emotional well-being.

He sighed. He hadn't wanted it to come to this. "As chief coroner of this county, Mrs. Duffy, I have the authority to have the body brought back to Los Angeles without your consent."

"*You* have the authority?" she shouted. "What are you trying to accomplish, Doctor? Don't you have any consideration for anyone but yourself?"

"Mrs. Duffy—" Parker tried to butt in, but the woman was on a roll.

"We'll see who has the authority! John will be buried in Chicago the day after tomorrow!"

The receiver was slammed down sharply in Parker's ear. He replaced his gently on its cradle and sat back considering his options. So much for a new day dawning. Perhaps he had read the omen wrong. Maybe it hadn't been an omen at all. He called Chicago information for the number of the coroner's office, and moments later was being greeted by the cheerful voice of Stander Collingsworth, medical examiner of Cook County.

Collingsworth was a jolly, apple-cheeked man who looked more like a glad-handing Chicago politician than the competent forensic pathologist he was. He had consulted Parker frequently over the years on points of forensic medicine, and the two had met in person several times at conventions of the National Association of Medical Examiners.

"So how are things out in the land of sun and sin?"

"Hot, Stander. In more ways than one. You probably know about the John Duffy case."

"Sure."

"The body was released and shipped last night to Wiebel Brothers Mortuary in Chicago. Some new evidence has developed that points to the possibility of foul play. But I need the body back to prove it."

"You have permission from the next of kin?"

"No. The widow refuses to cooperate."

"Hmmm." There was a pause. "What exactly is this new evidence?"

Parker explained and Collingsworth said, "Tell you

what, Eric. Send me what you have and I'll look it over. In the meantime, I'll go over to Wiebel Brothers myself and take a look at the body."

"I appreciate it, Stander. I'll express-mail the stuff today."

Parker called LASO Metro and left a message for Wolfe, then began putting together the packet for Collingsworth. He was almost finished when there was a knock on the door and Jacobi waddled in.

The investigator's excess flesh oozed over the arms of the chair as he lowered himself onto it. Although it was only a little past seven-thirty, the mustard stains on the man's shirt looked fresh.

"I thought you'd like to know what I found out over at Westbrook."

"I ran into Jonas Silverman last night. He told me you hadn't found anything."

Jacobi shrugged his corpulent shoulders. "When I left there yesterday, I hadn't. I talked to everybody involved in the McCullough surgery and ran into a stone wall. But last night I got a break. A scrub nurse I'd interviewed called and said she wanted to talk. She was afraid the surgeon in the case—Dr. Minkow—was going to wind up taking a bad rap for the whole thing, and she couldn't allow that."

"What rap?"

Jacobi grunted as he leaned forward and pulled a small spiral notebook out of his back pocket. He flipped it open and began reading. "McCullough was scheduled for surgery at eight that morning in OR four, but he was bumped by an emergency gunshot wound. The gunshot victim, one Scott Zukor, had been in a domestic quarrel and had taken a thirty-eight slug in the lower abdomen. The bullet pierced the bowel."

"*That* was where the gas gangrene came from," Parker anticipated.

Jacobi nodded and went on. "The surgeons did what they could for the kid and sewed him up. Enter McCullough. Because of the time squeeze—there were a couple more surgeries scheduled for that OR after McCullough—and because of a screw-up down at central supply, Minkow decided not to wait for new instruments, but to use the ones being sterilized in the room.

"Minkow starts the kidney transplant and everything is going along according to Hoyle until the anesthetist looks down on the floor and sees something. He immediately whispers something to the nurse who had sterilized the instruments and she turns white. What the anesthetist has seen is the paper indicator that was in the sterilizer with the instruments. Instead of being black, like it's supposed to be when the critical temperature is reached, the paper is still white. The nurse responsible is new and she'd taken out the instruments without checking. Dr. Minkow is told and he freaks, but there isn't anything he can do. He finishes up and ships McCullough off to recovery, but he knows he's just worked on a dead man."

"Did you check the sterilizer?"

"This is where it gets really interesting," Jacobi said. "I looked over all the equipment in the room. There's a new Castle sterilizer in that room. It was put in there three days after McCullough died. The scrub nurse told me that they'd had problems with the old sterilizer for three months. Half the time, they couldn't get the temperature up to two-sixty, the other half, it wouldn't stay there long enough. She says that several of the nurses and surgeons had complained about it repeatedly to Dr. Silverman, and had requested a new unit, but that he'd turned down the requests, saying the hospital couldn't afford it right now. He told them not to use the unit if there was a problem, to send the instruments down to central supply."

Parker felt angry, and at the same time saddened. That outburst last night had been born of panic—panic that it would be discovered that his administrative penny-pinching had killed a man. "Did you talk to Dr. Yee?"

"He wouldn't say much, but he was real nervous when I mentioned sepsis. I had the feeling he was hiding something." Jacobi scratched his fourth chin. "From what the nurse says, Silverman has been putting the pressure on, trying to keep the lid on it. I guess he's been phoning everybody involved, telling them to keep their mouths shut."

"You think one of those calls could have come to Dr. Yee?"

"If I were Silverman," Jacobi said, "Yee would be the first one I called."

Parker frowned thoughtfully. "Will this nurse go on the record? Get a statement from her today before she changes her mind," Parker told him. "Then go back to Westbrook and go through every memo from Jonas Silverman's office, as well as all purchase orders. If they won't come across with them, subpoena the records. I want the billing date for that sterilizer."

Jacobi hefted himself out of the chair and said, "Right. I'm also going to put another squeeze on Dr. Yee. I think he might be ready to crack."

Jacobi went out and Parker moved over to the window. He stared up the hill at the County Hospital and thought about calling Jonas and telling him how sorry he was about what he had to do, but he knew the man would never understand. It had gone too far for that. He just hoped that Silverman had not influenced Yee to deliberately falsify his autopsy findings. An administrative error was bad enough. It had lost a man's life and would end up costing the hospital money and credibility. But the other would end Silverman's career. Parker did not want to be responsible for that, but he didn't know what else he could do. He felt helpless against the forces within and outside himself. He could only play the scene out or be irrevocably lost to himself.

The flashing light on his phone broke into his thoughts. He was pleasantly surprised to hear Mia Stockton's voice bid him good morning. "I'm sorry to bother you," she said, "but I just had a break from shooting and I wanted to find out if it was true about Harvey."

"I'm afraid so."

"What happened?"

"He died of an overdose of cocaine and heroin."

"I knew Harvey was into coke, of course, but I had no idea he took heroin," she said, sounding genuinely surprised. "Was it an accident?"

"I'm not sure," Parker hedged. He didn't know whom she would be talking to today, and he didn't want the word to spread any faster than it already had. "I still have some questions I'd like to ask you. After last night, I've even added a couple to the list."

"Anytime."

"Tonight?"

"Fine."

He toyed with a thought, then asked, "Do you like Japanese food?"

"I love it."

"We could talk over dinner. I know of this great little Japanese restaurant in the Hollywood Hills."

"What's it called?"

"My place."

She laughed melodiously. It reminded Parker of wind chimes.

"I'm serious," he said earnestly. "I happen to be a gourmet Japanese cook."

"Really?" she asked, amused. "Where did you pick up that talent?"

"In Japan. My education was completed here, though, in cooking school." He paused. "Of course, if you would rather dine at a restaurant—"

"No," she said, laughing again. "This is something I'd like to see. What time and how do I get there?"

"I'll pick you up at seven."

"Just give me directions," she insisted. "I'll be there."

He did and hung up, wondering about the menu and the wisdom of the move. He *did* want to ask her more about Harvey and Duffy, but that was not the real reason he had invited her to dinner. He wanted to see her again, plain and simple. It had been a long time since he had been so attracted to a woman. Maybe Clemens was right: maybe it was time he had a little romance in his life.

He immediately dumped cold water on that thought. If totally self-confident about his work, Parker had always exhibited a kind of clumsy shyness in the affairs of romance. Some women had found it endearing, but as an actress, Mia Stockton was used to hearing lines written by professional writers and intoned by actors who knew how to deliver them. How could he compete with that? Then he thought of the concepts of *Life's Tough* and *Street Angels* and took heart.

20

For the next hour and a half Parker tended to administrative details. Signing release forms and death certificates. Answering correspondence from colleagues around the country requesting his opinion on technical points of forensic medicine. Arranging for the court-appointed exhumation of a deceased millionaire whose disinherited children were claiming he had died under "mysterious circumstances," in spite of the conclusion of "natural causes" by the attending physician, an employee of the dead millionaire's corporation. Discussing the details of several cases with deputy DA's who were mapping out their courtroom strategies.

At 1028 hours Jim Phillips called from downstairs. "We just got a case in from Westbrook I thought you'd want to know about. Braxton."

Parker sat upright. "I want the body prepared immediately for autopsy. Who's available? How about Schaffer?"

There was a moment while Phillips checked the roster. "I can arrange it."

"Fine. I'll assist myself."

Parker sat back and rubbed his forehead. The news was not unexpected; he had not given the woman much of a chance. He wondered if she had regained consciousness before she died. He hadn't been wondering long when Cindy buzzed him that Supervisor Tartunian was on the phone.

Tartunian initiated conversation in his usual manner, without bothering to say hello. "Parker? There will be a meeting in my office at ten A.M. on Friday. Be here."

Parker resented the imperiousness of the tone, and some of that resentment crept into his voice when he asked, "A meeting about what?"

"The future of the coroner's office."

"What about it?"

"Just be here," the supervisor snapped, and hung up.

The future of the coroner's office? What could the man possibly mean by that? There was an unmistakable undercurrent of threat in Tartunian's voice. Parker was still vaguely troubled by the call when he went downstairs.

The staff in Room A was busy with aneurysms and embolisms, cancers and thromboses when Parker walked in. He said good morning to each doctor, then went to table four, where Schaffer was standing beside the body of Emily Braxton, going over the hospital report. "'Morning, Chief," the young doctor said cheerfully.

Parker tried unsuccessfully to return the good cheer.

"I hear you saved this woman's life last night," Schaffer said.

It didn't take long for word to get around. "Apparently all I did was postpone her death."

"Was she a friend of yours?"

"No."

"Do you want to do the autopsy?" Schaffer asked. "I can assist—"

"No. I'll assist." Parker looked over the hospital report. Emily Braxton had remained in stable but critical condition until six-ten this morning, at which time her breathing became short and labored. Just after that, she had gone into cardiac arrest. Efforts to resuscitate failed and she had been pronounced dead at six-twenty-two. She had never regained consciousness.

Parker adjusted his mask as Schaffer moved around the table describing what he saw and shading in the burned areas on the outline drawing of a female form on his clipboard. The skin surface was extensively burned over the entire upper body—shoulders, arms, hands, head, neck, torso, and back—except for a conspicuous white zone of unburned area across the abdomen where the woman had been wearing a leather belt. The hair was nearly totally burned away and there were also burn areas on the upper thighs. Parker paused to add up the series of numbers Schaffer had jotted down alongside the drawing. "The total burn area is estimated at eighty-one percent. Thirty percent partial thickness, fifty-one percent full thickness."

Schaffer looked up Emily Braxton's nose with an

otoscope, noted the presence of black soot, then pried open the lips with two probes. "There is carbon material in the mouth and on the tongue," he said, then stopped. "Wait a minute."

He bent down, holding the magnifying glass close to the dead woman's mouth. There were at least twenty small black punched-out burns with small white raised edges distributed over the base of the tongue and on the interior mucosal portion of the lips. He handed the glass to Parker and stood back. "What do you think of those?"

Parker inspected the burns, then straightened. There was a puzzled look on his face. "Those look more like electrical than thermal burns."

"That's what I thought," Schaffer said.

"Better take some samples for the SEM," Parker told him.

Schaffer measured the burns and found them all to be the same size—0.3 centimeter in diameter. He counted twenty-two in all. He cut away those portions of the lips and tongue that showed the markings and turned the tissue samples over to Parker, who "fixed" them in a solution of formaldehyde. Because the specimens had to be freeze-dried before placing them in the specimen chamber of the scanning electron microscope, Parker sent an assistant to deliver them downstairs to Dr. Montoya, the specialist who operated the SEM, then resumed work.

After noting no evidence of trauma to the skull, he made his initial incision, and fifteen minutes later, Emily Braxton's lungs, bronchi, and larynx lay out and open on the table.

"There's her shortness of breath," Schaffer observed. "The airways are obstructed by severe edematous swelling of the lining membranes."

The rest of the autopsy only confirmed the obvious. At 1210 hours Schaffer intoned for the record that Emily Braxton had died of acute heart failure due to asphyxia resulting from inhalation injury.

While the fluid specimens were on their way up to toxicology, Schaffer and Parker went down to the subbasement, where the SEM was housed. Whereas traditional optical microscopes used light rays passed through a lens as a means of magnification, the image of the scanning electron microscope was achieved by scanning a specimen with electrons and projecting the resulting abstraction onto a television screen. The picture that appeared was a three-dimensional reproduction of the surface of the specimen magnified up to fifty thousand times. The instrument was so sensitive that a special underground room had been built to house it, to minimize vibrations that might prevent sharp imaging or error.

Dr. Montoya was waiting for them and already had the pictures on the screen when Parker and Schaffer arrived.

"I assumed you wanted the EDAX hooked up too." The EDAX, or energy-dispersion X-ray analyzer, provided a chemical analysis of a specimen by measuring the low-energy X rays given off by the various elements it was composed of. Parker nodded and turned his attention to the stereoscan screens on the wall.

The photographs showed a deep crater with irregular, slightly rolled edges, surrounded by numerous small blisters. Parker asked Montoya to enlarge a portion of the crater bed, and the small dark man kicked up the magnification.

Parker got close to the screen and pointed to a section with a pen. "See that honeycombed pattern? Electrocoagulated protein bubbles that have burst open. These are electrical burns, no doubt about it."

Montoya nodded and pointed to another pattern along the side of the crater, a series of tiny lines that blended together in a twist pattern. "That's your culprit right there. That pattern was made by an electrical wire."

"EDAX find any traces of copper?"

Montoya shook his head. "For metal transfer to occur, the flow of the current has to generate enough heat to melt the wire. Where the conductor is good—like the mucous membranes—the heat wouldn't be that great. I'd say what you had here was a regular old electrical cord and a wall socket."

Parker thought about the smashed lamp at the house. "If I bring you a sample of wire, you can match it up?"

"Is the pope Catholic?" Montoya said, smiling confidently.

In the elevator, Schaffer shook his head in wonderment and said, "We live in a copycat world. Whoever said people aren't influenced by TV violence should see that slide."

"What are you talking about?" Parker asked.

"I saw that on *Miami Vice* a couple of months ago."

"What?"

"*That.* A bunch of Colombian dope dealers kidnapped

this guy and tortured him by sticking an electrical wire in his mouth. After that, they dumped gas on him and lit it, to cover up the evidence. They didn't mention that you can determine the difference between electrical and thermal burns, though." He paused thoughtfully. "Why would somebody do something like that to that girl?"

Parker's mind was working fast. "Why did they do it in *Miami Vice*?"

"They wanted to know where a hidden dope shipment was."

"I think whoever tortured Emily Braxton might have wanted to know the same thing."

Schaffer got off on the security floor and Parker rode up to his office. The toxicological report on Brock was waiting on his desk and he opened the envelope anxiously.

Any doubts Parker might have had that Brock had been murdered vanished as he read. The heroin level in the decedent's blood had been 122 micrograms-ml, more than one hundred times the lethal dose. In addition, there were 9.8 micrograms-ml of cocaine, also a high dose, as well as ethanol, .07 percent. Alcohol and heroin had also been found in the stomach, indicating that he had taken some of the drug orally. The high dosage of heroin could be explained partially by the composition of the substance found in the balloon by the nightstand. Whereas most heroin purchased on the street was rarely more than one or two percent pure, the stuff on Brock's nightstand tested almost seventy percent pure. Whoever had injected Brock had been taking no chances.

As if on cue, Detective Wolfe returned Parker's call.

"You had yourself quite a night last night, from what I hear," Wolfe began. "Stroud called me this morning and told me all about it. Lucky for the woman you wandered over there."

"Not that lucky. She died this morning. We just finished the autopsy. Her death was no freebasing accident. She was set afire on purpose, after she was tortured."

"That's LAPD's baby," Wolfe said happily.

"But Brock is yours."

Parker ran down the autopsy findings and Wolfe said grudgingly, "That pretty much checks with what we found at the scene. There were almost zero prints in Brock's bedroom."

"Zero prints?"

"Yeah. Not even his own. Looks like whoever did it wiped the place down. He missed one, though. A partial on the plunger of the syringe."

"Have they identified it?"

"No. It isn't Brock's, that's all we know."

"Have you checked it against Emily Braxton's prints?"

"Not yet. I thought we might get lucky with Julio Sandoval, but it didn't match against any of his."

Parker's brows knitted. "Who is Julio Sandoval?"

"You haven't talked to Stroud this morning?"

"No."

"He got lucky with those numbers you gave him last night for that Corvette. One of the possibles the computer kicked out was Julio Sandoval. A real slimeball. His parents were Cuban émigrés back in the sixties. He's been arrested four times, twice for drug trafficking, once for felonious assault, once for murder. No convictions." There was a significant pause. "And get this: Sandoval's business number is in Brock's address book."

"Has he been picked up yet?"

"No. He didn't go to his office today. We'll get him, though."

"If Sandoval killed Brock, what about that print?"

"Maybe Sandoval wasn't alone," Wolfe speculated. "Maybe he brought along some muscle." He paused. "What'd you find out about that scuba gear?"

"I found out it doesn't fit Brock," Parker replied.

That went over about as well as Parker expected.

"Whaddya mean, it doesn't fit Brock?"

"Just what I said."

"What was it doing in his closet, then?"

"Good question," Parker said. "That fact does jibe with Patton's testimony. The scuba diver he described coming out of the water was taller and thinner than Brock."

"Eyewitness testimony sucks," Wolfe said almost belligerently.

"How is Kuttner taking this?"

"About like I figured," Wolfe said. "He's screaming bloody murder. He thinks the whole thing is a crock. I've had quite a few calls from the media about Brock, by the way. One reporter from the L.A. *Times* in particular."

"Alexis Saxby," Parker said intuitively.

"That's the one. She's been bugging me for an interview. I've been shining her on, but I don't know how long the stall is going to work."

"I'm trying to get Duffy's body back from Chicago now. I should know more then."

"How long?"

"A couple of days."

There was a harried sigh. "I'll try."

Parker hung up and Steenbargen strolled in casually and plopped down on the couch. Parker glanced irritatedly at his watch and asked, "Where have you been?"

"You wanted me to do some checking on Sol Grossman," the investigator said.

"And?"

"You were right. The man likes to put his clients' money in real estate. Duffy's last big investment was a condo project in Boise, Idaho, called Crestline Heights. The units—twenty-five of them—were supposed to be put on six acres of land purchased nine months ago for eight hundred thousand dollars by CH, Inc., a corporation whose principal shareholders were John Duffy and Sol Grossman. The eight-hundred-thousand equity—seven hundred thousand of which was Duffy's money, by the way—was used to secure a twenty-four-million-dollar construction loan taken out with Pacific California Bank. The loan is for eighteen months. The principal balance is due nine months from now."

"So?"

"When a construction loan is made, the money is deposited in an account from which checks are drawn for work completed. In order for the check to be okayed, the bank requires periodic on-site inspections, just to make sure the work is being done. As of this morning, there was eight million dollars in the Crestline account, which means that sixteen million has gone out for construction. Only, whoever has been doing Cal Pac's inspections hasn't been doing a very good job. I checked with Boise this morning, and all that has been put up so far is a wire fence and an outhouse. And that's all that's going to be put up for another three to four years."

"Why?" Parker asked, interested.

"Because the land CH, Inc. bought is O Zone."

"Smoggy?" Parker asked.

Steenbargen shook his head impatiently. "Not the gas. It's zoned O. Environmentally sensitive. Which means there is a three-to-four-year delay on any development on it."

"Grossman had to know that."

"You would think so," Steenbargen agreed. "The question is whether Duffy did. I checked Duffy's phone records. Ten days ago a call was made on his phone to the Diamond Construction Company in Boise. That's the company that's supposed to be building the condos. The conversation lasted for eight minutes. I talked to the head of the company"—he consulted his notes—"Dwayne Saugus. He denies knowing anything about the call and says nobody else in the office knows anything about it either." He paused. "Saugus refused to discuss dollar figures, but claims that Diamond has only been paid so far for the superficial grading and putting up the fence around the project site."

"That couldn't amount to sixteen million dollars," Parker observed. "Where did all the money go?"

"I was just on my way over to Grossman's office to ask him that very question," Steenbargen said. "I thought you might want to tag along and hear his answer."

"Sure. I want to make a stop somewhere first, though."

"You're the boss," Steenbargen said.

21

Steenbargen pushed open the front door and Parker ducked underneath the crime-scene tape and went inside.

The place was even more depressing in the light of day. The carpet was still sodden, the atmosphere was laden with the sharp, acidic smell of charcoal. The blackened walls and floor absorbed and weakened the meager sunlight that dribbled in through the windows and front door.

"Exactly what are we looking for here?" Steenbargen asked.

"Probably a standard electrical wire with a plug on one end and stripped at the other."

Parker went immediately to the tipped-over kitchen chair by the wall, bent down, and examined the smashed lamp on the floor. He took out a pen and turned over a piece of the base of the lamp. Protruding from it was a cleanly severed stub of wire. "This wire was cut." He eyed the socket in the baseboard nearby. "The other end was probably plugged in there."

Parker stared at the chair intently and let his mind work on the scene. "That chair is from the kitchen. The killer must have brought it in here, placed it near enough to the socket so the cord would reach, then tied Emily Braxton to it. There was loud music playing when I got here, probably to cover her screams. He most likely gagged her too. He could have pushed the wire through a hole in the gag into her mouth."

From the socket, the two men spread out through the room, their eyes glued to the scorched carpet. After covering the room fruitlessly three times, they split off into other rooms, backtracked, then alternated room assignments, just in case one of them, for some reason, repeatedly failed to notice something. After fifteen minutes they met back in the living room. "Nothing," Steenbargen said.

"He must have taken it with him," Parker said, and wandered into the kitchen.

Steenbargen followed and said, "If he was careful enough to take the wire and the gag, why would he leave the suitcase?"

"The suitcase was obviously locked. The killer had to make sure of the contents. Emily Braxton by that time was probably in no shape to tell him where the key was, so he took it into the kitchen and jimmied the locks. Once that was done, he couldn't lug the stuff out in the bag—it wouldn't stay closed."

"Which means he probably brought along his own bag or took the stuff out in something from here."

Parker opened the back door and stood on the back porch. "The killer must have untied the girl, dumped ether on her and lit it, then split out the back. She couldn't have been on fire long, probably only from the time I heard her scream, no longer than ten or twenty seconds." He peeled off his jacket and handed it to Steenbargen. "When your second hand gets to twelve, say, 'Go.' Then meet me out front."

"What are you going to do?"

"Get my running in. I've been lax the last couple of days."

Steenbargen pointed down at Parker's brown shoes. "In those?"

"I didn't bring my running shoes, but the killer probably didn't either. We'll allow for it, though, just in case he did."

Steenbargen focused his gaze on the face of his watch and yelled, "Go!"

Parker took off. He was at the back gate in three bounds, unlatched it, and sprinted down the alley. Fifty yards later, he hit the street, made a right, and ran to the corner. He made another right and crossed the street, pushing himself as hard as he could for the last twenty yards of sidewalk. When he got abreast of the approximate spot the Corvette had been parked, he shouted, "Stop!"

Parker's shirt was sticking to him and he was winded as he walked over to the car where Steenbargen was standing. "Twenty-four seconds."

"Allowing for the time it would have taken the guy to get out of the house, as well as the time it would have taken him to open his car door and get in, we're probably talking a minimum of thirty seconds." He shook his head. "That's too long."

"Maybe the guy is a world-class sprinter," Steenbargen said, handing Parker his jacket. "Or maybe he was just a lookout, and the guy who did the dirty work was parked in the alley."

Parker had to admit that was a possibility.

On the way over to Grossman's office, Parker filled in Steenbargen on the Brock and Braxton autopsies. When he finished, the investigator asked, "You think whoever shot up Brock planted the diving equipment at his place to make it look as if he killed Duffy?"

"Your guess is as good as mine."

"I'll check with NAUI when we get back to the office."

Most divers in the country were certified by NAUI— the National Association of Underwater Instructors. "Even if he wasn't certified," Parker pointed out, "he could have been self-taught. You don't have to be certified to buy scuba gear."

Steenbargen signaled and got off the freeway. "True. But if he bought a wetsuit, you'd think he'd buy one that fit."

Sol Grossman was just getting off the phone as his secretary showed Parker and Steenbargen into the office.

Grossman did not look overjoyed to see either of them, but he invited the men to sit down. "What is it now, Dr. Parker?" His demeanor was much less friendly than on the previous visit—almost hostile, in fact.

"Joan Duffy tells me you've advised her not to authorize a new examination of her husband's body."

Grossman folded his hands across his stomach and leaned back. "That's right."

"Any particular reason?"

The agent leaned forward. "I think you've got it backwards, Doctor. You're the one who's supposed to come up with a reason."

"I explained my reasons to her."

Grossman smiled sardonically. "That nonsense about a scuba diver!" He shook his head. "I really don't understand your motives in this, Parker. The way you've conducted this investigation from the beginning has been a disgrace. But this is really too much."

"What about your own motives, Mr. Grossman?"

The man's eyes took on a nasty glint. "What is that supposed to mean?"

"You wouldn't happen to have any personal motives for wanting to see Duffy's death remain an accident, would you?"

Grossman's face reddened. "I think you'd better explain that remark."

"You admitted that the night before Duffy died, you argued about money," Parker said.

"So?"

"So you left out a few details. Such as the fact that Duffy accused you of stealing and threatened to fire you."

The agent laughed derisively. "John threatened to fire me every other week. It meant nothing."

"What was the reason behind the threat this week? Crestline Heights?"

The redness in his cheeks paled, and some of the bluster

left his voice. "Why would John threaten to fire me over Crestline Heights? He stood to make a lot of money off that project."

"*If* the units were sold," Steenbargen cut in casually. "But to be sold, they first have to be built, which at the moment doesn't look too promising. Did you know when you bought the property in Idaho that it was O Zone?"

"We were assured by people in positions of power that a variance would be granted. So far, it hasn't. But I'm still hopeful."

"If a variance were granted tomorrow," Steenbargen said, "you still couldn't complete construction by the time the loan to CH, Inc. comes due."

"So I'll get an extension of the note," Grossman said. "The president of the bank is a friend of mine."

Steenbargen nodded. "Is he in on the Crestline deal too?"

Grossman scowled. "No. Just John and myself."

"Did Duffy know about the zoning restriction?" Parker asked.

"Of course."

"Ten days ago Duffy called Diamond Construction in Boise. He talked to someone there for eight minutes, but nobody in the office seems to remember taking the call. Would you happen to know what that was about?"

Grossman tried to look puzzled. "No."

Steenbargen pursed his lips and tugged on his mustache. He looked troubled. "Would it maybe have been to find out where the sixteen million dollars missing from the CH account at Cal Pac disappeared to?"

Grossman remained unruffled by the question. Parker had to hand it to the man—he was one cool customer. He was one of those few individuals who seemed to calm in combat conditions. "I don't know what you're talking about. Whatever money has been drawn from the construction account has gone for expenses. Plans, grading, fencing—"

"You can buy a lot of fence for sixteen million dollars," Steenbargen said. "The way I figure it—and please feel free to correct me if I'm wrong—is that you were counting on Duffy being too busy or too stoned to bother to check up on his money. That was probably one reason you picked Idaho for the project—it was nice and far away.

"The president of Cal Pac—your buddy—and the people at Diamond were probably in on it too. It would have been much easier that way. Diamond would have submitted grossly inflated invoices for payment and your buddy would have okayed them."

Steenbargen stopped for a moment to gauge Grossman's reaction, but there didn't seem to be any. "My guess is that you probably intended to leave the eight million dollars in the bank. That way, when the loan came due, you could pay off the interest on the note. That would have bought you maybe another year. When it was all eaten up, CH, Inc. would be bankrupted, the bank would foreclose on the property, Duffy would be out seven hundred thousand, and you and your cronies would split sixteen mil."

Grossman said warningly, "If I were you, Mr. Steenbargen, I would be very careful making statements like that. The county might wind up in court facing an expensive and embarrassing defamation suit." He paused. "I don't know why my business affairs are suddenly a subject of scrutiny by the coroner, but for your information, Duffy was not going to lose any money on the Crestline deal. Anytime he wanted out, I would have gladly taken him out. In fact, months ago, when we first started to encounter political problems in Boise, I offered to redeem John's CH stock at its original value, plus interest. That offer was made in front of witnesses, including Joan Duffy. John turned the offer down. He wanted to stick it out. The offer still stands for Joan, if she wants to get out."

Grossman stood up. "If you want to talk to me again, Dr. Parker, you can do it through my attorneys."

"I have one more question, Mr. Grossman," Parker said, smiling strangely. "Has Boodry invested in any of your real-estate projects?"

For the first time, Parker detected something in the man's eyes, a ripple of fear. "Good day, gentlemen."

"What do you think?" Steenbargen asked when they got outside.

Parker shook his head and frowned. "I don't know."

"What about this?" Steenbargen tried. "Duffy found out about the Crestline scam and threatened Grossman with legal action, so Grossman decided to get rid of him. He played on Brock's jealousy of the guy and his desperation to get his name in lights by promising to handle his career if Brock got rid of Duffy. Once Duffy was out of the way, Grossman had to get rid of Brock—"

"How about the wetsuit that didn't fit?" Parker said. "It

doesn't fly for me. For one thing, it made sense, what he was saying about giving Duffy his money back."

"You're right. Grossman didn't care about Duffy's seven hundred thousand. That was just a little something to prime the pump. He wanted the bank's millions. Even if Duffy found out about the scheme, it wouldn't have mattered to Grossman. Nobody would have been likely to do anything about it anyway."

Parker stared at him, puzzled. "What do you mean, nobody would do anything about it? It's fraud."

"Technically, maybe. But no prosecutor would touch it. The bank managers are adults. Nobody forced them to loan CH, Inc. the money. Grossman didn't perform, that's all. You can't prosecute someone for that."

"If the bank president was in on it—"

"It's conspiracy," Steenbargen said, nodding. "But try to prove it."

"I can't believe Grossman is going to get away with stealing millions." Parker frowned.

Steenbargen smiled vaguely. "Maybe he won't. The IRS has never heard of due process." He glanced at Parker curiously. "Who's this Boodry you were talking about?"

"Someone else who's never heard of due process."

Parker described his encounter with Boodry and Steenbargen chuckled. "Well, one thing for sure. If we're looking for someone to fit into that wetsuit, that leaves Grossman out."

"Not necessarily," Parker said. "He wouldn't have to stick his hands in mud to get them dirty."

"Meaning that if he knows wrestlers, he might know a diver?"

"It might be worth checking out. I'd also like to know if Grossman had any business dealings with Harvey Brock. Even if Brock and Braxton were killed as part of a dope burn, it doesn't explain their connection with Duffy's death. The three are connected in some way. I know it. The police aren't going to find the link. They aren't even going to look."

"Which leaves it up to us?" Steenbargen asked.

Parker said nothing. It seemed that the moment they got out of one chamber of the nautilus, they found themselves in another. He wondered how many more he had to explore before he got to the end.

=22=

Parker had just had time to change into his "outfit" before the doorbell rang. He went to the door wearing black trousers and black shoes, a black apron, and, to set off his short-sleeved white shirt, a black tie. He was also holding—at the moment, only for effect—black pot-holder mitts.

Mia Stockton laughed when she saw him. "What is this? *The Real Stuff?*"

"Absolutely authentic," Parker said, standing aside. "Brought all the way from Little Tokyo. Come in, please."

The scent of lilacs entered with her and he took her wrap. She looked around the place and said sincerely, "Cute house. Fantastic view."

"That's really why I bought it." He noted with satisfaction that she was wearing a body-hugging silk dress that showed all of her figure. He felt stirrings within himself he had not felt in quite a long time. "What would you like to drink?"

"In that getup, I wouldn't think you'd offer a choice," she said, still amused. "Some sake would be fine."

Luckily, the sake was already warmed. Ah, microwaves, Parker thought, wondering how he had ever coped without one.

When Parker came out of the kitchen, she was studying the unfinished landscape on the easel. "You paint."

"I dabble." He handed her the warmed sake and she moved over to the wall to examine Parker's favorite, *Guard Duty*, in which a black stallion stood on a windswept cliff overlooking a splendiferous harem. In that oil, for once, all the elements had come together and Parker had gotten everything just right, a miracle for an amateur. Mia looked at Parker with unabashed admiration. "This one—can you stand a compliment?—is terrific."

Yes, Parker thought. He could stand a compliment. He hadn't had many lately. But then, who was counting?

"I'm impressed. A Renaissance man."

He was warmed by her praise. "Friends," he said, raising his sake bowl in a toast. "I'm glad you could come. Welcome—and may you visit often."

The toast was interrupted by Boomer, who chose that moment to throw himself against the bedroom door and let loose with an unearthly howl.

"You didn't tell me you had a dog," Mia said, surprised.

"I don't, thank God. It's a birthday present for my son."

"Let him out."

"My son? He's not in there."

She made a face. "The dog."

Parker sighed. "You might regret those words." He went to the door and pulled it open. Despite repeated admonitions, Boomer proceeded to jump and slobber all over him, after which he adjourned to Mia, managing in the process to stick his nose three or four times into her most private parts.

"You teach him this?" Mia demanded, squealing.

"Only because he asked."

When Boomer finally settled down, Parker got him fed, watered, walked, patted and praised, and back in bed in record fashion, ignoring Mia's request that he be allowed to stay up. Boomer was the worst scene-stealer he'd ever met. He didn't need that kind of competition.

"How old is your boy?" Mia asked, laughing at his blatant purpose.

"Twelve. At least he will be next week."

"You have other children?"

"No."

"How long have you been divorced?"

"Six years."

"Your only marriage?"

He nodded.

"If I may be personal, what happened?"

Parker shrugged. "She accused me of bigamy. Said I was married to her and my job, and she was right. There were other problems. We'd grown apart. But the job was a big one."

Mia sipped her sake and asked, "Is she remarried?"

"No. She's done a great job with Ricky, though. She's a good mother."

"Maybe she still loves you and wants you back."

He shook his head ruefully. "No. We tried that once, for Ricky's sake, but it didn't work out. Too much had happened that couldn't be forgotten. Our marriage didn't do a lot for Eve's self-esteem. That's something I feel guilty about."

"We all do what we can," she said.

"I wish I could do more for her. She won't let me. Too proud. And bitter at me for choosing my work over her." He slid open the sliding glass door and they went out onto the balcony. They leaned on the railing and stared out at the shimmering lights. "You ever been married?"

She smiled and shook her head. "There hasn't been time. I didn't want to be accused of bigamy."

"How did you get into acting?"

She shrugged. "It was kind of a fluke, really. I graduated from the University of Indiana with a degree in telecommunications and dreams of being the next Leslie Stahl. Only Leslie Stahl was still around and the networks didn't want two. I wound up working as a weather girl on a small TV station in La Crosse, Wisconsin, and while I was there, I did some commercials for a local store that sold camping equipment.

"During one of the commercials, a trained bear we were using decided to become untrained and tore down the set. That commercial wound up on Dick Clark's *Commercial Bloopers* and a big commercial producer saw it and called me to audition for the part of a ditsy bank teller he was carrying through a series of commercials. I got the part and from that, I was hired as a regular on *Days of Night*, a daytime soap, and then Byron called about the *Life's Tough* role."

"Weather girl to star," Parker mused.

"The way things are going, maybe back to weather girl."

"What about the spin-off?"

"*Great Friends?* I've seen the script for the pilot. Byron's expectations may be a bit overblown. He has a tendency to do that where I'm concerned."

"He's got a thing for you?" Parker asked curiously.

"You might say that."

"Are you two dating or something?"

"Were. Past tense."

"How long past?"

She smiled. "Don't tell me *this* is part of your investigation."

Parker shook his head. "Purely personal. I like to get a feel for the competition."

Her laugh sounded like wind chimes. "The field is clear, at least where Byron is concerned. We stopped dating before I started seeing John."

"Were you two serious?"

She lifted an eyebrow. "My, you *are* nosy."

"Sorry. It's an occupational trait."

She smiled. "That's all right, I don't mind. He was serious, I wasn't. That was actually why I stopped seeing Byron. He was getting in too deep. We just weren't going anywhere. I couldn't make him understand that, that it had nothing to do with John."

"He blamed Duffy for breaking you up?"

She nodded. "That was another reason for the tension on the set the past season, and why John wanted off the show. He and Byron were always digging at each other. Especially after—" She cut herself off.

Parker picked up the cue. "After what?" Something made him ask: "Duffy thought Fenady sent that note to his wife, didn't he?"

She nodded grudgingly. "They had a big blowout about it. Byron denied it, but John didn't believe him. After that, John took every opportunity to rub Byron's nose in the fact that I'd dropped him for a married man. It wasn't true, but John threw it up to Byron as if it were."

"That must have set well with Fenady," Parker observed. "I talked to the man. He seems to have a colossal ego."

"He does," she said. "But it's typical of egos in the television industry—falsely inflated. Byron is a nice enough guy, don't get me wrong. But have you ever met anyone who never had an original thought? Everything they thought or did came from somewhere else?"

"Uh-huh."

"That's Byron. And it shows in his work. Every series he has ever done is recombinant."

"I know the biological definition of the term—"

"Same meaning," she said. "Something spliced together from a bunch of different shows. Byron is the master of recombinance. Only it isn't just in his shows. It's in his head. He thinks that way. Every clever little thing he says, he's stolen from someone else. That's why I think I was so smitten by John at first. He was so fresh and original."

Parker shrugged. "But you can't argue with success. The

public must want recycled garbage. Fenady has made a fortune selling it to them."

She shook her head. "Byron's back is against the wall. He needs a hit show. Badly."

"How badly could he need one?" Parker asked. "With all the successes he's had, he could buy an island and retire."

She cocked her head and fluffed her hair with the back of her hand. She looked lovely doing that, Parker thought. He was smitten. He just hoped he didn't end up like Fenady's shows—canceled.

"People think that just because a producer has some successful shows," she was saying, "he's automatically a millionaire. It doesn't work that way."

"How does it work?" He really didn't care. He just wanted to hear her talk.

"It isn't difficult to grasp," she assured him. "The network pays a licensing fee to a supplier—either a studio or an indie prod like Byron—"

"Here we go," Parker broke in. "Indie prod?"

She smiled. "Independent producer. A producer like Byron sells a concept to a network and the network commits to so many episodes at X dollars per episode. A few years ago, the networks were buying hour-long action shows, on the theory that that was what the public wanted to see.

"That type of show costs a bundle to produce, usually a lot more than the network licensing fee, so the producer is operating in the red. What he is counting on is that the show will get good enough ratings so that the network will renew it for next season. Once it has been on enough seasons—anywhere from three to five—the producer has enough episodes stockpiled to sell it for syndication."

"What if the show only runs two years?"

"The producer can get slaughtered. Which is why Byron is trying to switch to half-hour sitcoms like *Life's Tough*, and phase out big-budget shows like *Street Angels*. They're easier to syndicate and much easier to produce. If the unit cost can be kept within the licensing fees, anything else is gravy."

"What about *Life's Tough*? You think it will be syndicated?"

"That's hard to say. If we'd gotten canceled, I would have said no way. But with all the publicity and it being John's last work and all, who knows?" Her look turned serious. "What happened with Harvey?"

"He was murdered. Someone shot him full of heroin and tried to make it look like an accidental overdose. It was probably a drug burn."

"How terrible," she said, as if she really thought it was.

"That was one of the hazards of the business he was in. The life expectancy in the cocaine trade is considerably less than the national average."

"I suppose." She dropped her gaze and then looked back up, into his eyes. "It had nothing to do with John's death, then?"

"Why do you ask that?" Parker asked curiously.

She shrugged. "Just because they were friends, and their deaths coming so close together . . ."

Parker searched her face, trying to gauge if there was

something behind the surface, but if there was, she was not giving it away. "What connection would there be? Can you think of one?"

"Me? No." She handed him her cup and smiled. "May I have some more sake, please?"

To hell with forensics tonight, he thought. He was not going to squander this opportunity. He had never felt comfortable with the incipient testing stages of a relationship. This one, however, he felt strongly about. She was attractive, bright, witty, and independently successful—and he liked her a lot. Too much to let his job blow whatever chances he had. He took her cup and said, "You can sip and watch."

Parker led the way into the kitchen, where the ingredients for sukiyaki had already been rinsed and laid out on the counter. A slab of Spencer steak, half a Chinese cabbage, a bunch of green onions, and eight black mushrooms along with a cube of tofu and a package of yam noodles. Kelp stock was simmering on the stove and the rice cooker was steaming.

He poured out two more bowls of sake and Mia leaned against the counter and feigned alarm as he went to work with a razor-sharp knife. "Why this passion?"

"What passion?"

"To be a Japanese restaurant."

"I got into it when I was a kid," Parker explained, swiftly reducing the meat to thin slices. "In Tokyo. My father was an Army surgeon and he was stationed there a couple of years after World War II. We lived off-base with Japanese help and I hung around home a lot and there wasn't that much to do—did you ever watch *Leave It to Beaver* in Japanese?—so I spent an unusual amount of time in the kitchen. Ergo, Parker, the boy chef."

"Who is now making . . . ?"

". . . sukiyaki. The Japanese equivalent of a barbecue. There is no standard recipe, but form is very important. Hence my uniform. And my meditation."

"You're meditating now?"

"Yes."

"Thanks."

"Hence, also," Parker said, laughing with her, "the artistry. The object is not simply to cook and eat food. The object is to have an almost religious experience."

"Are we having one now?"

"Not yet, but soon. Watch for it. There will be signs." Parker finished chopping the vegetables and cut up the tofu, setting them aside with the meat and noodles. Then he made a stir-fry sauce by mixing sugar, sake, and soy sauce into the kelp stock.

Mia murmured one last "Mmmm" and went to set the table. Parker, watching while he cooked, noted that she had a good sense of what should be, going automatically to the places where dishes, chopsticks, and napkins were kept.

Everything came together at the same time—the sukiyaki ready, the rice cooked perfectly, the table set—and they sat down with mock but still oddly serious ceremony. Parker wondered if Mia felt the same way he did—that the simple dinner marked the start of something important.

"Incredible," Mia pronounced, taking her first bite. "I'm glad for your restricted childhood." She looked at him with the twinkle back in her eye. "What else did they teach you in lieu of *Beaver?*"

Parker considered. He ought to have a good answer for that, he thought, but he couldn't find one, no matter how much he sifted through his tofu. "Geometry."

Mia laughed. "You're kind of shy, aren't you?"

"Sometimes," Parker admitted.

"That's nice in a man."

"There's nothing wrong with it in a woman, either," Parker said, still busy with his tofu.

"You mean you think I'm forward?"

Parker finally looked up. "God, I hope so."

The dinner conversation stayed along those lines, playful, teasing. Afterward he turned on the stereo—Johnny Mathis—and they had brandy on the couch. Parker was surprised, and pleased, when she leaned over and kissed him gently, tenderly, on the mouth. She leaned back and smiled.

"Now you probably really think I'm forward."

"I don't think I can handle it."

"You're a nice man, Mr. Coroner. There's something very . . . I don't know, *real* about you. You have no idea how nice that can be to be around when you deal with unreal most of your waking hours."

His body tingled with anticipation as he leaned forward and kissed her again. Her back stiffened and then she seemed to melt into him as her tongue found its way into his mouth, searching, hungry. He stood, and without a word she slipped her hand into his and followed him into the bedroom.

Later, Parker would wish that he had kept track. Some sort of record of time, number, positions, and places. Something that had never occurred to him to do before, and which, with anyone else, might have seemed crude or crass. Not with Mia, though. With Mia, Parker thought, one should have a record, some kind of permanent declaration that this took place, and how and why it happened.

They made love for what seemed like hours, oblivious of everything except each other, the need and the fulfillment they found together. Parker couldn't get enough of her. He found himself aroused again and again. Magically, it was the same for her, coming with him each time, always a partner. After a while, for Parker at least, the images blurred, to be remembered mostly as a single instance, the time when—as in his one perfect painting—it finally all came together in one perfect act of love.

When they were done, they lay on top of the sheets, sweaty and sated, and Parker propped himself up on one elbow and gazed in awe at her magnificent body, wondering at his good fortune. He traced the outline of her chin with a forefinger, let it run down her neck, between her breasts.

She kissed his hand, sighed, and sat up. "I have to go. I have an early call tomorrow."

Parker watched her pleasurably as she slipped into her clothes. All her motions were achieved with a sensual, catlike grace, and he marveled at how much he could be aroused by simply watching a woman dress.

"Sure you have to go?"

"Yes," she said firmly.

"I'd like to see you again."

She picked up her dress and looked down at him. "I'd like that too."

"Saturday? We could make a day of it."

"You have to take your son out, remember?"

"I remember," he said. "I'd like you to meet him."

She smiled. "Call me Saturday."

Mia took her clothes into the bathroom and Parker pulled on a jogging suit instead of a robe. It was late and he didn't want her out in the street alone. He was in the kitchen getting a glass of water when she came out of the bedroom and kissed him tenderly on the cheek. "You're a gentle lover, Mr. Coroner. And a hell of a cook."

He told her he would call her tomorrow and walked her to her car. After she had gone, he went out onto his balcony and stared at the tapestry of lights, which seemed especially beautiful tonight. He realized he must have looked stupid, grinning like a Cheshire cat, but he didn't care. He felt as if something truly good had happened to him for the first time in a long while, and if the result of that feeling was looking stupid, it was a small price to pay.

=== 23 ===

Parker woke up at five-twenty-six, pulled on his sweats and Nikes and, accompanied by Boomer, went on the two-mile "grand circle." At the top of Sycamore, he stopped for a few moments to watch the sunrise, then trotted the downhill course home, feeling inspired and perspired.

At 0710 he arrived at the Forensic Science Center, and after checking on the day's schedule, went upstairs. Stander Collingsworth had already been at work several hours when Parker called and asked, "Stander, did you get the packet?"

"I got it."

"And?"

There was an uncomfortable pause. "You have a little political problem out there, Eric?"

It was Parker's turn to pause uncomfortably. "Why do you ask?"

"Since you called yesterday, I've had calls from Myron Feldman, Joan Duffy's attorney, as well as from his business manager, urging me to turn down your request. Not long after that, I got a call from your County Supervisor Tartunian. He asked me to delay my decision on the matter until tomorrow."

"On what grounds?"

"On the grounds that as of tomorrow afternoon, you wouldn't be coroner anymore."

Parker sat back, stunned. "Where would he get that idea?"

"I don't know, but he didn't seem to think there was any doubt about it. He said you would be resigning. Either that, or you would be fired."

It probably should have come as no surprise, but somehow, it did. Parker felt a constriction in his chest.

"I'm sorry, Eric," Collingsworth sympathized. "I hope you get it straightened out, whatever the problem is. I know how thankless this goddamn job can be."

"You're going to wait until tomorrow to make your decision?"

"I don't see that I have any choice," Collingsworth said. "Give me a call tomorrow and we'll take it from there."

Parker sat at his desk and stared out the window, trying to make sense of what was happening to him. It was crazy. How could they possibly fire him? On what grounds?

The phone rang. To Parker, it sounded like an alarm bell. "Hello?"

"Eric? Frank Fiore. Listen, I'm sending something over by deputy I think you should look at. It didn't come from me, though, understand?"

"What is it?" Parker asked numbly.

"A copy of the charges Tartunian intends to file against you if you don't resign as coroner. I told you he wanted your head. Well, he's going for it. I thought you should see them, so you could at least be prepared for what he's going to throw at you at that meeting tomorrow."

"What kind of charges?" Parker asked, confused.

"They're in the package I'm sending over," the mayor said. "They're strictly bullshit, but I thought you should be able to prepare yourself."

"Thanks, Mayor."

"Remember: you didn't get anything from me."

At 0820 hours Cindy entered with a sealed manila envelope and said, "A deputy from the mayor's office just delivered this."

Parker thanked her and waited until she had gone out before opening the envelope.

There were fifty-eight charges in all, among them being:

—That Parker had, in his six years of running the coroner's office, demonstrated administrative incompetence, resulting in a serious logjam of cases and possibly endangering the public health.

—That he had lost the confidence of his staff and medical colleagues.

—That he had consistently courted publicity for his own egomaniacal purposes, to the detriment of the department. (The DeWitt and Duffy cases were specifically cited.)

—That he had exhibited bizarre, erratic behavior in carrying out his duties. (His request of Tom Barnes that his students wear tuxedos to their upcoming class was mentioned as just one example.)

—That he had recklessly raised the specter of a county-wide panic by making "irresponsible public statements" about the possibility of an outbreak of bubonic plague in Los Angeles.

—That he had been heard to utter after a recent temblor of 5.6 that he wished a "major earthquake would hit," so that he could "show what the department could really do" and become an overnight celebrity.

—That he had tacitly threatened the life of the county administrative officer by offering to perform a "free autopsy on him while he was still alive."

Parker could scarcely believe it. The whole thing was ludicrous. What was not total fabrication had been twisted and pulled out of context to make him sound like a madman.

There was a knock at the door and Steenbargen stuck his head in. "Cindy says you left orders not to be disturbed, but I didn't think that meant me." He came in, took one look at Parker's expression, and asked, "What's wrong with you? You look as if your best friend just died."

"I've been informed that as of tomorrow I will no longer be coroner."

Steenbargen's brow furrowed. "What are you talking about?"

"Apparently Tartunian is going to give me the option of quitting or being fired."

"On what grounds?"

Parker held up the sheet of charges and tossed them on the desktop. Steenbargen picked them up, and as he read, his expression grew sanguine. When his eyes reached the bottom of the page, he looked up and said, "This is a crock."

"Sure."

"The only reason there's a logjam of cases is that they won't release funds—"

"You know that and I know that."

"And *they* know that," Steenbargen interjected angrily. "You can make mincemeat out of this crap. You can disprove every charge on here."

Parker smiled sheepishly. "Except the autopsy offer I made to Brewster."

Steenbargen shrugged. "What the hell. If the guy can't take a joke, fuck him. What about this 'plague' thing, and the bit with the tuxedos?"

Parker explained his statement to Brewster's deputy and his reasoning behind the formal-dress request, and Steenbargen said, "You have to hand it to them, they can move fast when they want to." He smiled at Parker searchingly. "What are you going to do about this?"

Parker sighed and shook his head. "I don't know."

Steenbargen leaned forward aggressively on the desk. "Whaddya mean, *you don't know?*"

"This department is my primary consideration," Parker told him. "It's obvious that Tartunian and Brewster want my scalp and they're willing to sacrifice everything I've worked to build up here to get it. I can't let that happen."

"You can't let them run over you," Steenbargen said. "If you resign and they publish those charges, everyone will believe they're true. Your reputation will be ruined. You *have* to fight."

"Even if I can prove every charge false, people will still believe they're true," Parker said. He sighed and slumped back in his chair. "What the hell. Maybe it's time. I'm tired."

Steenbargen pushed off the desk and tossed a hand casually in the air. "Yeah. What the hell. Maybe you're right. You're forty-five. You can always buy a nice little quiet farm somewhere away from it all, raise some chickens and pigs. Appomattox would be nice. That's an appropriate place for surrender."

The taunt stung, but Parker just frowned guiltily.

"You can't go out that way," Steenbargen told him, then grinned. "You wouldn't know how."

They were interrupted by Cindy, who buzzed him that a Detective Stroud was on the phone.

"Doc," Stroud said cheerfully, "I just thought you'd like to know that we picked up Sandoval. He was holed up at an address on Alvarado, along with two pounds of heroin, six pounds of rock cocaine, some PCP, and a stash of automatic weapons. We didn't have him in the car five minutes before he started singing for a deal."

The news perked up Parker a bit. "Did he cop out to the Brock and Braxton killings?"

"Naw. He admits he was there, all right, but he claims he never went in. According to him, the Braxton broad called him up about six and said she wanted to sell him back a load of coke he'd sold Brock the night before for twenty G's—for ten thousand. She said she needed the money bad, to get out of town, that somebody was trying to kill her. Sandoval says he went over to her place to see what it was all about, but when he got there, there was somebody else already in the house. He was waiting out front in his car, he says, when you pulled up. Then Braxton came out on fire, and he decided to get the hell out of there."

"That fits the facts," Parker admitted.

Stroud said, "The guy is a scumbag. He'd say anything to get out from under a murder rap."

"He admitted he was dealing to Brock?"

"Yeah. And large quantities. According to him, Brock was moving a couple of kilos a week to his hotsy-totsy movie-star clientele."

"Where would Brock get that kind of money?"

"Sandoval says Brock was just the front man, that he had a partner who was the banker. Some TV bigshot. I guess it was through the partner's studio connections that Brock was moving the shit."

"Does Sandoval know who this Mr. Big is?"

"Naw," the detective said. "He claims Brock never told him."

Parker thought about it. "He might be telling the truth." He told Stroud about his alley-run the afternoon before. "If there was someone else in the house, he could have been parked in the alley. That spilled coke out back proves that the killer went out the back door—"

"I hate to disappoint you, Doc," Stroud broke in, "but that wasn't coke out back."

That stopped Parker momentarily. "What was it?"

There was a rustling of papers. "Dihydroxyaluminum sodium carbonate, cornstarch, corn syrup, magnesium stearate, and sugar. And that's how you spell relief."

"Huh?"

"A Rolaid."

"A Rolaid," Parker repeated as the realization struck him.

"Yeah. Somebody must have dropped one and stepped on it."

After a few seconds: "Doc, you still there?"

"I'll get back to you," Parker said hurriedly, and hung up. He called Wolfe at Metro. "You got a match on that partial print yet?"

"No."

"Try matching it to Byron Fenady's."

"Fenady? Are you kidding?"

"Do I sound like I'm kidding?"

"What makes you think it was Fenady?"

"A Rolaid was found on the porch behind her house. Fenady eats Rolaids like candy." Parker realized how stupid it sounded as soon as it came out.

"Half this division eats Rolaids like candy," Wolfe scoffed.

"Sandoval told Stroud that Brock was moving large quantities of cocaine through the studio," Parker argued. "He also told him that Brock had a banker—some TV bigshot. I think that banker was Fenady."

"Fenady? A dope dealer?" Wolfe said doubtfully. "The man is a heavyweight producer. Why would he bother with that sort of garbage? It had to be small-time shit for him—"

"Maybe at one time, but not lately. Fenady has had a lot of shows canceled over the past few years and his company is in trouble. My guess is that he went into the dope business to keep everything afloat until he gets a major hit on the air."

"We're going to move on somebody like Fenady, we have to have better than guesswork. Can you put Fenady and Brock together?"

"Maybe."

"Maybe ain't good enough," Wolfe said. "Look, this guy ain't any two-bit street hustler. He won't take being bounced too easy. He has friends. *Big* friends. Before I even approached him, I'd have to have a hell of a lot more than some maybes and a Rolaid."

"You have a print."

"I have a *partial* print," Wolfe corrected him. "Even if they match up, we only have four points of identification. We like to have *ten* before going to court with it. I've gone to the DA with less, but I wouldn't even think of it with a heavy hitter like Fenady. If you get me some proof, a for-sure motive, something concrete that put Fenady and Brock together, that might be different."

"Okay," Parker said. "I'll get you your proof."

Wolfe must have picked up on the frustration in Parker's voice, because he said, "Look, Dr. Parker, if you're right about this guy, going off half-cocked isn't going to help put him away. First things first. I'll see if I can get a comparison on the prints, and if we get a match, we'll go from there. We have to build a case. It takes time—"

"I don't have any time," Parker told him, and hung up. He called Mia at the *Life's Tough* set and was told she was in the middle of a scene and couldn't come to the phone. He put the receiver down without leaving his name and said to Steenbargen, "Come on."

The investigator stared at him curiously. "Where?"

Parker picked up the sheet of charges and waved them in the air angrily. "To make Tartunian choke on these." He grinned. "You're right. I could never go out like that."

24

Mia stepped out of the bliss of the klieg-lighted living room and smiled radiantly when she saw Parker. She stood on tiptoes to kiss him on the cheek, and Parker introduced Steenbargen. They shook hands and she said, "What brings you two out to television land?"

"Business," Parker said solemnly.

She said in a semimocking tone, "I assumed that from the deadly serious look on your face."

"I have to ask you some questions," Parker said. "Is there someplace private we can talk?"

She told the director she would be in shouting range and led them away from the living room, across a floor covered with black electrical cables. Stepping over them, Parker felt as if he were negotiating a snake pit. When they were out of hearing range of the crew, she stopped and asked: "This okay?"

Parker nodded. "You told me last night that Fenady's production company is in trouble. How bad?"

"I don't really know," she said. "It's just the scuttlebutt. Byron doesn't talk about it to me. All I know is that he's been on edge lately."

"Was Fenady friendly with Harvey Brock?"

She looked at him searchingly, trying to determine the purpose behind his question. "What do you mean, 'friendly'?"

"Did you ever see them together?"

She thought about it before answering. "Yes."

"Where?"

"At Byron's house a couple of times."

"What was he doing there?"

She shrugged nonchalantly. "Byron said he was dropping off some story ideas."

"Was that *after* Brock had been thrown off the set?"

"Yes."

"Fenady was willing to do business with a known cocaine dealer, and even have him to his house?"

"I asked Byron the same question," she said.

"What did he say?"

She lifted one shoulder. "That he would accept a treatment from the devil himself if it would help him boost ratings. I have to admit, every once in a while Harvey did come up with a good idea for an episode."

"Did you ever see Fenady and Emily Braxton together?"

"Harvey's girlfriend? Yeah. I've seen her around a few times."

"Around the studio?" Parker asked intently.

"Yeah," she said, looking at him strangely.

"Lately?"

"A few times. Why?"

Parker exchanged glances with Steenbargen and asked, "Does Fenady use cocaine?"

She pulled her head back and said, "Whoa. You're getting into an area I don't feel comfortable discussing. The man *is* my employer."

Parker turned up his hands pleadingly. "You're going to have to trust me, Mia—"

"That cuts both ways," she said, her voice taking on a chill.

"I can't tell you right now," Parker said. "Not until I get a few more things nailed down. I'll tell you as soon as I can. I promise."

Her expression turned pouty and she looked away.

Parker said, "I wouldn't even be asking you these questions if they weren't extremely important."

She looked doubtfully at Steenbargen.

"Mike here is my right arm," Parker assured her. "Whatever you trust me with, you can trust him with." He repeated the question, a little more insistently: "Does Fenady use cocaine?"

She mulled it over. "This is not for public consumption."

"Of course not."

"If I hear one word of this conversation repeated—" she began warningly.

"You won't," Parker assured her.

Her look was still doubtful, but she said, "I don't know

291

what it has to do with anything, but the answer is yes, he does."

"Heavily?"

"I don't know what that means. Your definition and someone else's definition might be different. He's been tooting more lately, since things started going sour with the show. It gives him an edge against the fear. At least he thinks it does."

"Duffy knew all about Brock's dope business," Parker went on. "Did he ever mention Brock having a partner? A money man?"

"We didn't discuss Harvey's business," she replied a bit tartly.

"Duffy seemed pretty confident he was going to be able to walk away from *Life's Tough* without any problem. Did he say how he was going to accomplish that?"

"No."

"Did he ever mention how he was going to get Fenady to release him from his contract?"

"No."

"You never discussed it with him?"

She mulled it over, then said, "I wouldn't call it a discussion. A week or so ago, John brought up the subject of leaving the show again and I remarked that Byron would never let him go. He just got this strange look on his face, almost a smirk, and said Byron would release him all right, that he would *have* to."

"Did he say what he meant by that?"

She shook her head. "No. I assumed it was just the drugs talking."

"One more question," Parker said. "Does Fenady know how to scuba-dive?"

Her eyes, which were blue again, blinked confusedly. "Why would you want to know that?"

"I promised I'd let you know as soon as I can, and I will," Parker assured her.

She was not overjoyed with that answer, but said, "He produced a series a few years ago—*Sea Hunter*. The technical adviser on the show taught him."

Parker tried not to let any emotion show on his face. "Is Fenady around?"

"Somewhere," she said. "He stopped by the set earlier. You might try his office."

Parker caught the uneasiness in her eyes and smiled gently. "Trust me."

Someone called out Mia's name and she said, "I have to go back to work."

Parker told her he would see her later, and when she was gone, said to Steenbargen, "Call Wolfe. Tell him what we've got and see if he'll try to get warrants for Fenady's house and office. I'll meet you over there."

"Right," Steenbargen said, and started off.

The offices of Fenady Productions were on the second floor of an unelaborate battleship-gray wooden building left over from the studio's heyday. A gray-haired secretary who also looked as if she were part of the building's historical legacy interrupted her typing long enough to tell Parker that Fenady was over at building number four, going over plans for a set that was to be built for *Street Angels*.

On his way over to the building, Parker debated his options. He could wait for Wolfe to issue the search warrants, in which case he might be waiting a long time. Even with Mia's testimony, he knew Wolfe would tread carefully with a man of Fenady's stature. And if that happened, there was a good chance that Parker's career—and this case along with it—would slip into quiet oblivion. Parker had to make sure there were grounds for a warrant, grounds that Wolfe couldn't ignore.

Building four was another huge hangar, but there was little glamour in its interior. Its concrete floor was covered with sawdust and its hollow vastness was filled with stacks of paneling, planks of board, and worktables, only two of which were being used. Fenady was bent over one of them looking at a set of plans with a short, balding man in a carpenter's apron. He looked up and said, "Well, well, the morgue comes calling. What brings you around, Dr. Parker?"

"You, Mr. Fenady."

Fenady straightened. "Well, you found me. What do you want?"

"For you to listen to a story," Parker said with false enthusiasm. "It kept me up all night. I thought it was so good I had to hunt you down personally and tell it to you. It's just your kind of property. It's a murder mystery."

Fenady's eyes narrowed. "Look, Parker, I really don't have time—"

"Please, Mr. Fenady," Parker implored. "It won't take long. I know you'll like it. It's all about this big-time TV producer whose production company begins to flounder when his shows start to get canceled because of falling ratings." He stopped and asked teasingly, "You want me to go on?"

There was a wary glint in Fenady's eyes now. Trying to look casual, he glanced at his watch and said, "Go ahead. I have a few minutes." He looked at the carpenter, then pointed to another worktable a few yards away. "Let's go over there."

They walked over to a worktable where someone had left a saber saw. Fenady told him to continue.

"The producer runs into a small-time comic, a friend of the star of one of his series, who supplements his meager income from nightclubs by selling cocaine. The producer immediately hits on an idea of how to keep his empire afloat by turning the comic's penny-ante operation into a big one. He will be the banker and give the comedian access to the lot and steer him into show-biz connections who will buy in quantity, while the comic takes the visible risks as front man."

He paused to make sure he had Fenady's attention and then continued: "It's a good arrangement—profitable for everyone—but then the front man gets caught by studio security selling. The producer pretends to be enraged, and he really is, not because the front man has been selling coke on the lot, but because he got caught and spoiled everything. But he has to make things look good, so he bars the comic from the lot and hushes up the matter. To keep the lucrative trade going, the producer and the comic decide to use the comic's girlfriend for the role of salesperson. That works out okay for a while, but then they run into another snag. The star of the producer's show, who is dissatisfied with his role and wants out of his contract, finds out about the producer's arrangement with his friend and threatens to expose things unless the producer releases him. Does it work for you so far?" Parker asked.

"You said something about a murder mystery," Fenady said, trying to sound disinterested. He looked at his watch again.

"So I did," Parker said. "The producer decides to do in the star—"

Fenady shook his head. "Why didn't he just let the guy go? The murder motive is weak—"

"Several reasons," Parker said, studying the man's face. "One, the deed is actually half a labor of love, because the producer always hated the star, ever since he took the producer's girlfriend—the costar on the series—away from him. They'd had a couple of rows about it, a particularly nasty one in which the star accused the producer of sending poison-pen letters about his extramarital affairs to his wife.

"Two, the star had been acting squirrelly of late—he liked his cocaine even better than most of his buddy's customers—and he couldn't be trusted to keep his mouth shut, especially considering his animosity for the producer. And three, up to that time the producer could not afford to let the guy walk. He needed the show the star is in to last another season so that it would go into syndication. But when he gets word that the series is being canceled, the producer realizes there is little chance of syndication—unless the star is dead. The star is suddenly worth more dead than alive because the show, being the star's last work, suddenly becomes a marketable item."

"This is beginning to sound screwy," Fenady said.

"Just bear with me and listen to the rest," Parker said. "The producer is a scuba diver. He learned from the technical adviser on one of his old TV shows. He knows the star swims in the ocean at a certain time every morning, so he slips into the water in his diving gear, attaches a special weight belt to the guy, waits for him to drown, and removes it. But just like Murphy's law, as the producer is getting into his car, he is spotted by his comedian-partner, who just happened to be making a dope delivery to the star that morning. The comic puts two and two together and comes up with an idea, a little blackmail scheme of his own.

"The comic, who has always dreamed of making it big, but could never really get to second base with his stuff, tells the producer that he will keep his mouth shut about seeing him at the beach if the producer will put him in a show of his own. The star was nothing to the comic anyway—he'd treated him like dirt—and the little guy saw his chance to seize the day. The producer has other ideas, however.

"He strings the comic along, then goes over to his apartment and slips some heroin into his drink. When the guy passes out, he injects him with a lethal dose, trying to make it look as if the guy died speedballing. Then he leaves his diving gear in the comic's closet to try to throw suspicion for the star's death onto him. See, the producer is nervous. He's read an article in the papers about the star's 'accidental' death possibly being a murder, a possibility reinforced by a pesky coroner who mentions a possible witness at the scene."

Fenady said nothing, but ran his hand along the edge of the table.

"But the producer has one mess to clean up to cover his tracks completely—the comic's girlfriend. Not only does she know about the dope, but she knows about Duffy. She has to go. But before she goes, the producer decides to get the last load of dope he paid for just a few nights before. She resists telling him, but he finally gets it out of her by sticking an electrical wire in her mouth. The producer has gotten that bit from a *Miami Vice* episode he saw a few months before. See, not only is the guy a murderer, he's a plagiarist. Every idea he's ever had, he's stolen from someone else."

That remark seemed to get Fenady. His lips compressed and his eyes glittered sharply as he pulled a pack of Rolaids from his pocket.

"You dropped one of those there, you know."

Fenady's entire face tightened. "What?"

"A Rolaid. You dropped one at Emily Braxton's. Careless."

Fenady looked at the Rolaids as if they had betrayed him, and put them back into his pocket.

"You were careless at Brock's too," Parker told him. "You left one of your prints on the plunger of the syringe you used."

Fenady stared at him, trying to determine if he was

lying. He could see by the steely look in the coroner's eyes that he was not.

Fenady tried to look properly outraged. "What are you, nuts?"

"No," Parker said. "You are. Not nuts enough to get off on an insanity plea, or even enough to argue diminished capacity, but nuts, nevertheless. Not only is there physical evidence, but there are witnesses that put you and Brock together. The cops are on their way with warrants right now. Once they find that cocaine, it's scaled. It's over, Fenady. You're history."

Fenady's shoulders slumped and he turned his back on Parker and leaned on the edge of the table. He stood like that for a moment in silent defeat, and then, without warning, he wheeled around. Parker did not see the saber saw until it was too late. Light exploded in his head and then a lot of sharp pain, and Parker was falling. Luckily, the floor stopped him.

A loud buzzing noise started up in his head suddenly, and he looked up, dazed, to see that the noise was not in his head at all, but in Fenady's hand. With great effort he rolled away as the vibrating blade of the saber saw came down on the concrete where his head had been, and broke off with a loud *chink!*

Parker scuttled backward across the sawdust-covered floor like a disoriented crab and Fenady started after him with a crazed look in his eyes, but then one of the carpenters yelled, and the producer's head snapped around.

The two workmen were frozen by their worktables, staring at Fenady in horror. The producer looked down at the saw in his hand, dropped it, and ran.

The bald carpenter ran over and helped Parker to his feet. "You okay? What in the hell got into him? He looked like he was trying to kill you."

Parker touched his head. His hand came away bloody. "He was." He swayed dizzily and the man tried to steady him, but Parker brushed away the attempt to help and started out the door.

By the time Parker got outside, Fenady was two hundred yards ahead, at the end of the alley that ran between two soundstages. He turned and saw Parker coming, opened the door of one of the buildings, and disappeared inside. Parker lurched by a couple of strolling extras, but being residents in the land of make-believe, they didn't give the blood-spattered man a second glance. Parker got to the door and yanked it open and plunged into the building. His head still had not cleared and it took him a few seconds to realize he was not hallucinating when he plowed into the seven-foot green lizard-man dressed in a metallic silver jumpsuit.

"Watch it, asshole," the lizard-man said, but Parker ignored him and kept going.

He pushed his way through some technicians and found himself in the interior of an alien spaceship piloted by shiny robots with pulsating red eyes.

"What the hell is that guy doing there?" an angry voice bellowed. "Somebody get him out of there!"

Parker stepped out of the ring of blinding lights and scanned the crowd as a burly security man stepped up and grabbed his arm. Parker flashed his badge and said, "Police business. You see a man run in here?"

The man pointed to the other side of the building, and Parker's gaze followed the finger to a strip of daylight showing through a closing door.

Five yards beyond the door, Parker found himself on the tenement-lined street he had strolled on before, except this time it was full of people. A streetcar clanged and rolled by and pedestrians shouldered their way rudely by him.

From his camera dolly-throne, the irate director stood up and pointed at Parker. "You! Don't goddamn stand there. Move!" He noticed the blood on Parker's head and shouted, "This isn't a goddamn battle scene! What's the blood for?"

Parker's eyes swept the street and caught a glimpse of Fenady's blue shirt, at the end, trying to hide in the foot traffic. Fenady glanced over his shoulder and saw Parker, and started running again. When he turned left at the end of the corner, Parker knew where he was going.

The crew for *Street Angels* was setting up for a shot on a long street of parked cars. Fenady stopped by one of the dollies, said something to the cameraman, then looked back at Parker and grinned strangely. Fenady waved at him, then sprinted to the pink Maserati and jumped in. The car's engine roared to life, its tires squealed, and it shot off like a bullet as Parker reached the camera dolly.

"What in the hell is he doing?" The director came up shouting to the cameraman, whose camera was rolling.

"I don't know," the man answered.

The Maserati made a 360-degree turn at the end of the street, then sat for a few seconds idling before Fenady punched the accelerator. Tires smoked as the sleek car laid a long patch of rubber and came hurtling by the cameras. Parker caught a glimpse of Fenady's face as he passed, his lips curled back in a death's-head grimace, his eyes full of madness. Then the car was by them, a blur.

The director threw up his arms. "Will someone please tell me what's going on?"

All eyes on the set were focused on the back of the pink car, waiting for the flash of brake lights, as it neared the end of the simulated street, going better than seventy. They were still waiting when the sports car veered sharply to the right and plowed head-on into a parked truck, exploding into a shower of glass and metal.

A cloud of thick dust obscured the view of the accident, but Parker didn't have to see to know that there would be no need to hurry to get there.

"My God," the director said, his mouth open, his eyes wide, uncomprehending.

Everyone on the set was frozen, silent, watching the dust settle, and then there was a mad scramble for cars.

The cameraman shook his head. "Awesome. Fucking awesome."

Parker asked him, "What did he say to you?"

The man looked down at Parker and blinked. "He told me he was going to show us how he wanted it done."

"That's all?"

The man shook his head. "No. He said to be sure to get it on the first take, that it was going to guarantee the show a fifty-share."

=== 25 ===

"You're sure this is what you want?" Pat Clemens asked.

"Yes," Parker replied.

"You're absolutely, positively sure," Clemens asked dubiously.

"Yes."

The pretty dark-haired secretary put down the phone and showed them all of her even white teeth. "Supervisor Tartunian will see you now."

On his way past her desk, Clemens ogled the woman appreciatively. "Cute," he said to Parker as they went through the door.

Tartunian sat behind the mahogany desk in the large plush office. Brewster, the CAO, and Supervisor Willis sat in cushy high-backed leather chairs flanking the desk.

Tartunian was the only one of the trio who was coatless. He wore a white shirt rolled up at the sleeves. He looked athletically trim for a man in his late forties. His black hair was devoid of gray and his square-jawed face was tanned and weathered from lots of golf and sailing and whatever other outdoor activities required a lot of money and leisure time that Parker never had.

Brewster's face and hair were as red as they always were. The man looked as if he were perpetually angry. Willis was bald and pale. His wire-framed glasses sat well down on his narrow nose and his suit hung limply on his narrow-shouldered frame. He hadn't been on the board that long and Parker had heard little about him except that he was pro-development, and rumors that a lot of his money had come from real-estate investments in Tartunian's district.

"Dr. Parker," Tartunian began.

"This is Pat Clemens, my attorney," Parker said.

Tartunian smiled. "This isn't a hearing—"

"Perhaps not officially," Clemens interjected. "But we have been informed that you have compiled a list of 'charges' which you intend to bring against Dr. Parker." The contempt was thick in Clemens' voice when he used the word "charges." "It is only correct and proper, in that case, that he should have legal representation present."

"We haven't called this meeting to present any charges," Tartunian protested.

"Really?" Clemens asked. "Then what did you call it for?"

"If you would sit down, gentlemen, I'll tell you."

Parker and Clemens took chairs facing the tribunal. Parker felt like a heretic appearing before some grim-faced

Inquisitional body, and he was grateful for his friend's re-assuring presence.

Tartunian cleared his throat and began: "We have asked you here, Doctor, to discuss certain complaints we have received about you from within and without your department. Complaints of administrative incompetence, unprofessionalism, and instances of bizarre behavior exhibited by you unfitting for a representative of county government. On the basis of these allegations, some members of the board have called for your immediate resignation. After a lengthy debate, however, it has been decided to take a less drastic course of action."

"The headlines this morning wouldn't have had anything to do with that decision, would they?" Parker asked.

Behind the thick glasses, Willis' eyes darted over to Tartunian, then quickly back to Parker. They never seemed to light on anything for more than a second or two before taking off again.

"I presume you're talking about the Duffy case," Tartunian remarked grudgingly. "Congratulations on a brilliant piece of work."

A police search of Fenady's house had turned up a large cocaine stash, and a check of his phone records had established a more-than-casual acquaintance with Brock. In a front-page article in the L.A. *Times*, Alexis Saxby had quoted Detective Sergeant Mitchell James as saying that he was certain that more evidence would be turned up and that a solid case would be built, linking Fenady's suicide to the triple murder. In the interview, the detective had shunted a good deal of the credit for breaking the case to Parker.

"Thanks," Parker said sourly. "The case was solved only through the diligent backing and support of the board."

Tartunian scowled. "We aren't here to pick over our past differences, Doctor. We're here to find a reasonable solution to this problem."

"What problem?"

"Come off it, Doctor," Brewster cut in. "You can't deny you have a major problem. When you took over as coroner, the average time elapsed between a body being taken to the morgue and its release was three days. That's up to six now. You have bodies stacked up in the hallways—"

"We have bodies stacked up because *you* won't release any funds," Parker shot back.

"Because you have consistently overspent your budget allocations," Brewster interjected in an argumentative tone.

Parker was restrained by Clemens' hand on his knee.

"Gentlemen, please," Tartunian broke in. When Parker had settled back in his chair, he said, "What we propose, Doctor, is a probation period of one year. During that time, you will maintain a low public profile, stick to the business at hand, and carry out the duties of your office with decorum and dignity. I realize you and Mr. Brewster have experienced some problems working with each other. To facilitate the operation of your department and coordinate with the CAO, an administrative officer will be appointed to handle the day-to-day budget matters and administrative details of the Forensic Science Center."

Parker leaned forward. "In other words, you're putting a leash on me. I'll be just another pathologist while your puppet runs the show." He shook his head. "Thanks, but no thanks."

Tartunian's face hardened. "I don't think you realize what we're offering you here."

"Yes, I do. You don't think I can see through this ruse, Tartunian? You want to get rid of me just as badly as you did before, only you can't right now, not with the Duffy case splattered all over the front page of the *Times*. You want my head because of your son, and Brewster wants my head because he sees me as a threat to his little political fiefdom, and the rest of the board wants it because I've shot my mouth off in public one too many times about politicians being nothing but liars and thieves."

Tartunian's lips compressed and his face reddened beneath the tan. Clemens jumped in between the two men, who stared at each other like two dogs about to fight. "Supervisor, Dr. Parker does not wish to stay on as coroner under your conditions. But not because of any charges you intend to level at him. We have seen those so-called charges and we hold them to be totally false. I have no doubt, if this ever got to the stage of a civil-service hearing, Dr. Parker would be totally vindicated, and you gentlemen would wind up with a lot of political egg on your faces.

"In the interim, however, Dr. Parker feels that you would continue to tighten your chokehold on the Forensic Science Center, in an effort to get to him. He does not want that. He has spent too long and put too much of his life building it up. Therefore, he wishes to resign. No fuss, no publicity." He paused meaningfully and said, "He promises he won't even tell the media about your friendship with Fenady, Supervisor, or your call to Chicago, which the public might erroneously construe as an attempt to put a lid on the investigation of John Duffy's death."

Tartunian's frown deepened. "What's the catch?"

Clemens coughed into his hand. "Not one. Three. Number one, if one word of these libelous allegations about Dr. Parker becomes public, all agreements are off. The county will be sued for slander and libel and everything will be made public. Everything."

"Go on," Tartunian said.

"Number two, Dr. Parker names his successor."

"Who?"

"Dr. James Phillips, his current chief of operations."

Tartunian's expression softened a bit. "I'll have to confer with the board, but I'm sure the choice will be agreeable to the other members. What else?"

"Dr. Parker wants access to the facilities of the Forensic Science Center whenever he needs them."

That made the three of them sit up. "What for?"

"Research," Parker spoke up. "I will be going into private practice."

"As what?" Brewster asked.

"Forensic consultant."

Willis shook his head doubtfully. "I don't see how we could reconcile giving a private citizen access to equipment paid for by public funds—"

Clemens said, "For a nominal fee, the county could retain Dr. Parker as a special consultant. I've been over the statutes."

"How nominal?" Brewster asked.

"That's for you to decide," Parker told them. "Who knows? Someday you might need an expert outside opinion."

"Your competence as a pathologist has never been in question," Willis offered. "Only your competence as an administrator." He hesitated and looked at his colleagues. "I, for one, would have no objection to such an arrangement."

"It's possible," Tartunian admitted thoughtfully.

"Then we have a deal?" Clemens asked.

"I'll give you an answer by four o'clock," Tartunian said. "But I'd say, yes, we have a deal."

Outside, Clemens asked Parker once more in a concerned voice, "You're sure this is what you want?"

The truth was, Parker's feelings were gravely mixed, but he said, "I'm sure, Pat. Things couldn't go on the way they were. Thanks for being there."

Clemens nodded. "I'll be by tonight. We'll do the grand circle."

"Sure," Parker said.

=== 26 ===

Parker was cleaning out his desk when Steenbargen walked in.

"Need a hand?"

"Thanks," Parker said, smiling.

They began to load six years into four medium-size cardboard boxes.

"What are you going to do?" Steenbargen asked as they worked.

Parker shrugged. "I don't know. Maybe buy that farm you were talking about."

"I have a better idea," Steenbargen said, and reached inside his jacket pocket. He pulled out a business card and handed it to Parker. "What do you think?"

The card read: "DR. ERIC C. PARKER—Coroner at Large."

In smaller print, down in the right-hand corner, was: "Michael Steenbargen—Chief Investigator."

"What is this?"

"Our business card," Steenbargen said, smiling broadly. "Like it?"

"It's gorgeous, but what is this stuff at the bottom?"

"My name. I quit this morning."

The news upset Parker. "You can't quit. You only have four years to go until retirement—"

"I couldn't retire any more than you. What am I going to do, buy a farm and raise chickens? No way."

"But you'll lose your benefits—"

"Some, not all. But I look at it this way: this sort of opportunity doesn't come up every day. If I wait for four years until I retire, you'll have another investigator, and I'll have to look for something else. This is saving me time and money." He paused. "Anyway, this place wouldn't be the same without you."

Cindy, who had been conspicuously absent when Parker arrived at the office, stuck her head in. "I just heard the news. I can't tell you how sorry I am, Dr. Parker. Do you need any help?"

Parker frowned. "I think you've already helped enough, Cindy, thanks."

She touched her throat and tried to look perplexed, but the trapped look in her eyes gave her away. "What do you mean?"

"There was too much in those charges that he couldn't have known without having a man inside. Or I should say, woman."

Her eyes widened and she shook her head. "I . . . I don't know what you mean."

"You know what I mean," Parker said. "You were his source. That bit with the tuxedos tipped it for me. There was nobody else who could have gotten that information to him that fast." He hesitated. "What did he offer you? A promotion?"

She broke down and started to cry. "I didn't want to do it, I really didn't. But he threatened to have me transferred to *Van Nuys* unless I cooperated. I couldn't face the thought of fighting that traffic every day. It would have meant an hour extra on the freeway *every day*—"

"I'll be goddamned," Steenbargen said, shaking his head.

"Get out of here," Parker told her, disgusted. She went out, sobbing, and Parker said in wonderment, "Sold out for a clear freeway lane."

"I think this might be a blessing in disguise," Steenbargen declared. "I think we both might be better off out of here."

The phone rang. Parker picked it up.

"Doc, you're a fucking genius!" a voice exclaimed.

"Pardon me?" Parker said, puzzled.

"About that shoe. It was a transvestite, all right. We got the creep! Name is Rupert Evans."

"Who is this?"

"Burke," the man said. "Homicide."

Parker remembered then.

"I started pulling in hookers I knew and a couple of them told me about this drag queen that had been working the neighborhood. They hadn't seen him around in the last couple of nights, but last night he popped up and one of them pointed him out. All I had to do was put the cuffs on the creep and he broke down and started to cry. Laid it all out, how he was picked up by the victim and was going down on him, when the guy reaches down and gropes him. I guess the guy freaked out and started to wail on Evans, who tried to get out of the car. That checks out with Evans' face. He's pretty banged up. Anyway, the john won't let Evans out of the car, and to defend himself, Evans takes off his high-heeled shoe and starts swinging. The next thing he knows, the shoe is sticking out of the john's forehead. We found the shoe at Evans' apartment. The lab found traces of blood on the heel that match with the victim's."

"Good work," Parker said as enthusiastically as he could.

"I just thought you'd like to know," Burke said.

"Thanks," Parker said, meaning it. Little victories. You took them where you could get them.

Parker hung up and the phone rang again. This time, Cindy picked it up. She put the caller on hold, then said, "It's Dr. Silverman. He sounds mad."

"Tell him," Parker said, savoring the moment, "tell him to call the new coroner if he has a problem."

Parker loaded the boxes into his car and said good-bye to his tearful colleagues and staff. On his way out, he stopped off at the library and was looking over the exhibits one last time, lost in his memories, when a noise behind him made him turn.

"I'm sorry to disturb you, Doctor," Emmett Jackson apologized.

"That's all right, Emmett."

"I heard the news."

Parker nodded.

"I just wanted to tell you that I've decided not to go into dentistry. I've decided to go into forensic medicine."

"That's great, Emmett," Parker said, genuinely pleased. "I'm really happy and pleased for you. It's a good decision." He reached forward and took Emmett's oversize hand. "Good luck."

"Thank you."

Parker felt his mood change as he watched Emmett leave. He had planned to stay longer among the glass cases, savoring the memories, but then he decided that, like Emmett, his place was in the future, not the past. Without looking backward, he headed for the door.

27

Saturday dawned bright and clear. The first day of the rest of my life, Parker thought, feeling good about it, but apprehensive too. This was the day that Boomer got presented to Ricky and Eve—and anything could happen.

With Ricky, it was a sure thing, of course. Ricky was going to go crazy over Boomer. But Eve? Parker wasn't too sure. From time to time she had talked about getting a dog. She said she wouldn't mind the company and she'd feel safer. But she never did anything about it, which would indicate, for whatever reason, that she really didn't want one.

"Step on a slug, it could go any way," Parker told Boomer, leaving the freeway at Chatsworth. "She may love you, which means you get to have a swimming pool. Or she may hate you, which means you're stuck with me and the tub."

Boomer grinned and wagged his tail, happy with either prospect.

"The kid," Parker said. "Have I told you about the kid? He's our secret weapon. When he sees you, he's going to go ape, and when she sees him going ape, which is what we are counting on, the plan is that's going to melt her heart. So forget her, concentrate on the kid, okay? The kid is the key."

Boomer wagged his tail some more.

"So you'll recognize the kid," Parker said, "he looks a little like me, younger of course, but the same steel-blue eyes, penetrating like he could see right through you, so you better watch out. Blond hair, a handsome face, and a crooked grin. His mother's nose, freckles, and high forehead. His father's walk, slightly knock-kneed. You getting all this?"

"Ruff," Boomer barked, which Parker accepted as a yes.

"Now, something else," Parker said. "Mia? The lady you met the other night? I really like her. I'm going to be seeing her again, and if there ever was a good time to tell Ricky and Eve, it's got to be this morning, provided they're both crazy about you. The idea is, I'll just slide in on your coattails, so to speak. Make the two of you one package. I'll say something like, 'Well, you guys finally got yourself a dog, and guess what, I got myself a lady friend.' And they'll look up from hugging and petting you and they'll say, 'Oh, yeah? Who?' and I'll say, 'You've probably seen her, she's a TV star.'"

"Ruff."

Parker pulled up in front of a Tudor stucco. Every time

he saw it, he had the same thought: that it could use a little paint . . . too bad there wasn't a man around the house. And then he would remember that it could have used a little paint even when there had been a man around.

Some things worked out, some things didn't, Parker thought. The important thing was to keep trying.

He was going to honk the horn, then changed his mind and got out of the car, thinking this time, at least, he'd better do things right.

All Pan books are available at your local bookshop or newsagent, or can be ordered direct from the publisher. Indicate the number of copies required and fill in the form below.

Send to: **CS Department, Pan Books Ltd., P.O. Box 40, Basingstoke, Hants. RG21 2YT.**

or phone: 0256 469551 (Ansaphone), quoting title, author and Credit Card number.

Please enclose a remittance* to the value of the cover price plus: 60p for the first book plus 30p per copy for each additional book ordered to a maximum charge of £2.40 to cover postage and packing.

*Payment may be made in sterling by UK personal cheque, postal order, sterling draft or international money order, made payable to Pan Books Ltd.

Alternatively by Barclaycard/Access:

Card No. | | | | | | | | | | | | | | | | | | | |

Signature:

Applicable only in the UK and Republic of Ireland.

While every effort is made to keep prices low, it is sometimes necessary to increase prices at short notice. Pan Books reserve the right to show on covers and charge new retail prices which may differ from those advertised in the text or elsewhere.

NAME AND ADDRESS IN BLOCK LETTERS PLEASE:

....

Name ————————————————————————————

Address ————————————————————————————

————————————————————————————

————————————————————————————

————————————————————————————

3/87